THE HOME AND THE WORLD

RABINDRANATH TAGORE was born in 1861, into one of the fore-most families of Bengal. He was the fourteenth child of Deben-dranath Tagore, who headed the Brahmo Samaj (a Hindu reform movement). The family house at Jorasanko in Calcutta was a hive of cultural and intellectual activity. Tagore was educated by private tutors, and first visited Europe in 1878. He started writing at an early age, and his talent was recognized by Bankimchandra Chatterjee, the leading writer of the day. In the 1890s Tagore lived mainly in rural East Bengal, managing family estates. In the early 1900s he was involved in the Swadeshi campaign against the British, but withdrew when the movement turned violent. In 1912 he came to England with *Gitanjali*, an English translation of some of his religious lyrics. It was acclaimed by W. B. Yeats and later published by Macmillan, leading directly to his winning the Nobel Prize for Literature in 1913. In the 1920s and 1930s he made extensive lecture tours of America, Europe and the Far East. Proceeds from these tours, and from his Western publications, went to Visva-Bharati, the school and international university he creat-ed at Santiniketan, a hundred miles north-west of Calcutta.

Tagore was a controversial figure at home and abroad: at home because of his ceaseless innovations in poetry, prose, drama and music; abroad because of the stand he took against militarism and nationalism. In 1919 he protested against the Amritsar Massacre by returning the knighthood that the British had given him in 1915. He was close to Mahatma Gandhi, who called him the 'Great Sentinel' of modern India; but he gener-ally held himself aloof from politics. His own translations (*Collected Poems and Plays of Rabindranath Tagore*, 1936) have not proved sufficient to sustain the worldwide reputation he enjoyed in his lifetime; but as a Bengali writer his eminence is unchallenged. His works run to thirty-two large volumes. They contain some sixty collections of verse; novels such as *Gora* and *The Home and the World*; experimental plays such as *The Post Office* and *Red Oleanders*; and essays on a host of religious, social and literary topics. He also wrote over 2,000 songs, which have become the national music of Bengal, and include the national anthems of both India and Bangladesh. Late in life he took up painting, exhibiting in Moscow, Berlin, Paris, London and New York. He died in 1941.

ANITA DESAI was born in 1937. Her father was Bengali and her mother German, and she was educated in Delhi. Her published work includes *Fire on the Mountain* (1977), which won the Royal Society of Literature's Winifred Holtby Memorial Prize and the 1978 National Academy of Letters Award; *Games At Twilight* (1978); *Clear Light of Day* (1980), shortlisted for that year's Booker Prize for Fiction; *In Custody* (1984), also shortlisted for the Booker Prize and filmed by Merchant Ivory; *Baumgartner's Bombay* (1988); and *Journey to Ithaca* (1995). Anita Desai is the author of two books for children, *The Peacock Garden* (1979) and *The Village by the Sea* (1982), which won the *Guardian* Award for Children's Fiction and was subsequently made into a film. Her latest novel, *Fasting, Feasting* (1999), was shortlisted for the Booker Prize, and was followed in 2000 by a collection of short stories, *Diamond Dust*. Anita Desai holds Fellowships at the Royal Society of Literature in London, the American Academy of Arts and Letters in New York, Girton College and Clare Hall in Cambridge. She won Italy's Moraria Prize in 1999. She lives in Cambridge, Massachusetts, and teaches in the Writing Program of the Massachusetts Institute of Technology.

WILLIAM RADICE was born in 1951 in London. He has pursued a double career as a poet and as a scholar and translator of Bengali, and has written or edited nearly thirty books. In addition to his translations of Tagore for Penguin, his publications include eight books of his own poems, *Teach Yourself Bengali* (1994), *Myths and Legends of India* (2001) and *A Hundred Letters from England* (2003). He has also translated from German (Martin Kämpchen's *The Honey-Seller and Other Stories*, 1995, and Sigfrid Gauch's autobiographical novel *Traces of My Father*, 2002) and Italian (Puccini's *Turandot* for English National Opera). He wrote the libretto for Param Vir's Tagore-based chamber opera *Snatched by the Gods* (1992). He has contributed regularly to BBC radio, has lectured widely in South Asia, North America and Europe, and has been given literary prizes in India and Bangladesh. William Radice is Senior Lecturer in Bengali at SOAS, University of London, and from 1999 to 2002 was Head of the Departments of South and South East Asia. He lives in London and Northumberland.

RABINDRANATH TAGORE

The Home and the World

Translated by SURENDRANATH TAGORE
Introduction by ANITA DESAI
Preface by WILLIAM RADICE

PENGUIN BOOKS

PENGUIN BOOKS

Published by the Penguin Group
Penguin Books Ltd, 80 Strand, London WC2R 0RL, England
Penguin Group (USA) Inc., 375 Hudson Street, New York, New York 10014, USA
Penguin Group (Canada), 10 Alcorn Avenue, Toronto, Ontario, Canada M4V 3B2
(a division of Pearson Penguin Canada Inc.)
Penguin Ireland, 25 St Stephen's Green, Dublin 2, Ireland (a division of Penguin Books Ltd)
Penguin Group (Australia), 250 Camberwell Road, Camberwell, Victoria 3124,
Australia (a division of Pearson Australia Group Pty Ltd)
Penguin Books India Pvt Ltd, 11 Community Centre,
Panchsheel Park, New Delhi – 110 017, India
Penguin Group (NZ), cnr Airborne and Rosedale Roads, Albany,
Auckland 1310, New Zealand (a division of Pearson New Zealand Ltd)
Penguin Books (South Africa) (Pty) Ltd, 24 Sturdee Avenue, Rosebank 2196, South Africa

Penguin Books Ltd, Registered Offices: 80 Strand, London WC2R 0RL, England

www.penguin.com

First published in serial form in India 1915
First published in book form in India 1916
This translation first published in Great Britain by Macmillan 1919
Published in Penguin Books 1985
Published with a new Preface, Additional Notes, Chronology and Further Reading in
Penguin Classics 2005

028

Printed and bound in Great Britain by Clays Ltd, Elcograf S.p.A.
Typeset in Palatino VIP

ISBN-13: 978-0-140-44986-0

www.greenpenguin.co.uk

Contents

Contents

Preface

The Home and the World is a great modern novel that has waited a long time to come into its own. As with many works of art and literature that break new ground, responses to it – in Bengal, India and the West – have often been confused and misinformed, and critics have only gradually acquired the insight and background knowledge that such a complex work of fiction requires. Even its admirers have felt obliged to make apologies for it, to find interest and strength in it but also flaws. But with a writer as great and deliberate as Tagore, what initially seems imperfect is no longer so when one understands better what he was trying to do.

Can a fully sympathetic reading apply as much to the English translation by Surendranath Tagore as to the original Bengali text? The first thing that non-Bengali readers need to know is that *The Home and the World*, published serially as *At Home and Outside* in the *Modern Review* in 1918–19 and in book form by Macmillan in 1919, is in many ways a different book from *Ghare Baire*, which appeared serially in the journal *Sabuj Patra* from May 1915 to February 1916, in book form (with cuts) in 1916, and in a new edition (with cuts restored) in 1920.

The differences between the two texts are not primarily to do with the quality of the translation, though for many years it was conventional for Bengali commentators on the book to lay part of the blame for hostile Western reactions to *The Home and the World* on Surendranath's work. In recent years, critics with access to both languages have become more respectful of

Surendranath's achievement, more aware of what a challenge the Bengali text presents to any translator, more willing to read his English not as 'dated' but as representative of its provenance and period. Moreover, the research of Tagore's leading contemporary biographer (Prasanta Kumar Paul) has revealed that Tagore himself had more of a hand in the translation than was previously thought. In a letter to Macmillan of 5 November 1918, he wrote:

> My nephew Surendranath has translated the latest novel of mine which I think you will find fully acceptable. A large part of it I have done myself and it has been carefully revised.

This gives the translation an enhanced authenticity, as Tagore was by no means so attentive to Macmillan's editions of his other novels and collections of short stories.

Surendranath Tagore (1872–1940) was the son of Tagore's elder brother Satyendranath, who was famous for being the first Indian to qualify for the Indian civil service. Surendranath, like his father, studied for a while in England, acquiring a training in the life insurance business. He was briefly involved in secret revolutionary activity against the British, but abandoned that for the kind of 'constructive Swadeshi'[1] that his uncle Rabindranath favoured. He was co-founder of the Hindusthan Co-operative Insurance Company. Earlier, he and his cousin Balendranath had been engaged in a sugar-cane and jute business on the estates in north Bengal where Rabindranath acquired in the 1890s an experience that lay directly behind the character of Nikilesh in *The Home and the World*. During the Swadeshi agitation against Lord Curzon's announcement in 1905 of the partition of Bengal, Surendranath helped to found a weaving school in Kushtia.

Surendranath's relationship with Rabindranath was thus very close, and in the celebrated letters that Tagore wrote in the 1890s to Surendranath's sister Indira, describing his life in rural Bengal, 'Suri' or 'Suren' is often mentioned. He was a gifted writer, contributing to journals such as *Sabuj Patra* and

1. See Additional Notes, p. 207.

Sadhana that published Tagore's work, and writing versions of stories from the *Mahabharata* that Rabindranath brought out in book form. Like many members of the Tagore family, he was intellectually and artistically distinguished, and his translation of *Ghare Baire* reflects that distinction. It is a highly sophisticated piece of work, deserving respect, not patronage.

Was there a correlation between the cuts that were made in the first Bengali edition of the book, and the cuts in Surendranath's translation that are the most marked difference between it and the (full) Bengali original? This does not yet seem to have been researched; nor have I seen any speculation on whether those cuts were made partly in response to the barrage of readers' complaints that Tagore received when the novel first appeared serially in *Sabuj Patra*. Sensitive to criticism as he was, it may be that the cuts stemmed partly, at least, from a temporary loss of nerve.

Early criticism of the book by Bengalis was essentially moralistic. There was much in the subject matter of the book – the adulterous affair between Bimala and Sandip, Sandip's iconoclastic assaults on convention and orthodoxy, Nikhilesh's 'unpatriotic' rejection of aspects of the Swadeshi campaign – to shock the reading public. So exasperated was Tagore by his readers' apparent inability to read the book as a novel, as a work of fiction rather than a tract, that he published in *Sabuj Patra* a rejoinder – in the form of a reply to a letter from an anonymous lady reader – before the serialization was complete. Three years later – between the book publication of the cut and the complete texts – he published another article in a similar vein, in the journal *Prabasi*. An English version of the first of these articles appeared in the *Modern Review* in 1918, during the serial publication in that journal of the English translation of the book. Calling the article in English 'The Object and Subject of a Story', Tagore roundly condemns criticism that is no more than 'a judgement of the proprieties which are necessary for orthodoxy', and acidly points out:

> There are a crowd of heroines in Shakespeare's dramas, but their excellence is not judged according to their peculiar English qualities; and even the most fanatical Christian theologians desist

from awarding them marks, in order of merit, according to their degree of Christianity.

In his second article, he is particularly scathing of those who conclude that he is himself hostile to Rama's wife Sita because Sandip, in the novel, makes disparaging remarks about Sita.

The furore in Bengal about *Ghare Baire* when it first appeared – so intense that Tagore's biographer Prabhat Kumar Mukherjee wrote (in 1936) that 'of all the works of Rabindranath, *Ghare Baire* has probably provoked the largest number of critics, literary or otherwise' – is important to recall, not for what the critics said but for their perception of the book's novelty and daring. It was seen to be – and indeed it was – avant-garde, and the journal in which it appeared, *Sabuj Patra* ('Green Leaves'), edited by Pramatha Chaudhuri, Tagore's friend and the husband of his niece Indira, aimed generally to 'jolt the reader's mind and shake it'. When Surendranath's translation was published, and with the consolidation of Tagore's presence in the English language in the interwar years, the radicalism of the book was overlooked. Even Bengali critics, when writing in English, tended to see it as a period piece, connected more in its social ambience to the late nineteenth century than to the twentieth century Swadeshi campaign that formed its immediate background. As late as 1994, Ashish Nandy in *The Illegitimacy of Nationalism: Rabindranath Tagore and the Politics of Self*, a study that has been very influential in the understanding of Tagore's reservations about nationalism, surprisingly says: '*Ghare-Baire* is a nineteenth-century novel, written in a nineteenth-century style. It is only chronologically a product of this century.' Maybe Satyajit Ray's film, with its beautifully reconstructed nineteenth-century *zamindari* interiors, has helped to sustain this impression.

In prose style alone, however, *Ghare Baire* has to be seen as a modern, twentieth-century work, for it was the first Bengali novel to be written in the *calit bhasha*, the form of Bengali that has now become the norm, as opposed to the nineteenth-century *sadhu bhasha* in which Tagore also excelled in his earlier prose works. Nineteenth-century writers had experimented with the *calit bhasha* in dialogue, and Tagore first used it in print in a collection of letters he wrote during his first visit to England (1878–80). But it was only with his *Sabuj Patra* phase that he switched to making it his main prose vehicle, first in *Strir Patra* ('The Wife's Letter', 1914), a short story that took sides with an oppressed wife, then in *Ghare Baire* itself.

The effect of the switch might be imagined by supposing that abbreviated English verb forms – can't, won't, I'm, etc. – had been studiously avoided in English prose, until a single pioneering writer in the early twentieth century suddenly started to use them – abandoning the full forms completely. But the style of *Ghare Baire* is a breakthrough not only in verb endings and pronouns: it is startlingly terse and epigrammatic, in a manner that Tagore had developed in *Caturanga*, a novella first published a year before *Ghare Baire*. Of this book, Kaiser Haq wrote in a Preface to his definitive translation (*Quartet*, Heinemann, 1993):

> Transitions in plot and character development are abrupt, descriptions are compressed into minimalist dimensions, the terse language flashes suddenly into image and epigram. Such devices have become part of the inherited repertoire of the contemporary writer, but if we remember that before book publication in 1916 *Quartet* was serialised in 1914–15, when literary modernism was in its infancy, we will better appreciate its daring originality.

The same can be said of *The Home and the World*.

The modernism of the novel is veiled in Surendranath's version not so much by his prose style, which often copes with the subtlety and complexity of the original remarkably well, but by his organization of the book into chapters. For the sharing of the narrative between several characters Tagore did have a precedent in *Rajani* (1875), a novel by the pioneering nineteenth-century novelist Bankimchandra Chatterjee. In Bankim's novel, however, the narrative is like a relay race – one character takes over when another leaves off. In *Ghare Baire* the same events are told from three points of view. In 'The Form of *The Home and the World*', included in an excellent volume of essays on the book edited by P. K. Datta (*Rabindranath Tagore's* The Home and the World: *A Critical Companion*, 2003), Tapobrata Ghosh rightly argues that 'the three characters of *Ghare Baire* are given full control over their own autobiographies. But in the English version, the power of the characters to write their own autobiographies is limited by the intervention of the masterful author.' Is it because the structure of the book, in the English, chapterized version, seems fussily at odds with its relatively simple plot that the style has seemed to many florid and wordy, when in fact it is dense and compact? A translation that kept the headings of the original – 'Bimala's autobiography', 'Nikhilesh's autobiography', 'Sandip's autobiography', rather than 'Bimala's story' (i.e. narrative), etc. as at present, might instantly make a different and more experimental impression.

A new wave in the study and interpretation of both *Ghare Baire* and *The Home and the World* has to be dated from Satyajit Ray's magnificent film of 1984, if only because the inevitable arguments in Bengal about the differences between the film and the book made people read and think about it closely, while admirers of the film abroad were drawn to investigation of its source and political background. The film also revealed new kinds of relevance in the book, confirming its classic status. Indrani Majumdar, in her updated edition of Marie Seton's book on Ray (*Portrait of a Director: Satyajit Ray*, 1971), recalls that the scene (which is not in the book) where Bimala's English companion Miss Gilby expresses pain at being physically ill-treated by people she thought were friendly seemed poignantly comparable to Indira Gandhi's assassination by her Sikh bodyguards. More recent audiences – and readers of the book – might well find, in Sandip's reckless ideology and Nikhilesh's horror of Hindu–Muslim conflict, foreshadowings of the crises in Ayodhya in 1992 and Gujarat in 2002. At the end of the film, Ray's decision to leave no doubt – by showing Bimala transmuted into a widow – that Nikhilesh was killed in the riot, whereas in the book his fate is left open, initially caused some annoyance; but it strikes many now as a comment by Ray on the tragic implications of the book – the struggle for survival, during Ray's own lifetime and beyond, of the liberal, tolerant outlook embodied in Nikhilesh.

The majority of recent critical essays have explored the binaries that have not only been such a focus in post-colonial literary criticism but are inherent in the very title of *Ghare Baire*. Home and world, man and woman, love and domesticity, nationalism and colonialism, tradition and modernity: most studies circle round one or more of these oppositions, and with each circuit come to embrace more of the novel's complexity. Historical scholarship, as in Sumit Sarkar's seminal study, *The Swadeshi Movement in Bengal, 1903–1908* (1973), has enriched our understanding of the book's ideological background. Biographical studies such as Ashish Nandy's exploration, in *The Illegitimacy of Nationalism*, of Tagore's friendship with the Shakta-turned-Catholic-turned-revolutionary Brahmabandhab Upadhyay (the model, Nandy argues, for the heroes and the villains in all of Tagore's political novels), have helped us to see why Nikhilesh needs Sandip while at the same time rejecting him. Religious studies, which have made striking progress recently in interpreting Bengali Shaktism and Tantricism, show us how Tagore, through Sandip's relationship with Bimala, probed deeply and critically into forms of Hinduism that he found dangerously irrational and nihilistic.

What aspects of the book still need to be explored? There is scope, I think – given that the translation itself has classic status and is unlikely to be wholly supplanted by a new translation – for closer comparison of the two texts than has been attempted even by Bengali specialists in English. The cuts are revealing and sometimes startling – such as one where Sandip gloatingly recalls his previous romantic conquests. There are additions too: the last paragraph on p. 84, for example, is not in the original. Some changes of detail, such as Longfellow's poems being changed in the English to Mrs Hemans's poems (p. 56), or 'Vinolia soap'[1] changed to 'Pears' soap' (p. 81), indicate discussion and collaboration between Rabindranath and Surendranath, for no translator is likely to make such changes

---

1. The name in the original may be fictitious – with echoes perhaps of 'vanilla' and 'oil'.

himself. Some trimming of minor characters, and the removal altogether of a second sister-in-law, were followed by Ray in his film, suggesting that the English was his source as well as the Bengali. (But note how subtly Ray preserves the wise presence of Chandranath Babu, Nikhilesh's old teacher: he may not have as much to say as in the Bengali text, but he intervenes strongly at crucial junctures.) The most interesting points of comparison, however, which if investigated by critics would clarify for non-Bengali readers the patterns of thought in the book, are in the translation of abstract terms. In many ways the book is an argument about truth. Whose truth is truer? Nikhilesh's? Sandip's? What kind of truth must Bimala finally accept? The truth of *sakti* (female power), or the truth of conjugality? Is truth simply objective reality, or does it have a moral or spiritual dimension? There is one Bengali word for truth – *satya* – and as a leitmotif running through the book 'Truth' in the English version works quite well. But Sandip often uses 'Truth' and 'Life' and other such terms iron-ically. In debates with Nikhilesh he will talk about *satya-jinis*, 'the Truth-thing', i.e. the idealistic Truth that Nikhilesh cares about, inferior to what Sandip, as a radical worshipper of Nature, understands as the real, raw truth. For other terms used in the English, we often find a variety of words in Bengali, all with different nuances. 'Passion', for example, can be *iccha* ('wish'), *prabritti* ('instinct'), or *kshudha* ('hunger'). Then there are English words used in the Bengali, such as 'art' or 'affinity' or 'modern' – all with nuances that may be hard to translate but that can be analysed and explained.

Probing such details would bring more to the fore the sheer intellectualism of the book. Lyrical and poetic though it is at times, it is above all a novel of ideas. Sandip may be a villain, but he is a very intellectual villain. His violent and unscrupulous nationalism is as rationally thought out as the political terrorism of today. This has not always been well understood by critics and biographers of Tagore. Krishna Kripalani, in his authoritative English biography in 1962, called Sandip 'the Machiavellian patriot, the unscrupulous politician, the splendid wind-bag and shameless seducer'. Yet Bhabani Bhattacharya, a leading figure in the modernist *Kallol* movement in Bengal in the 1930s, found in Sandip's acute self-knowledge the virtue of honesty: 'He never tried to deceive himself, and in his honesty lies the source of his power.' For me, in his cerebration as well as his villainy, he is akin to Edmund in *King Lear* ('Thou, Nature, art my goddess ...').

Ultimately, as with Shakespeare's tragedies, to understand these patterns deepens the book's pathos and enhances its relevance. Female readers may identify with Bimala and see the story as essentially her tragedy (though to some feminists it is disappointing that she should eventually opt for husband and home, rather than Sandip and the world). Male readers today may find acute relevance in what Sumit Sarkar has called its 'two masculinities': the dilemma of a man – Nikhilesh – who may be an aristocrat but who is in other respects a 'new man' who wants his wife to have autonomy. If Nikhilesh, as a generous and constructive landowner, is in part a self-portrait of Tagore himself, his failings (of which he is all too aware) also project anxiety about power and virility that are resonant today to an extent that even Tagore might not have foreseen.

'O Lord, sound once again those flute strains which you played for me, long ago, standing at the rosy edge of my morning sky – and let all my complexities become simple and easy.' Thus prays Bimala, in extremis, before the book's dénouement and final tragedy. Understanding of *The Home and the World* may have grown over the eighty-five years since it was published. But of one thing we can be sure: increased understanding will not – any more than for Bimala – bring escape from complexity. Because Tagore's novel is both great and modern, it will always have new things to say.

WILLIAM RADICE
Northumberland, 2004

Chronology

1858 The British Crown takes over the Government of India, following the Mutiny of 1857.

1861 Tagore born in Calcutta, in the family house at Jorasanko.

1873 Goes with his father Debendranath Tagore on a tour of the Western Himalayas.

1875 His mother dies.

1877 Starts to publish regularly in his family's monthly journal, *Bharati*.

1878 First visit to England.

1880 His book *Sandhya Sangit* (Evening Songs) acclaimed by Bankimchandra Chatterjee, the leading writer of the day.

1883 Controversy over Lord Ripon's Ilbert bill, to permit Indian judges to try Englishmen, intensifies antagonism between British and Indians.

Tagore marries.

1884 His sister-in-law Kadambari commits suicide.

1885 First Indian National Congress meets at Bombay.

1886 Tagore's daughter Madhurilata (Bela) born.

1888 His son Rathindranath born.

1890 His father puts him in charge of the family estates.

Second, brief visit to England.

Starts to write prolifically for a new family journal, *Sadhana*.

1898 Sedition Bill; arrest of Bal Gangadhar Tilak; Tagore reads his paper *Kantha-rodh* (The Throttled) at a public meeting in Calcutta.

1901 Marriage of his elder daughters Bela and Renuka (Rani).

Inauguration of the Santiniketan School.

1902 His wife dies.

1903 Rani dies.

1904 Satischandra Ray, his assistant at Santiniketan, dies.

1905 Swadeshi agitation against Lord Curzon's proposal to partition Bengal, with Tagore playing a leading part.

His father dies.

1907 His younger son Samindra dies.

1908 Thirty-five revolutionary conspirators in Bombay and Bengal arrested.

1909 Indian Councils Act, increasing power of provincial councils, attempts to meet Indian political aspirations.

1910 Bengali *Gitanjali* published.

1912 Third visit to England; first visit to America; publication of the English *Gitanjali*.

1913 Tagore awarded the Nobel Prize for Literature.

1914 230,000 Indian troops join the first winter campaign of the Great War.

1915 Tagore's first meeting with Gandhi.

He receives a knighthood.

1916 Home Rule League formed by Annie Besant and B. G. Tilak.

Tagore goes to Japan and the USA; lectures on *Nationalism* and *Personality*.

1917 E. S. Montagu, Secretary of State, declares the development of self-government in India to be official policy.

Tagore reads his poem 'India's Prayer' at the Indian National Congress in Calcutta.

1918 Rowlatt Act against Sedition provokes Gandhi's first civil disobedience campaign.

Tagore's eldest daughter Bela dies.

German-Indian Conspiracy Trial in San Francisco implicates him: he sends a telegram to President Wilson asking for protection 'against such lying calumny'.

1919 Gen. Reginald Dyer's Amritsar Massacre; Tagore returns his knighthood.

1920 Death of Tilak leaves Gandhi undisputed leader of the nationalist movement. Tagore travels to London, France, Holland, America.

1921 Back to London, France, Switzerland, Germany, Sweden, Germany again, Austria, Czechoslovakia.

After meeting with Gandhi in Calcutta, Tagore detaches himself from the Swaraj (home rule) campaign.

Visva-Bharati, his university at Santiniketan, inaugurated.

1922 Gandhi sentenced to six years imprisonment.

Tagore tours West and South India.

1923 Congress party under Motilal Nehru and C. R. Das ends its boycott of elections to the legislatures established by the Government of India Act (1919).

1924 Tagore travels to China and Japan.

After only two months at home, sails for South America: stays with Victoria Ocampo in Buenos Aires.

1925 Returns via Italy.

Gandhi visits Santiniketan; Tagore again refuses to be actively involved in Swaraj, or in the charka (spinning) cult.

Bengal Criminal Law Amendment Act crushes new terrorist campaign in Bengal.

1926 Tagore travels to Italy, Switzerland (staying with Romain Rolland at Villeneuve), Austria, England, Norway, Sweden, Denmark, Germany (meets Einstein), Czechoslovakia, Bulgaria, Greece, Egypt.

1927 Extensive tour of South-east Asia.

1928 Starts painting.

1929 To Canada, Japan, Saigon.

1930 To England (via France) to deliver Hibbert Lectures at Manchester College, Oxford (*The Religion of Man*); to Germany, Switzerland, Russia, back to Germany, USA.

Exhibitions of his paintings in Birmingham, London and several European capitals.

Gandhi's 'salt-march' from Ahmedabad to the coast inaugurates new civil disobedience campaign.

1932 Tagore travels (by air) to Iran and Iraq.

His only grandson Nitindra dies.

Gandhi declares fast-unto-death in jail in Poona; later breaks his fast with Tagore at his bedside.

1934–6 Tours of Ceylon and India with a dance-troupe from Santiniketan.

1935 Government of India Act emerges from Round Table Conferences of 1930–32, with all-India Federation and provincial autonomy as its main aims.

1937 Tagore delivers Convocation Address to Calcutta University, in Bengali.

Starts Department of Chinese Studies at Visva-Bharati.

Congress Party ministries formed in most states.

Tagore falls seriously ill in September.

1939 Congress ministries resign on grounds that the British Government has failed to make an acceptable declaration of its war aims.

1940 Tagore's last meeting with Gandhi, at Santiniketan.

Death of C. F. Andrews, Tagore's staunch friend and supporter at Santiniketan.

Oxford University holds special Convocation at Santiniketan to confer Doctorate on Tagore.

Muslim League under Jinnah demands separate state for Muslims.

1941 Tagore dies in Calcutta.

1942 Congress Party calls on Britain to 'quit India' immediately.

1946 Congress forms interim Government under Jawaharlal Nehru.

1947 Viscount Mountbatten announces partition: India and Pakistan become independent dominions.

1948 Assassination of Gandhi.

1950 India is declared a Republic.

Introduction

Georg Lukács condemned *The Home and the World* as 'a petit bourgeois yarn of the shoddiest kind' and said of Tagore that he was 'a wholly insignificant figure ... whose creative powers do not even stretch to a decent pamphlet. He lacks the imagination even to calumniate convincingly and effectively, as Dostoevsky, say, partly succeeded in doing in his counter-revolutionary novel, *Possessed* ... He survives by sticking scraps of the *Upanishads* and the *Bhagvadgita* into his works amid the sluggish flow of his own tediousness ...'

E. M. Forster, incapable of such savage vituperation, said more mildly but equally devastatingly that 'the World proved to be a sphere ... for a boarding-house flirtation that masks itself in patriotic talk'. He deplored the novel's language for its 'Babu sentences' and said that Tagore 'meant the wife to be seduced by the World, which is, with all its sins, a tremendous lover; she is actually seduced by a West Kensingtonian Babu'.

Such criticism has to be taken into account because it was levelled at the winner of the Nobel Prize for Literature, because Tagore had often been compared to Tolstoy as well as considered a precursor of Gandhi; Romain Rolland had described a meeting between Tagore and Gandhi as one between 'a philosopher and an apostle, a St Paul and a Plato'. Nevertheless, when *The Home and the World* was published in India in 1915 it was attacked by readers who thought it betrayed Tagore's essential pusillanimity and insincerity in fighting colonial rule and felt that he wrote it to curry favour with the rulers – a gibe that was given the lie when Tagore renounced his knighthood in protest against the massacre at Amritsar in 1919.

It is unlikely that the novel itself, as a piece of fiction, created such a furore. The truth is that it was itself a participant in the political storm that had gathered over India in the first decade of the century and of which Tagore was at the vortex. If it still reads as highly controversial matter, nearly forty years after the end of colonial rule in India and almost eighty years since the time in which the novel was set, it is because it has remained so astonishingly relevant. Indeed it has become increasingly so as the terrorist movement that Tagore described when it was in its infancy as a movement of romantic idealism, impractical and misdirected, has developed into a tough, utterly professional system and a threat in all parts of the world.

It would be unfair to read the book merely as a romantic novel, without informing oneself of the historical facts of the period to which it belongs. Following Lord Curzon's arbitrary division of Bengal in 1905, under the diabolically successful British tactic of 'divide and rule', a protest movement was born. This was Swadeshi, the policy of boycotting British goods with the aim of encouraging indigenous industry and cottage crafts. Tagore welcomed the movement and was an active participant – he wrote fiery pamphlets in its favour, composed patriotic songs that swept Bengal then and are still sung today (Ezra Pound was not far from the truth when he said, 'Tagore has sung Bengal into a nation'), and in the days of his youthful enthusiasm even played a part in establishing a weaving centre and a matchstick factory, though he later admitted in his autobiography that 'the matches refused to light and the loom expired after manufacturing a solitary towel'. Yet the sight of excited crowds gloating over bonfires of imported cloth sickened him; he pitied the students who were hoodwinked into giving up their schools and colleges to become followers of dubious political leaders; the riots horrified him and he began to feel there was something basically wrong with the movement.

Introduction

To his dismay it proved – unlike the Gandhism of a later age – an elitist movement, run by the educated and landowning classes, the *bhadralok* of Bengal, who had no connection with and little consideration for the labouring classes. Tagore felt that the boycott of cheap British goods in favour of expensive and poorly made Indian goods was harming the interests of the poor, to whom Swadeshi was an abstract, distant and meaningless term. The sufferers were chiefly Muslim peasants and traders who became resentful of wealthy Hindu landowners and politicians who could easily afford the luxury of idealism in the form of bonfires into which British goods were flung. From sulky non-participation they graduated to protest through riots and murders, and Tagore was horrified to find that the movement that had been conceived to fight the communalist forces set free by the British had itself become violently communal. At this stage he withdrew from the fray; his critics called this a desertion and a betrayal of the cause, and denied that the boycott of English goods was affecting the poor adversely, since these were goods they could not in any case afford. Instead he occupied himself with constructive work in the villages on his central Bengal estates and educational experiments in his school at Santiniketan. The historian Sumit Sarkar has pointed out that in those early years of the century he 'anticipated almost every basic principle of what later became a nationwide mass movement of non-violent non-cooperation under the dynamic leadership of Mahatma Gandhi'.

Of course Tagore was no Gandhi, having neither the latter's genius for leadership nor his strategic ability. His disillusionment with the cause and his reply to his critics were embodied in the novel *The Home and the World*, which illustrates the battle he had had to fight in his own mind, and the extent to which he had both won and lost.

It is easy to see that Tagore felt the greatest empathy with his Tolstoyan hero, Nikhil, a wealthy landowner who is altruistic, benevolent, rational and Westernized in his ideas, but draws back from 'progress' as exemplified by Sandip, the revolutionary who stops at nothing – neither robbery nor murder – to achieve his ends. Nikhil is a highly idealized portrait of an enlightened humanist who faces hostility, isolation and ridicule because of his opposition to the violent means employed by the more charismatic but unscrupulous revolutionary. He might be almost too good to be believable if Tagore did not manage to convince one of his undeniable decency.

In his bitterness against the terrorist movement, Tagore created in Sandip a scoundrel so blatant that even a fervent admirer, William Rothenstein, gave away in a letter to Tagore his true if unconscious reaction in the words: 'Your book is a masterpiece of simple and uncompromising statement. And you have done the whole thing with a simple box of figures – not more than a Punch and Judy showman uses for his own little drama.' Sandip is vain, arrogant, bullying, greedy and nihilistic; he resembles nothing so much as the conventional blackguard of the Indian stage or the Bombay cinema, stroking his handlebar moustache as he gloats over a bag of gold and a cowering maiden. Yet Lukács made a grave error in thinking him 'a contemptible caricature of Gandhi'; Tagore was one of Gandhi's earliest admirers, and Gandhi was, of course, always a votary of non-violence who never countenanced terrorism for any reason. Nor was Sandip by any stretch of the imagination a representative of those crusading romantics who were, Lukács thought, 'without question motivated by the purest idealism and self-sacrifice'. Tagore offended both by painting Nikhil in tones of unalloyed gold and depicting Sandip in an unrelieved shade of black. Readers tended not to notice that Nikhil was by no means a conservative, being led by ideas that were rational and progressive, or that Sandip was not only immoral but also attractively virile and charismatic.

The novel is a dramatization of the tension between the two, representing the clash between the old and the new, realism and idealism, the means and the end, good and evil. The conflict comes out into the open when its focus becomes Nikhil's wife Bimala (extraordinary that Forster should have read her relationship with Sandip as 'a boarding-house flirtation'). It is clear that the figure of Bimala represents Bengal to Tagore. She is referred to frequently as 'Mother' by one character or the other, suggesting that she is Durga, the mother-goddess and favourite deity of Bengal. Her husband offers her gold, jewels and tender love; Sandip offers his worship; and revolutionaries bow before her and touch her feet in obeisance. When Tagore writes of how her adoring husband begs Bimala to leave the *zenana* to which custom has kept her confined and come out into 'the world', he seems to be coaxing Bengal out of the orthodoxy and superstition he so hated into the light of the modern age, to make her a fit deity for independent India. (In a film Satyajit Ray has made of the novel, this is one of the most significant scenes, played almost in slow motion.) Once she emerges into the outer world of which she is so utterly ignorant and where she is so disastrously unsure, she betrays Nikhil and his confidence in her by not merely throwing herself passionately into the Swadeshi movement but also falling in love with its proponent, Sandip. Nikhil's elderly 'master', who watches this development with pain, and Nikhil's widowed sister-in-law, who treats him like a beloved younger brother, urge him to send Sandip away before more harm is done; but Nikhil refrains from doing so, as he knows Bimala's feelings would continue to cling to Sandip if he were banished. He wants her to choose between the two of them, freely and without coercion, and return to him of her own accord or not at all.

The drama comes to a head over the matter of a small fortune that Sandip demands of Bimala as a way of establishing his power over her. This leads to disastrous complications, and the novel ends in scenes of unbearable tension and horrific violence. Bimala realizes now that the path Sandip has shown her is evil; she draws back from it, but by then it is tragically too late.

A dramatic tale, yet not particularly dramatic in the telling. Tagore was a prophet and a teacher rather than a novelist – even his biographer, Krishna Kripalani, admitted that 'Tagore was no Tolstoy or Balzac ... the poet, the singer and the teacher constantly meddled with the novelist' – and it was the idea that allured him, not the plot. Therefore events with highly dramatic potential are set aside in a line or two, action takes place off-stage, as it were, and whole pages are given over to rhetorical display, presented with such rococo elaboration as to make the novel seem like an ornate edifice of Victorianism. It was from these passages that Forster unearthed such 'Babu sentences' as 'Passion is beautiful and pure as the lily that rises out of slimy soil; it rises superior to its defilement and needs no Pears' soap to wash it clean' – and there may be readers who find it difficult to proceed with such convoluted prose. The blame can be laid upon the translation – when John Masefield read some of Tagore's plays, he felt they would fail if staged because, as he said, 'Our people could not get effects out of dialogue of that kind; the plant won't transplant.' Doubtless a more modern and colloquial translation could be made to suit the altered tastes of the times, but the truth is that Bengali is a highly rhetorical language. Bengalis are as given to impassioned and extravagant speech as they are to radical politics, and Tagore wrote political essays from which he took whole sentences to place in the mouth of the central character, Nikhil. Clearly it was to him a natural, not a contrived or literary, language. It belonged to its period, the Victorian. It was of a piece with such architecture as the Victoria Terminus in Bombay, and with the dark, looming furniture, fussy costumes and domestic trappings of that age, and must be seen in this context.

In spite of this, and in spite of the predominance and suffocating weight of so much polemic, there are extraordinary flashes of light and colour, as if created by the striking of flints, as well as touches of tenderness and childishness which lighten the lowering clouds of the prevalent mood of disaster and give the novel variation and vivacity. Bimala appears in a white sari with a gold border, or her 'earthen-red sari with a broad blood-red border'; 'her complexion is dark, but it is the lustrous darkness of a sword-blade, keen and scintillating'. The 'little red ribbon which peeps through the luxuriant masses of her hair, with its flash of secret longing, it is the lolling tongue of the red storm cloud'; and there is always the auspicious vermilion mark on her forehead. The reader can appreciate the ardour in the words, 'It seemed to me that the gold border of her sari was her own inner fire flaming out and twining around her. There is the flame we want, visible fire!' Sandip is described in tones of darkness, sporadically and luridly lit: 'Sandip's hungry eyes burnt like lamps of worship before my shrine'; 'the sovereigns shone out. And in a moment the black covering seemed to be lifted from Sandip's countenance also.' Nikhil sorrowfully says of himself, 'I am not a flame, only a black coal, which has gone out. That is what the story of my life shows – my row of lamps has remained unlit.' It is significant that Satyajit Ray begins his film of the novel with flickers of fire upon a dark screen.

Tagore's feeling for nature is so deep and intense that it is more than a literary device. It is entirely natural for him to use it continually as a metaphor for human actions and emotions, as when Bimala says of herself, with such acute self-perception, 'So long I had been like a small river at the border of a village. But the tide came up from the sea, and my breast heaved; my banks gave way and the great drum-beats of the sea were echoed in my mad current.'

Whenever Tagore writes of the common people of his beloved land, the Bengal countryside, the prose takes on a simplicity and directness absent from his account of the aristocratic protagonists. Panchu – who suffers equally at the hands of wealthy moneylenders and the fiery revolutionaries who profess to be his redeemers – is a minor character in the novel, merely one of the hundreds of peasants on Nikhil's vast estates, but the merest reference to him seems to open windows and let in fresh air from the rice fields and mango groves outside. Again, in a passage of pure lyricism Nikhil recalls the childhood games he played with his sister-in-law when she entered his home as a bride of nine years: how he would steal delicacies from the storeroom for her dolls' wedding feast, or fetch green guavas off the trees for her to cut and spice for him; how she would give him secret offerings of treats behind their elders' backs. Here Tagore clearly had in mind his own relationship with his adored sister-in-law, Kadambari Devi. One of the most tragic events of Tagore's life was her youthful suicide; it gave his feeling for her a particular intensity and poignancy that illuminates these lines. The relationship between Bimala and Sandip's young disciple, Amulya, has about it a similarly pure radiance. Such passages have a naturalness to them, a simplicity and truthfulness that lighten the sombre drama at the heart of the novel and make it breathe with life. There is nothing static, earthbound or lifeless about it, for all its weightiness; it has the complexity and tragic dimensions of Tagore's own times, and ours.

ANITA DESAI
1985

Further Reading

Works by Tagore

Only books that are in print or easily available in libraries are listed here. For a survey article that includes a list of older translations, see *Encyclopedia of Literary Translation into English*, 2 vols., ed. Olive Classe (London and Chicago: Fitzroy Dearborn Publishers, 2000). For more bibliography, and information about Tagore's Bengali writings, see the Further Reading lists in *Selected Poems* and *Selected Short Stories* of Tagore (Penguin, 2005).

Collected Poems and Plays (London: Macmillan, 1936). This book comprises the English translations that Tagore did himself, but without any annotation or information.

The English Writings of Rabindranath Tagore, ed. Sisir Kumar Das (New Delhi: Sahitya Akademi, Vol. 1 (*Poems*), 1994; Vol. 2 (*Plays, Stories, Essays*), 1996; Vol. 3 (*A Miscellany*), 1996. This edition is richly introduced and annotated.

Glimpses of Bengal: Selected Letters, newly trans. after Surendranath Tagore's translation of 1921 by Krishna Dutta and Andrew Robinson and with an introduction by Andrew Robinson (London: Papermac, 1991).

Gora (novel), trans. Sujit Mukherjee, with an introduction by Meenakshi Mukherjee (New Delhi: Sahitya Akademi, 1997).

He (fantasy fiction), trans. Kalyan Kundu and Anthony Loynes (London: The Tagore Centre UK, 2003).

My Reminiscences, Surendranath Tagore's translation of 1912, revised and introduced by Andrew Robinson (London: Papermac, 1991).

Nationalism (lectures), new edn with an introduction by E. P. Thompson (London: Papermac, 1991).

Quartet (novella), trans. Kaiser Haq (Oxford: Heinemann, 1993).

Rabindranath Tagore: An Anthology, ed. Krishna Dutta and Andrew Robinson (London: Picador, 1997).

Selected Poems, trans. with an introduction by William Radice (Harmondsworth: Penguin Books, 1985, revised 1987, 1993; new edns 1994, 2005; Delhi: Penguin Books India, 1995).

Selected Short Stories (various translators), ed. Sukanta Chaudhuri (New Delhi: Oxford University Press, 2000).

Selected Short Stories, trans. with an introduction by William Radice (Harmondsworth: Penguin Books, 1991, revised 1994; new edn 2005; Delhi: Penguin Books India, 1995).

Selected Stories, trans. Krishna Dutta and Mary Lago (London: Macmillan, 1991).

Three Companions (novellas), trans. Sujit Mukherjee (Hyderabad and London: Sangam Books, by arrangement with Orient Longman, 1992).

About Tagore

The list is limited mainly to recent books and articles. Fuller bibliographies can be found in the books by Krishna Dutta and Andrew Robinson.

Chatterjee, Bhabatosh, *Rabindranath Tagore and Modern Sensibility* (New Delhi: Oxford University Press, 1996).

Chaudhuri, Nirad C., *Thy Hand, Great Anarch! India 1921–1952* (London: The Hogarth Press, 1987), especially Book 2, Chapter 5, pp. 595–636: 'Tagore; the lost great man of India'.

Das Gupta, Uma (ed.), *A Difficult Friendship: Letters of Edward Thompson and Rabindranath Tagore 1913–1940* (New Delhi: Oxford University Press, 2003).

Datta, P. K. (ed.), *Rabindranath Tagore's* The Home and the

World: *A Critical Companion* (New Delhi: Permanent Black, 2003). A first-rate collection of esssays.

Dutta, Krishna and Andrew Robinson, *Rabindranath Tagore: The Myriad-Minded Man* (London: Bloomsbury, 1995; New York: St Martin's Press, 1996).

Dutta, Krishna and Andrew Robinson (eds.), *Selected Letters of Rabindranath Tagore*, with a foreword by Amartya Sen (Cambridge and New York: Cambridge University Press, 1997).

Hogan, Patrick Colm and Lalita Pandit (eds.), *Rabindranath Tagore: Universality and Tradition* (Cranbury, NJ, London, UK, and Mississauga, Ontario: Associated University Presses, 2003). Includes two essays on *The Home and the World*. Kathleen Koljian's insights into the links between Bimala and Bengali Shaktism are particularly useful.

Kripalani, Krishna, *Rabindranath Tagore: A Biography* (London: Oxford University Press, and New York: Grove Press, 1962; revised edn, Calcutta: Visva-Bharati, 1980).

Kundu, Kalyan, Sakti Bhattacharya and Kalyan Sircar (eds.), *Imagining Tagore: Rabindranath Tagore and the British Press (1912–1941)* (Kolkata: Sahitya Samsad in collaboration with The Tagore Centre UK, 2000).

Lago, Mary M. (ed.), *Imperfect Encounter: Letters of William Rothenstein and Rabindranath Tagore 1911–1941* (Cambridge, Mass.: Harvard University Press, 1972).

Radice, William, 'Rabindranath Tagore', in *Oxford Dictionary of National Biography*, Vol. 53 (Oxford: Oxford University Press, 2004).

Robinson, Andrew, *Satyajit Ray: The Inner Eye* (London: André Deutsch, 1989).

Sahitya Akademi (ed.), *Rabindranath Tagore 1861–1961: A Centenary Volume* (New Delhi: Sahitya Akademi, 1961, reprinted 1986). Introduction by Jawaharlal Nehru; memoirs by several of Tagore's associates; essays on all aspects of Tagore's life and work; essays on Tagore in other lands; bibliography of Tagore's Bengali and English works (with dates); chronicle of his life compiled by Prabhat Kumar Mukherjee (Tagore's biographer in Bengali) and Kshitis Roy.

Seton, Marie, *Portrait of a Director: Satyajit Ray* (London: Dobson Books, 1971; new edn with an afterword by Indrani Majumdar, New Delhi: Penguin Books India, 2003).

Thompson, Edward, *Rabindranath Tagore: Poet and Dramatist* (London and New York: Oxford University Press, 1926; second edn 1948; new edn with an introduction by Harish Trivedi, New Delhi: Oxford University Press, 1989).

The
Home
and the
World

Chapter One

※

Bimala's Story

I

MOTHER, today there comes back to mind the vermilion mark[1] at the parting of your hair, the *sari*[2] which you used to wear, with its wide red border, and those wonderful eyes of yours, full of depth and peace. They came at the start of my life's journey, like the first streak of dawn, giving me golden provision to carry me on my way.

The sky which gives light is blue, and my mother's face was dark, but she had the radiance of holiness, and her beauty would put to shame all the vanity of the beautiful.

Everyone says that I resemble my mother. In my childhood I used to resent this. It made me angry with my mirror. I thought that it was God's unfairness which was wrapped round my limbs – that my dark features were not my due, but had come to me by some misunderstanding. All that remained for me to ask of my God in reparation was, that I might grow up to be a model of what woman should be, as one reads it in some epic poem.

When the proposal came for my marriage, an astrologer was sent, who consulted my palm and said, 'This girl has good signs. She will become an ideal wife.'

And all the women who heard it said: 'No wonder, for she resembles her mother.'

I was married into a Rajah's house. When I was a child, I was quite familiar with the description of the Prince of

1. The mark of Hindu wifehood and the symbol of all the devotion that it implies.
2. The *sari* is the dress of the Hindu woman.

17

the fairy story. But my husband's face was not of a kind that one's imagination would place in fairyland. It was dark, even as mine was. The feeling of shrinking, which I had about my own lack of physical beauty, was lifted a little; at the same time a touch of regret was left lingering in my heart.

But when the physical appearance evades the scrutiny of our senses and enters the sanctuary of our hearts, then it can forget itself. I know, from my childhood's experience, how devotion is beauty itself, in its inner aspect. When my mother arranged the different fruits, carefully peeled by her own loving hands, on the white stone plate, and gently waved her fan to drive away the flies while my father sat down to his meals, her service would lose itself in a beauty which passed beyond outward forms. Even in my infancy I could feel its power. It transcended all debates, or doubts, or calculations: it was pure music.

I distinctly remember after my marriage, when, early in the morning, I would cautiously and silently get up and take the dust[1] of my husband's feet without waking him, how at such moments I could feel the vermilion mark upon my forehead shining out like the morning star.

One day, he happened to awake, and smiled as he asked me: 'What is that, Bimala? What *are* you doing?'

I can never forget the shame of being detected by him. He might possibly have thought that I was trying to earn merit secretly. But no, no! That had nothing to do with merit. It was my woman's heart, which must worship in order to love.

My father-in-law's house was old in dignity from the days of the *Badshahs*. Some of its manners were of the Moguls and Pathans, some of its customs of Manu and Parashar. But my husband was absolutely modern. He was the first of the house to go through a college course and take his M.A. degree. His elder brother had died young, of drink, and had left no children. My husband did not drink and was not given to dissipation. So foreign to the family was this abstinence, that to many it hardly seemed decent! Purity, they imagined, was

1. Taking the dust of the feet is a formal offering of reverence and is done by lightly touching the feet of the revered one and then one's own head with the same hand. The wife does not ordinarily do this to the husband.

only becoming in those on whom fortune had not smiled. It is the moon which has room for stains, not the stars.

My husband's parents had died long ago, and his old grandmother was mistress of the house. My husband was the apple of her eye, the jewel on her bosom. And so he never met with much difficulty in overstepping any of the ancient usages. When he brought in Miss Gilby, to teach me and be my companion, he stuck to his resolve in spite of the poison secreted by all the wagging tongues at home and outside.

My husband had then just got through his B.A. examination and was reading for his M.A. degree; so he had to stay in Calcutta to attend college. He used to write to me almost every day, a few lines only, and simple words, but his bold, round handwriting would look up into my face, oh, so tenderly! I kept his letters in a sandalwood box and covered them every day with the flowers I gathered in the garden.

At that time the Prince of the fairy tale had faded, like the moon in the morning light. I had the Prince of my real world enthroned in my heart. I was his queen. I had my seat by his side. But my real joy was, that my true place was at his feet.

Since then, I have been educated, and introduced to the modern age in its own language, and therefore these words that I write seem to blush with shame in their prose setting. Except for my acquaintance with this modern standard of life, I should know, quite naturally, that just as my being born a woman was not in my own hands, so the element of devotion in woman's love is not like a hackneyed passage quoted from a romantic poem to be piously written down in round hand in a schoolgirl's copy-book.

But my husband would not give me any opportunity for worship. That was his greatness. They are cowards who claim absolute devotion from their wives as their right; that is a humiliation for both.

His love for me seemed to overflow my limits by its flood of wealth and service. But my necessity was more for giving than for receiving; for love is a vagabond, who can make his flowers bloom in the wayside dust, better than in the crystal jars kept in the drawing-room.

My husband could not break completely with the old-time traditions which prevailed in our family. It was difficult, therefore, for us to meet at any hour of the day we pleased.[1] I knew exactly the time that he could come to me, and therefore our meeting had all the care of loving preparation. It was like the rhyming of a poem; it had to come through the path of the metre.

After finishing the day's work and taking my afternoon bath, I would do up my hair and renew my vermilion mark and put on my *sari*, carefully crinkled; and then, bringing back my body and mind from all distractions of household duties, I would dedicate it at this special hour, with special ceremonies, to one individual. That time, each day, with him was short; but it was infinite.

My husband used to say, that man and wife are equal in love because of their equal claim on each other. I never argued the point with him, but my heart said that devotion never stands in the way of true equality; it only raises the level of the ground of meeting. Therefore the joy of the higher equality remains permanent; it never slides down to the vulgar level of triviality.

My beloved, it was worthy of you that you never expected worship from me. But if you had accepted it, you would have done me a real service. You showed your love by decorating me, by educating me, by giving me what I asked for, and what I did not. I have seen what depth of love there was in your eyes when you gazed at me. I have known the secret sigh of pain you suppressed in your love for me. You loved my body as if it were a flower of paradise. You loved my whole nature as if it had been given you by some rare providence.

Such lavish devotion made me proud to think that the wealth was all my own which drove you to my gate. But vanity such as this only checks the flow of free surrender in a woman's love. When I sit on the queen's throne and claim homage, then the claim only goes on magnifying itself; it is never satisfied. Can there be any real happiness for a woman

1. It would not be reckoned good form for the husband to be continually going into the zenana, except at particular hours for meals or rest.

in merely feeling that she has power over a man? To surrender one's pride in devotion is woman's only salvation.

It comes back to me today how, in the days of our happiness, the fires of envy sprung up all around us. That was only natural, for had I not stepped into my good fortune by a mere chance, and without deserving it? But providence does not allow a run of luck to last for ever, unless its debt of honour be fully paid, day by day, through many a long day, and thus made secure. God may grant us gifts, but the merit of being able to take and hold them must be our own. Alas for the boons that slip through unworthy hands!

My husband's grandmother and mother were both renowned for their beauty. And my widowed sister-in-law was also of a beauty rarely to be seen. When, in turn, fate left them desolate, the grandmother vowed she would not insist on having beauty for her remaining grandson when he married. Only the auspicious marks with which I was endowed gained me an entry into this family – otherwise, I had no claim to be here.

In this house of luxury, but few of its ladies had received their meed of respect. They had, however, got used to the ways of the family, and managed to keep their heads above water, buoyed up by their dignity as *Ranis* of an ancient house, in spite of their daily tears being drowned in the foam of wine, and by the tinkle of the dancing girls' anklets. Was the credit due to me that my husband did not touch liquor, nor squander his manhood in the markets of woman's flesh? What charm did I know to soothe the wild and wandering mind of men? It was my good luck, nothing else. For fate proved utterly callous to my sister-in-law. Her festivity died out, while yet the evening was early, leaving the light of her beauty shining in vain over empty halls – burning and burning, with no accompanying music!

His sister-in-law affected a contempt for my husband's modern notions. How absurd to keep the family ship, laden with all the weight of its time-honoured glory, sailing under the colours of his slip of a girl-wife alone! Often have I felt the lash of scorn. 'A thief who had stolen a husband's love!' 'A sham hidden in the shamelessness of her new-fangled finery!'

The many-coloured garments of modern fashion with which my husband loved to adorn me roused jealous wrath. 'Is not she ashamed to make a show-window of herself – and with her looks, too!'

My husband was aware of all this, but his gentleness knew no bounds. He used to implore me to forgive her.

I remember I once told him: 'Women's minds are so petty, so crooked!' 'Like the feet of Chinese women,' he replied. 'Has not the pressure of society cramped them into pettiness and crookedness? They are but pawns of the fate which gambles with them. What responsibility have they of their own?'

My sister-in-law never failed to get from my husband whatever she wanted. He did not stop to consider whether her requests were right or reasonable. But what exasperated me most was that she was not grateful for this. I had promised my husband that I would not talk back at her, but this set me raging all the more, inwardly. I used to feel that goodness has a limit, which, if passed, somehow seems to make men cowardly. Shall I tell the whole truth? I have often wished that my husband had the manliness to be a little less good.

My sister-in-law, the Bara Rani,[1] was still young and had no pretensions to saintliness. Rather, her talk and jest and laugh inclined to be forward. The young maids with whom she surrounded herself were also impudent to a degree. But there was none to gainsay her – for was not this the custom of the house? It seemed to me that my good fortune in having a stainless husband was a special eyesore to her. He, however, felt more the sorrow of her lot than the defects of her character.

1. *Bara* = Senior; *Chota* = Junior. In joint families of rank, though the widows remain entitled only to a life-interest in their husbands' share, their rank remains to them according to seniority, and the titles 'Senior' and 'Junior' continue to distinguish the elder and younger branches, even though the junior branch be the one in power.

II

My husband was very eager to take me out of *purdah*.[1]

One day I said to him: 'What do I want with the outside world?'

'The outside world may want you,' he replied.

'If the outside world has got on so long without me, it may go on for some time longer. It need not pine to death for want of me.'

'Let it perish, for all I care! That is not troubling me. I am thinking about myself.'

'Oh, indeed. Tell me what about yourself?'

My husband was silent, with a smile.

I knew his way, and protested at once: 'No, no, you are not going to run away from me like that! I want to have this out with you.'

'Can one ever finish a subject with words?'

'Do stop speaking in riddles. Tell me . . .'

'What I want is, that I should have you, and you should have me, more fully in the outside world. That is where we are still in debt to each other.'

'Is anything wanting, then, in the love we have here at home?'

'Here you are wrapped up in me. You know neither what you have, nor what you want.'

'I cannot bear to hear you talk like this.'

'I would have you come into the heart of the outer world and meet reality. Merely going on with your household duties, living all your life in the world of household conventions and the drudgery of household tasks – you were not made for that! If we meet, and recognize each other, in the real world, then only will our love be true.'

'If there be any drawback here to our full recognition of each other, then I have nothing to say. But as for myself, I feel no want.'

'Well, even if the drawback is only on my side, why shouldn't you help to remove it?'

1. The seclusion of the zenana, and all the customs peculiar to it, are designated by the general term 'Purdah', which means Screen.

Such discussions repeatedly occurred. One day he said: 'The greedy man who is fond of his fish stew has no compunction in cutting up the fish according to his need. But the man who loves the fish wants to enjoy it in the water; and if that is impossible he waits on the bank; and even if he comes back home without a sight of it he has the consolation of knowing that the fish is all right. Perfect gain is the best of all; but if that is impossible, then the next best gain is perfect losing.'

I never liked the way my husband had of talking on this subject, but that is not the reason why I refused to leave the zenana. His grandmother was still alive. My husband had filled more than a hundred and twenty per cent of the house with the twentieth century, against her taste; but she had borne it uncomplaining. She would have borne it, likewise, if the daughter-in-law[1] of the Rajah's house had left its seclusion. She was even prepared for this happening. But I did not consider it important enough to give her the pain of it. I have read in books that we are called 'caged birds'. I cannot speak for others, but I had so much in this cage of mine that there was not room for it in the universe – at least that is what I then felt.

The grandmother, in her old age, was very fond of me. At the bottom of her fondness was the thought that, with the conspiracy of favourable stars which attended me, I had been able to attract my husband's love. Were not men naturally inclined to plunge downwards? None of the others, for all their beauty, had been able to prevent their husbands going headlong into the burning depths which consumed and destroyed them. She believed that I had been the means of extinguishing this fire, so deadly to the men of the family. So she kept me in the shelter of her bosom, and trembled if I was in the least bit unwell.

His grandmother did not like the dresses and ornaments my husband brought from European shops to deck me with. But she reflected: 'Men will have some absurd hobby or other, which is sure to be expensive. It is no use trying to check

1. The prestige of the daughter-in-law is of the first importance in a Hindu household of rank.

their extravagance; one is glad enough if they stop short of ruin. If my Nikhil had not been busy dressing up his wife there is no knowing whom else he might have spent his money on!' So whenever any new dress of mine arrived she used to send for my husband and make merry over it.

Thus it came about that it was her taste which changed. The influence of the modern age fell so strongly upon her, that her evenings refused to pass if I did not tell her stories out of English books.

After his grandmother's death, my husband wanted me to go and live with him in Calcutta. But I could not bring myself to do that. Was not this our House, which she had kept under her sheltering care through all her trials and troubles? Would not a curse come upon me if I deserted it and went off to town? This was the thought that kept me back, as her empty seat reproachfully looked up at me. That noble lady had come into this house at the age of eight, and had died in her seventy-ninth year. She had not spent a happy life. Fate had hurled shaft after shaft at her breast, only to draw out more and more the imperishable spirit within. This great house was hallowed with her tears. What should I do in the dust of Calcutta, away from it?

My husband's idea was that this would be a good opportunity for leaving to my sister-in-law the consolation of ruling over the household, giving our life, at the same time, more room to branch out in Calcutta. That is just where my difficulty came in. She had worried my life out, she ill brooked my husband's happiness, and for this she was to be rewarded! And what of the day when we should have to come back here? Should I then get back my seat at the head?

'What do you want with that seat?' my husband would say. 'Are there not more precious things in life?'

Men never understand these things. They have their nests in the outside world; they little know the whole of what the household stands for. In these matters they ought to follow womanly guidance. Such were my thoughts at that time.

I felt the real point was, that one ought to stand up for one's rights. To go away, and leave everything in the hands of the enemy, would be nothing short of owning defeat.

But why did not my husband compel me to go with him to Calcutta? I know the reason. He did not use his power, just because he had it.

III

If one had to fill in, little by little, the gap between day and night, it would take an eternity to do it. But the sun rises and the darkness is dispelled – a moment is sufficient to overcome an infinite distance.

One day there came the new era of *Swadeshi*[1] in Bengal; but as to how it happened, we had no distinct vision. There was no gradual slope connecting the past with the present. For that reason, I imagine, the new epoch came in like a flood, breaking down the dykes and sweeping all our prudence and fear before it. We had no time even to think about, or understand, what had happened, or what was about to happen.

My sight and my mind, my hopes and my desires, became red with the passion of this new age. Though, up to this time, the walls of the home – which was the ultimate world to my mind – remained unbroken, yet I stood looking over into the distance, and I heard a voice from the far horizon, whose meaning was not perfectly clear to me, but whose call went straight to my heart.

From the time my husband had been a college student he had been trying to get the things required by our people produced in our own country. There are plenty of date trees in our district. He tried to invent an apparatus for extracting the juice and boiling it into sugar and treacle. I heard that it was a great success, only it extracted more money than juice. After a while he came to the conclusion that our attempts at reviving our industries were not succeeding for want of a bank of our own. He was, at the time, trying to teach me political economy. This alone would not have done much harm, but he also took it into his head to teach his countrymen ideas of thrift, so as to pave the way for a bank; and then he

---

1. The Nationalist movement, which began more as an economic than a political one, having as its main object the encouragement of indigenous industries.

actually started a small bank. Its high rate of interest, which made the villagers flock so enthusiastically to put in their money, ended by swamping the bank altogether.

The old officers of the estate felt troubled and frightened. There was jubilation in the enemy's camp. Of all the family, only my husband's grandmother remained unmoved. She would scold me, saying: 'Why are you all plaguing him so? Is it the fate of the estate that is worrying you? How many times have I seen this estate in the hands of the court receiver! Are men like women? Men are born spendthrifts and only know how to waste. Look here, child, count yourself fortunate that your husband is not wasting himself as well!'

My husband's list of charities was a long one. He would assist to the bitter end of utter failure anyone who wanted to invent a new loom or rice-husking machine. But what annoyed me most was the way that Sandip Babu used to fleece him on the pretext of *Swadeshi* work. Whenever he wanted to start a newspaper, or travel about preaching the Cause, or take a change of air by the advice of his doctor, my husband would unquestioningly supply him with the money. This was over and above the regular living allowance which Sandip Babu also received from him. The strangest part of it was that my husband and Sandip Babu did not agree in their opinions.

As soon as the *Swadeshi* storm reached my blood, I said to my husband: 'I must burn all my foreign clothes.'

'Why burn them?' said he. 'You need not wear them as long as you please.'

'As long as I please! Not in this life . . .'

'Very well, do not wear them for the rest of your life, then. But why this bonfire business?'

'Would you thwart me in my resolve?'

'What I want to say is this: Why not try to build up something? You should not waste even a tenth part of your energies in this destructive excitement.'

'Such excitement will give us the energy to build.'

'That is as much as to say, that you cannot light the house unless you set fire to it.'

Then there came another trouble. When Miss Gilby first

27

came to our house there was a great flutter, which afterwards calmed down when they got used to her. Now the whole thing was stirred up afresh. I had never bothered myself before as to whether Miss Gilby was European or Indian, but I began to do so now. I said to my husband: 'We must get rid of Miss Gilby.'

He kept silent.

I talked to him wildly, and he went away sad at heart.

After a fit of weeping, I felt in a more reasonable mood when we met at night. 'I cannot,' my husband said, 'look upon Miss Gilby through a mist of abstraction, just because she is English. Cannot you get over the barrier of her name after such a long acquaintance? Cannot you realize that she loves you?'

I felt a little ashamed and replied with some sharpness: 'Let her remain. I am not over anxious to send her away.'

And Miss Gilby remained.

But one day I was told that she had been insulted by a young fellow on her way to church. This was a boy whom we were supporting. My husband turned him out of the house. There was not a single soul, that day, who could forgive my husband for that act – not even I. This time Miss Gilby left of her own accord. She shed tears when she came to say goodbye, but my mood would not melt. To slander the poor boy so – and such a fine boy, too, who would forget his daily bath and food in his enthusiasm for *Swadeshi*.

My husband escorted Miss Gilby to the railway station in his own carriage. I was sure he was going too far. When exaggerated accounts of the incident gave rise to a public scandal, which found its way to the newspapers, I felt he had been rightly served.

I had often become anxious at my husband's doings, but had never before been ashamed; yet now I had to blush for him! I did not know exactly, nor did I care, what wrong poor Noren might, or might not, have done to Miss Gilby, but the idea of sitting in judgement on such a matter at such a time! I should have refused to damp the spirit which prompted young Noren to defy the Englishwoman. I could not but look upon it as a sign of cowardice in my husband, that he should fail to understand this simple thing. And so I blushed for him.

And yet it was not that my husband refused to support *Swadeshi*, or was in any way against the Cause. Only he had not been able whole-heartedly to accept the spirit of *Bande Mataram*.[1]

'I am willing,' he said, 'to serve my country; but my worship I reserve for Right which is far greater than my country. To worship my country as a god is to bring a curse upon it.'

1. Lit.: 'Hail Mother'; the opening words of a song by Bankim Chatterjee, the famous Bengali novelist. The song has now become the national anthem, and *Bande Mataram* the national cry, since the days of the *Swadeshi* movement.

Chapter Two

*

Bimala's Story

IV

THIS was the time when Sandip Babu with his followers came to our neighbourhood to preach *Swadeshi*.

There is to be a big meeting in our temple pavilion. We women are sitting there, on one side, behind a screen. Triumphant shouts of *Bande Mataram* come nearer: and to them I am thrilling through and through. Suddenly a stream of barefooted youths in turbans, clad in ascetic ochre, rushes into the quadrangle, like a silt-reddened freshet into a dry river-bed at the first burst of the rains. The whole place is filled with an immense crowd, through which Sandip Babu is borne, seated in a big chair hoisted on the shoulders of ten or twelve of the youths.

Bande Mataram! Bande Mataram! Bande Mataram! It seems as though the skies would be rent and scattered into a thousand fragments.

I had seen Sandip Babu's photograph before. There was something in his features which I did not quite like. Not that he was bad-looking – far from it: he had a splendidly handsome face. Yet, I know not why, it seemed to me, in spite of all its brilliance, that too much of base alloy had gone into its making. The light in his eyes somehow did not shine true. That was why I did not like it when my husband unquestioningly gave in to all his demands. I could bear the waste of money; but it vexed me to think that he was imposing on my husband, taking advantage of friendship. His bearing was not that of an ascetic, nor even of a person of moderate means, but foppish all over. Love of comfort seemed to . . . any number of such reflections come back to me today, but let them be.

When, however, Sandip Babu began to speak that afternoon, and the hearts of the crowd swayed and surged to his words, as though they would break all bounds, I saw him wonderfully transformed. Especially when his features were suddenly lit up by a shaft of light from the slowly setting sun, as it sunk below the roof-line of the pavilion, he seemed to me to be marked out by the gods as their messenger to mortal men and women.

From beginning to end of his speech, each one of his utterances was a stormy outburst. There was no limit to the confidence of his assurance. I do not know how it happened, but I found I had impatiently pushed away the screen from before me and had fixed my gaze upon him. Yet there was none in that crowd who paid any heed to my doings. Only once, I noticed, his eyes, like stars in fateful Orion, flashed full on my face.

I was utterly unconscious of myself. I was no longer the lady of the Rajah's house, but the sole representative of Bengal's womanhood. And he was the champion of Bengal. As the sky had shed its light over him, so he must receive the consecration of a woman's benediction . . .

It seemed clear to me that, since he had caught sight of me, the fire in his words had flamed up more fiercely. Indra's[1] steed refused to be reined in, and there came the roar of thunder and the flash of lightning. I said within myself that his language had caught fire from my eyes; for we women are not only the deities of the household fire, but the flame of the soul itself.

I returned home that evening radiant with a new pride and joy. The storm within me had shifted my whole being from one centre to another. Like the Greek maidens of old, I fain would cut off my long, resplendent tresses to make a bowstring for my hero. Had my outward ornaments been connected with my inner feelings, then my necklet, my armlets, my bracelets, would all have burst their bonds and flung

1. The Jupiter Pluvius of Hindu mythology.

themselves over that assembly like a shower of meteors. Only some personal sacrifice, I felt, could help me to bear the tumult of my exaltation.

When my husband came home later, I was trembling lest he should utter a sound out of tune with the triumphant paean which was still ringing in my ears, lest his fanaticism for truth should lead him to express disapproval of anything that had been said that afternoon. For then I should have openly defied and humiliated him. But he did not say a word . . . which I did not like either.

He should have said: 'Sandip has brought me to my senses. I now realize how mistaken I have been all this time.'

I somehow felt that he was spitefully silent, that he obstinately refused to be enthusiastic. I asked how long Sandip Babu was going to be with us.

'He is off to Rangpur early tomorrow morning,' said my husband.

'Must it be tomorrow?'

'Yes, he is already engaged to speak there.'

I was silent for a while and then asked again: 'Could he not possibly stay a day longer?'

'That may hardly be possible, but why?'

'I want to invite him to dinner and attend on him myself.'

My husband was surprised. He had often entreated me to be present when he had particular friends to dinner, but I had never let myself be persuaded. He gazed at me curiously, in silence, with a look I did not quite understand.

I was suddenly overcome with a sense of shame. 'No, no,' I exclaimed, 'that would never do!'

'Why not!' said he. 'I will ask him myself, and if it is at all possible he will surely stay on for tomorrow.'

It turned out to be quite possible.

I will tell the exact truth. That day I reproached my Creator because he had not made me surpassingly beautiful – not to steal any heart away, but because beauty is glory. In this great day the men of the country should realize its goddess in its womanhood. But, alas, the eyes of men fail to discern the goddess, if outward beauty be lacking. Would Sandip Babu find the *Shakti* of the Motherland manifest in me? Or would he simply take me to be an ordinary, domestic woman?

That morning I scented my flowing hair and tied it in a loose knot, bound by a cunningly intertwined red silk ribbon. Dinner, you see, was to be served at midday, and there was no time to dry my hair after my bath and do it up plaited in the ordinary way. I put on a gold-bordered white *sari*, and my short-sleeve muslin jacket was also gold-bordered.

I felt that there was a certain restraint about my costume and that nothing could well have been simpler. But my sister-in-law, who happened to be passing by, stopped dead before me, surveyed me from head to foot and with compressed lips smiled a meaning smile. When I asked her the reason, 'I am admiring your get-up!' she said.

'What is there so entertaining about it?' I enquired, considerably annoyed.

'It's superb,' she said. 'I was only thinking that one of those low-necked English bodices would have made it perfect.' Not only her mouth and eyes, but her whole body seemed to ripple with suppressed laughter as she left the room.

I was very, very angry, and wanted to change everything and put on my everyday clothes. But I cannot tell exactly why I could not carry out my impulse. Women are the ornaments of society – thus I reasoned with myself – and my husband would never like it, if I appeared before Sandip Babu unworthily clad.

My idea had been to make my appearance after they had sat down to dinner. In the bustle of looking after the serving the first awkwardness would have passed off. But dinner was not ready in time, and it was getting late. Meanwhile my husband had sent for me to introduce the guest.

I was feeling horribly shy about looking Sandip Babu in the face. However, I managed to recover myself enough to say: 'I am so sorry dinner is getting late.'

He boldly came and sat right beside me as he replied: 'I get a dinner of some kind every day, but the Goddess of Plenty keeps behind the scenes. Now that the goddess herself has appeared, it matters little if the dinner lags behind.'

He was just as emphatic in his manners as he was in his public speaking. He had no hesitation and seemed to be accustomed to occupy, unchallenged, his chosen seat. He claimed the right to intimacy so confidently, that the blame would seem to belong to those who should dispute it.

I was in terror lest Sandip Babu should take me for a shrinking, old-fashioned bundle of inanity. But, for the life of me, I could not sparkle in repartees such as might charm or dazzle him. What could have possessed me, I angrily wondered, to appear before him in such an absurd way?

I was about to retire when dinner was over, but Sandip Babu, as bold as ever, placed himself in my way.

'You must not,' he said, 'think me greedy. It was not the dinner that kept me staying on, it was your invitation. If you were to run away now, that would not be playing fair with your guest.'

If he had not said these words with a careless ease, they would have been out of tune. But, after all, he was such a great friend of my husband that I was like his sister.

While I was struggling to climb up this high wave of intimacy, my husband came to the rescue, saying: 'Why not come back to us after you have taken your dinner?'

'But you must give your word,' said Sandip Babu, 'before we let you off.'

'I will come,' said I, with a slight smile.

'Let me tell you,' continued Sandip Babu, 'why I cannot trust you. Nikhil has been married these nine years, and all this while you have eluded me. If you do this again for another nine years, we shall never meet again.'

I took up the spirit of his remark as I dropped my voice to reply: 'Why even then should we not meet?'

'My horoscope tells me I am to die early. None of my forefathers have survived their thirtieth year. I am now twenty-seven.'

He knew this would go home. This time there must have been a shade of concern in my low voice as I said: 'The blessings of the whole country are sure to avert the evil influence of the stars.'

'Then the blessings of the country must be voiced by its

34

goddess. This is the reason for my anxiety that you should return, so that my talisman may begin to work from today.'

Sandip Babu had such a way of taking things by storm that I got no opportunity of resenting what I never should have permitted in another.

'So,' he concluded with a laugh, 'I am going to hold this husband of yours as a hostage till you come back.'

As I was coming away, he exclaimed: 'May I trouble you for a trifle?'

I started and turned round.

'Don't be alarmed,' he said. 'It's merely a glass of water. You might have noticed that I did not drink any water with my dinner. I take it a little later.'

Upon this I had to make a show of interest and ask him the reason. He began to give the history of his dyspepsia. I was told how he had been a martyr to it for seven months, and how, after the usual course of nuisances, which included different allopathic and homoeopathic misadventures, he had obtained the most wonderful results by indigenous methods.

'Do you know,' he added, with a smile, 'God has built even my infirmities in such a manner that they yield only under the bombardment of *Swadeshi* pills.'

My husband, at this, broke his silence. 'You must confess,' said he, 'that you have as immense an attraction for foreign medicine as the earth has for meteors. You have three shelves in your sitting-room full of . . .'

Sandip Babu broke in: 'Do you know what they are? They are the punitive police. They come, not because they are wanted, but because they are imposed on us by the rule of this modern age, exacting fines and inflicting injuries.'

My husband could not bear exaggerations, and I could see he disliked this. But all ornaments are exaggerations. They are not made by God, but by man. Once I remember in defence of some untruth of mine I said to my husband: 'Only the trees and beasts and birds tell unmitigated truths, because these poor things have not the power to invent. In this men show their superiority to the lower creatures, and women beat even men. Neither is a profusion of ornament unbecoming for a woman, nor a profusion of untruth.'

As I came out into the passage leading to the zenana I found my sister-in-law, standing near a window overlooking the reception rooms, peeping through the venetian shutter.

'You here?' I asked in surprise.

'Eavesdropping!' she replied.

v

When I returned, Sandip Babu was tenderly apologetic. 'I am afraid we have spoilt your appetite,' he said.

I felt greatly ashamed. Indeed, I had been too indecently quick over my dinner. With a little calculation, it would become quite evident that my non-eating had surpassed the eating. But I had no idea that anyone could have been deliberately calculating.

I suppose Sandip Babu detected my feeling of shame, which only augmented it. 'I was sure,' he said, 'that you had the impulse of the wild deer to run away, but it is a great boon that you took the trouble to keep your promise with me.'

I could not think of any suitable reply and so I sat down, blushing and uncomfortable, at one end of the sofa. The vision that I had of myself, as the *Shakti* of Womanhood, incarnate, crowning Sandip Babu simply with my presence, majestic and unashamed, failed me altogether.

Sandip Babu deliberately started a discussion with my husband. He knew that his keen wit flashed to the best effect in an argument. I have often since observed, that he never lost an opportunity for a passage at arms whenever I happened to be present.

He was familiar with my husband's views on the cult of *Bande Mataram*, and began in a provoking way: 'So you do not allow that there is room for an appeal to the imagination in patriotic work?'

'It has its place, Sandip, I admit, but I do not believe in giving it the whole place. I would know my country in its frank reality, and for this I am both afraid and ashamed to make use of hypnotic texts of patriotism.'

36

'What you call hypnotic texts I call truth. I truly believe my country to be my God. I worship Humanity. God manifests Himself both in man and in his country.'

'If that is what you really believe, there should be no difference for you between man and man, and so between country and country.'

'Quite true. But my powers are limited, so my worship of Humanity is continued in the worship of my country.'

'I have nothing against your worship as such, but how is it you propose to conduct your worship of God by hating other countries in which He is equally manifest?'

'Hate is also an adjunct of worship. Arjuna won Mahadeva's favour by wrestling with him. God will be with us in the end, if we are prepared to give Him battle.'

'If that be so, then those who are serving and those who are harming the country are both His devotees. Why, then, trouble to preach patriotism?'

'In the case of one's own country, it is different. There the heart clearly demands worship.'

'If you push the same argument further you can say that since God is manifested in us, our *self* has to be worshipped before all else; because our natural instinct claims it.'

'Look here, Nikhil, this is all merely dry logic. Can't you recognize that there is such a thing as feeling?'

'I tell you the truth, Sandip,' my husband replied. 'It is my feelings that are outraged, whenever you try to pass off injustice as a duty, and unrighteousness as a moral ideal. The fact, that I am incapable of stealing, is not due to my possessing logical faculties, but to my having some feeling of respect for myself and love for ideals.'

I was raging inwardly. At last I could keep silent no longer. 'Is not the history of every country,' I cried, 'whether England, France, Germany, or Russia, the history of stealing for the sake of one's own country?'

'They have to answer for these thefts; they are doing so even now; their history is not yet ended.'

'At any rate,' interposed Sandip Babu, 'why should we not follow suit? Let us first fill our country's coffers with stolen goods and then take centuries, like these other countries, to

37

answer for them, if we must. But, I ask you, where do you find this "answering" in history?'

'When Rome was answering for her sin no one knew it. All that time, there was apparently no limit to her prosperity. But do you not see one thing: how these political bags of theirs are bursting with lies and treacheries, breaking their backs under their weight?'

Never before had I had any opportunity of being present at a discussion between my husband and his men friends. Whenever he argued with me I could feel his reluctance to push me into a corner. This arose out of the very love he bore me. Today for the first time I saw his fencer's skill in debate.

Nevertheless, my heart refused to accept my husband's position. I was struggling to find some answer, but it would not come. When the word 'righteousness' comes into an argument, it sounds ugly to say that a thing can be too good to be useful.

All of a sudden Sandip Babu turned to me with the question: 'What do *you* say to this?'

'I do not care about fine distinctions,' I broke out. 'I will tell you broadly what I feel. I am only human. I am covetous. I would have good things for my country. If I am obliged, I would snatch them and filch them. I have anger. I would be angry for my country's sake. If necessary, I would smite and slay to avenge her insults. I have my desire to be fascinated, and fascination must be supplied to me in bodily shape by my country. She must have some visible symbol casting its spell upon my mind. I would make my country a Person, and call her Mother, Goddess, Durga – for whom I would redden the earth with sacrificial offerings. I am human, not divine.'

Sandip Babu leapt to his feet with uplifted arms and shouted 'Hurrah!' – The next moment he corrected himself and cried: '*Bande Mataram.*'

A shadow of pain passed over the face of my husband. He said to me in a very gentle voice: 'Neither am I divine: I am human. And therefore I dare not permit the evil which is in me to be exaggerated into an image of my country – never, never!'

Sandip Babu cried out: 'See, Nikhil, how in the heart of a

woman Truth takes flesh and blood. Woman knows how to
be cruel: her virulence is like a blind storm. It is beautifully
fearful. In man it is ugly, because it harbours in its centre the
gnawing worms of reason and thought. I tell you, Nikhil, it
is our women who will save the country. This is not the time
for nice scruples. We must be unswervingly, unreasoningly
brutal. We must sin. We must give our women red sandal
paste with which to anoint and enthrone our sin. Don't you
remember what the poet says:

> *Come, Sin, O beautiful Sin,*
> *Let thy stinging red kisses pour down fiery red wine into our*
> *   blood.*
> *Sound the trumpet of imperious evil*
> *And cross our forehead with the wreath of exulting*
> *   lawlessness,*
> *O Deity of Desecration,*
> *Smear our breasts with the blackest mud of disrepute,*
> *   unashamed.*

Down with that righteousness, which cannot smilingly bring
rack and ruin.'

When Sandip Babu, standing with his head high, insulted
at a moment's impulse all that men have cherished as their
highest, in all countries and in all times, a shiver went right
through my body.

But, with a stamp of his foot, he continued his declamation:
'I can see that you are that beautiful spirit of fire, which burns
the home to ashes and lights up the larger world with its
flame. Give to us the indomitable courage to go to the bottom
of Ruin itself. Impart grace to all that is baneful.'

It was not clear to whom Sandip Babu addressed his last
appeal. It might have been She whom he worshipped with
his *Bande Mataram*. It might have been the Womanhood of his
country. Or it might have been its representative, the woman
before him. He would have gone further in the same strain,
but my husband suddenly rose from his seat and touched
him lightly on the shoulder saying: 'Sandip, Chandranath
Babu is here.'

I started and turned round, to find an aged gentleman at

39

the door, calm and dignified, in doubt as to whether he should come in or retire. His face was touched with a gentle light like that of the setting sun.

My husband came up to me and whispered: 'This is my master, of whom I have so often told you. Make your obeisance to him.'

I bent reverently and took the dust of his feet. He gave me his blessing saying: 'May God protect you always, my little mother.'

I was sorely in need of such a blessing at that moment.

Nikhil's Story

I

One day I had the faith to believe that I should be able to bear whatever came from my God. I never had the trial. Now I think it has come.

I used to test my strength of mind by imagining all kinds of evil which might happen to me – poverty, imprisonment, dishonour, death – even Bimala's. And when I said to myself that I should be able to receive these with firmness, I am sure I did not exaggerate. Only I could never even imagine one thing, and today it is that of which I am thinking, and wondering whether I can really bear it. There is a thorn somewhere pricking in my heart, constantly giving me pain while I am about my daily work. It seems to persist even when I am asleep. The very moment I wake up in the morning, I find that the bloom has gone from the face of the sky. What is it? What has happened?

My mind has become so sensitive, that even my past life, which came to me in the disguise of happiness, seems to wring my very heart with its falsehood; and the shame and sorrow which are coming close to me are losing their cover of privacy, all the more because they try to veil their faces. My heart has become all eyes. The things that should not be seen, the things I do not want to see – these I must see.

The day has come at last when my ill-starred life has to

reveal its destitution in a long-drawn series of exposures. This penury, all unexpected, has taken its seat in the heart where plenitude seemed to reign. The fees which I paid to delusion for just nine years of my youth have now to be returned with interest to Truth till the end of my days.

What is the use of straining to keep up my pride? What harm if I confess that I have something lacking in me? Possibly it is that unreasoning forcefulness which women love to find in men. But is strength a mere display of muscularity? Must strength have no scruples in treading the weak underfoot?

But why all these arguments? Worthiness cannot be earned merely by disputing about it. And I am unworthy, unworthy, unworthy.

What if I *am* unworthy? The true value of love is this, that it can ever bless the unworthy with its own prodigality. For the worthy there are many rewards on God's earth, but God has specially reserved love for the unworthy.

Up till now Bimala was my home-made Bimala, the product of the confined space and the daily routine of small duties. Did the love which I received from her, I asked myself, come from the deep spring of her heart, or was it merely like the daily provision of pipe water pumped up by the municipal steam-engine of society?

I longed to find Bimala blossoming fully in all her truth and power. But the thing I forgot to calculate was, that one must give up all claims based on conventional rights, if one would find a person freely revealed in truth.

Why did I fail to think of this? Was it because of the husband's pride of possession over his wife? No. It was because I placed the fullest trust upon love. I was vain enough to think that I had the power in me to bear the sight of truth in its awful nakedness. It was tempting Providence, but still I clung to my proud determination to come out victorious in the trial.

Bimala had failed to understand me in one thing. She could not fully realize that I held as weakness all imposition of force. Only the weak dare not be just. They shirk their responsibility of fairness and try quickly to get at results through the short-cuts of injustice. Bimala has no patience with patience. She loves to find in men the turbulent, the angry, the unjust. Her respect must have its element of fear.

I had hoped that when Bimala found herself free in the outer world she would be rescued from her infatuation for tyranny. But now I feel sure that this infatuation is deep down in her nature. Her love is for the boisterous. From the tip of her tongue to the pit of her stomach she must tingle with red pepper in order to enjoy the simple fare of life. But my determination was, never to do my duty with frantic impetuosity, helped on by the fiery liquor of excitement. I know Bimala finds it difficult to respect me for this, taking my scruples for feebleness – and she is quite angry with me because I am not running amuck crying *Bande Mataram*.

For the matter of that, I have become unpopular with all my countrymen because I have not joined them in their carousals. They are certain that either I have a longing for some title, or else that I am afraid of the police. The police on their side suspect me of harbouring some hidden design and protesting too much in my mildness.

What I really feel is this, that those who cannot find food for their enthusiasm in a knowledge of their country as it actually is, or those who cannot love men just because they are men – who needs must shout and deify their country in order to keep up their excitement – these love excitement more than their country.

To try to give our infatuation a higher place than Truth is a sign of inherent slavishness. Where our minds are free we find ourselves lost. Our moribund vitality must have for its rider either some fantasy, or someone in authority, or a sanction from the pundits, in order to make it move. So long as we are impervious to truth and have to be moved by some hypnotic stimulus, we must know that we lack the capacity for self-government. Whatever may be our condition, we shall either need some imaginary ghost or some actual medicine-man to terrorize over us.

The other day when Sandip accused me of lack of imagination, saying that this prevented me from realizing my country in a visible image, Bimala agreed with him. I did not say anything in my defence, because to win in argument does not lead to happiness. Her difference of opinion is not due to any inequality of intelligence, but rather to dissimilarity of nature.

They accuse me of being unimaginative – that is, according to them, I may have oil in my lamp, but no flame. Now this is exactly the accusation which I bring against them. I would say to them: 'You are dark, even as the flints are. You must come to violent conflicts and make a noise in order to produce your sparks. But their disconnected flashes merely assist your pride, and not your clear vision.'

I have been noticing for some time that there is a gross cupidity about Sandip. His fleshly feelings make him harbour delusions about his religion and impel him into a tyrannical attitude in his patriotism. His intellect is keen, but his nature is coarse, and so he glorifies his selfish lusts under high-sounding names. The cheap consolations of hatred are as urgently necessary for him as the satisfaction of his appetites. Bimala has often warned me, in the old days, of his hankering after money. I understood this, but I could not bring myself to haggle with Sandip. I felt ashamed even to own to myself that he was trying to take advantage of me.

It will, however, be difficult to explain to Bimala today that Sandip's love of country is but a different phase of his covetous self-love. Bimala's hero-worship of Sandip makes me hesitate all the more to talk to her about him, lest some touch of jealousy may lead me unwittingly into exaggeration. It may be that the pain at my heart is already making me see a distorted picture of Sandip. And yet it is better perhaps to speak out than to keep my feelings gnawing within me.

II

I have known my master these thirty years. Neither calumny, nor disaster, nor death itself has any terrors for him. Nothing could have saved me, born as I was into the traditions of this family of ours, but that he has established his own life in the centre of mine, with its peace and truth and spiritual vision, thus making it possible for me to realize goodness in its truth.

My master came to me that day and said: 'Is it necessary to detain Sandip here any longer?'

His nature was so sensitive to all omens of evil that he had at once understood. He was not easily moved, but that day he felt the dark shadow of trouble ahead. Do I not know how well he loves me?

At tea-time I said to Sandip: 'I have just had a letter from Rangpur. They are complaining that I am selfishly detaining you. When will you be going there?'

Bimala was pouring out the tea. Her face fell at once. She threw just one enquiring glance at Sandip.

'I have been thinking,' said Sandip, 'that this wandering up and down means a tremendous waste of energy. I feel that if I could work from a centre I could achieve more permanent results.'

With this he looked up at Bimala and asked: 'Do you not think so too?'

Bimala hesitated for a reply and then said: 'Both ways seem good – to do the work from a centre, as well as by travelling about. That in which you find greater satisfaction is the way for you.'

'Then let me speak out my mind,' said Sandip. 'I have never yet found any one source of inspiration suffice me for good. That is why I have been constantly moving about, rousing enthusiasm in the people, from which in turn I draw my own store of energy. Today you have given me the message of my country. Such fire I have never beheld in any man. I shall be able to spread the fire of enthusiasm in my country by borrowing it from you. No, do not be ashamed. You are far above all modesty and diffidence. You are the Queen Bee of our hive, and we the workers shall rally around you. You shall be our centre, our inspiration.'

Bimala flushed all over with bashful pride and her hand shook as she went on pouring out the tea.

Another day my master came to me and said: 'Why don't you two go up to Darjeeling for a change? You are not looking well. Have you been getting enough sleep?'

I asked Bimala in the evening whether she would care to have a trip to the Hills. I knew she had a great longing to see the Himalayas. But she refused . . . The country's Cause, I suppose!

I must not lose my faith: I shall wait. The passage from the narrow to the larger world is stormy. When she is familiar with this freedom, then I shall know where my place is. If I discover that I do not fit in with the arrangement of the outer world, then I shall not quarrel with my fate, but silently take my leave . . . Use force? But for what? Can force prevail against Truth?

Sandip's Story

I

The impotent man says: 'That which has come to my share is mine.' And the weak man assents. But the lesson of the whole world is: 'That is really mine which I can snatch away.' My country does not become mine simply because it is the country of my birth. It becomes mine on the day when I am able to win it by force.

Every man has a natural right to possess, and therefore greed is natural. It is not in the wisdom of nature that we should be content to be deprived. What my mind covets, my surroundings must supply. This is the only true understanding between our inner and outer nature in this world. Let moral ideals remain merely for those poor anaemic creatures of starved desire whose grasp is weak. Those who can desire with all their soul and enjoy with all their heart, those who have no hesitation or scruple, it is they who are the anointed of Providence. Nature spreads out her riches and loveliest treasures for their benefit. They swim across streams, leap over walls, kick open doors, to help themselves to whatever is worth taking. In such a getting one can rejoice; such wresting as this gives value to the thing taken.

Nature surrenders herself, but only to the robber. For she delights in this forceful desire, this forceful abduction. And so she does not put the garland of her acceptance round the lean, scraggy neck of the ascetic. The music of the wedding march is struck. The time of the wedding I must not let pass. My heart therefore is eager. For, who is the bridegroom? It is I. The bridegroom's place belongs to him who, torch in hand, can come in time. The bridegroom in Nature's wedding hall comes unexpected and uninvited.

Ashamed? No, I am never ashamed! I ask for whatever I want, and I do not always wait to ask before I take it. Those who are deprived by their own diffidence dignify their privation by the name of modesty. The world into which we are born is the world of reality. When a man goes away from the market of real things with empty hands and empty stomach, merely filling his bag with big sounding words, I wonder why he ever came into this hard world at all. Did these men get their appointment from the epicures of the religious world, to play set tunes on sweet, pious texts in that pleasure garden where blossom airy nothings? I neither affect those tunes nor do I find any sustenance in those blossoms.

What I desire, I desire positively, superlatively. I want to knead it with both my hands and both my feet; I want to smear it all over my body; I want to gorge myself with it to the full. The scrannel pipes of those who have worn themselves out by their moral fastings, till they have become flat and pale like starved vermin infesting a long-deserted bed, will never reach my ear.

I would conceal nothing, because that would be cowardly. But if I cannot bring myself to conceal when concealment is needful, that also is cowardly. Because you have your greed, you build your walls. Because I have my greed, I break through them. You use your power: I use my craft. These are the realities of life. On these depend kingdoms and empires and all the great enterprises of men.

As for those *avatars* who come down from their paradise to talk to us in some holy jargon – their words are not real. Therefore, in spite of all the applause they get, these sayings of theirs only find a place in the hiding corners of the weak. They are despised by those who are strong, the rulers of the world. Those who have had the courage to see this have won success, while those poor wretches who are dragged one way by nature and the other way by these *avatars*, they set one foot in the boat of the real and the other in the boat of the unreal, and thus are in a pitiable plight, able neither to advance nor to keep their place.

There are many men who seem to have been born only with an obsession to die. Possibly there is a beauty, like that of a sunset, in this lingering death in life which seems to fascinate them. Nikhil lives this kind of life, if life it may be called. Years ago, I had a great argument with him on this point.

'It is true,' he said, 'that you cannot get anything except by force. But then what *is* this force? And then also, what *is* this getting? The strength I believe in is the strength of renouncing.'

'So you,' I exclaimed, 'are infatuated with the glory of bankruptcy.'

'Just as desperately as the chick is infatuated about the bankruptcy of its shell,' he replied. 'The shell is real enough, yet it is given up in exchange for intangible light and air. A sorry exchange, I suppose you would call it?'

When once Nikhil gets on to metaphor, there is no hope of making him see that he is merely dealing with words, not with realities. Well, well, let him be happy with his metaphors. We are the flesh-eaters of the world; we have teeth and nails; we pursue and grab and tear. We are not satisfied with chewing in the evening the cud of the grass we have eaten in the morning. Anyhow, we cannot allow your metaphor-mongers to bar the door to our sustenance. In that case we shall simply steal or rob, for we must live.

People will say that I am starting some novel theory just because those who are moving in this world are in the habit of talking differently though they are really acting up to it all the time. Therefore they fail to understand, as I do, that this is the only working moral principle. In point of fact, I know that my idea is not an empty theory at all, for it has been proved in practical life. I have found that my way always wins over the hearts of women, who are creatures of this world of reality and do not roam about in cloud-land, as men do, in idea-filled balloons.

Women find in my features, my manner, my gait, my

speech, a masterful passion – not a passion dried thin with the heat of asceticism, not a passion with its face turned back at every step in doubt and debate, but a full-blooded passion. It roars and rolls on, like a flood, with the cry: '*I want, I want, I want.*' Women feel, in their own heart of hearts, that this indomitable passion is the lifeblood of the world, acknowledging no law but itself, and therefore victorious. For this reason they have so often abandoned themselves to be swept away on the flood-tide of my passion, recking naught as to whether it takes them to life or to death. This power which wins these women is the power of mighty men, the power which wins the world of reality.

Those who imagine the greater desirability of another world merely shift their desires from the earth to the skies. It remains to be seen how high their gushing fountain will play, and for how long. But this much is certain: women were not created for these pale creatures – these lotus-eaters of idealism.

'Affinity!' When it suited my need, I have often said that God has created special pairs of men and women, and that the union of such is the only legitimate union, higher than all unions made by law. The reason of it is, that though man wants to follow nature, he can find no pleasure in it unless he screens himself with some phrase – and that is why this world is so overflowing with lies.

'Affinity!' Why should there be only *one*? There may be affinity with thousands. It was never in my agreement with nature that I should overlook all my innumerable affinities for the sake of only one. I have discovered many in my own life up to now, yet that has not closed the door to one more – and that one is clearly visible to my eyes. She has also discovered her own affinity to me.

And then?

Then, if I do not win I am a coward.

Chapter Three

❋

Bimala's Story

VI

I WONDER what could have happened to my feeling of shame. The fact is, I had no time to think about myself. My days and nights were passing in a whirl, like an eddy with myself in the centre. No gap was left for hesitation or delicacy to enter.

One day my sister-in-law remarked to my husband: 'Up to now the women of this house have been kept weeping. Here comes the men's turn.

'We must see that they do not miss it,' she continued, turning to me. 'I see you are out for the fray, Chota[1] Rani! Hurl your shafts straight at their hearts.'

Her keen eyes looked me up and down. Not one of the colours into which my toilet, my dress, my manners, my speech, had blossomed out had escaped her. I am ashamed to speak of it today, but I felt no shame then. Something within me was at work of which I was not even conscious. I used to overdress, it is true, but more like an automaton, with no particular design. No doubt I knew which effort of mine would prove specially pleasing to Sandip Babu, but that required no intuition, for he would discuss it openly before all of them.

One day he said to my husband: 'Do you know, Nikhil, when I first saw our Queen Bee, she was sitting there so demurely in her gold-bordered *sari*. Her eyes were gazing inquiringly into space, like stars which had lost their way, just as if she had been for ages standing on the edge of some

1. Bimala, the younger brother's wife, was the *Chota* or Junior Rani.

darkness, looking out for something unknown. But when I saw her, I felt a quiver run through me. It seemed to me that the gold border of her *sari* was her own inner fire flaming out and twining round her. That is the flame we want, visible fire! Look here, Queen Bee, you really must do us the favour of dressing once more as a living flame.'

So long I had been like a small river at the border of a village. My rhythm and my language were different from what they are now. But the tide came up from the sea, and my breast heaved; my banks gave way and the great drum-beats of the sea waves echoed in my mad current. I could not understand the meaning of that sound in my blood. Where was that former self of mine? Whence came foaming into me this surging flood of glory? Sandip's hungry eyes burnt like the lamps of worship before my shrine. All his gaze proclaimed that I was a wonder in beauty and power; and the loudness of his praise, spoken and unspoken, drowned all other voices in my world. Had the Creator created me afresh, I wondered? Did he wish to make up now for neglecting me so long? I who before was plain had become suddenly beautiful. I who before had been of no account now felt in myself all the splendour of Bengal itself.

For Sandip Babu was not a mere individual. In him was the confluence of millions of minds of the country. When he called me the Queen Bee of the hive, I was acclaimed with a chorus of praise by all our patriot workers. After that, the loud jests of my sister-in-law could not touch me any longer. My relations with all the world underwent a change. Sandip Babu made it clear how all the country was in need of me. I had no difficulty in believing this at the time, for I felt that I had the power to do everything. Divine strength had come to me. It was something which I had never felt before, which was beyond myself. I had no time to question it to find out what was its nature. It seemed to belong to me, and yet to transcend me. It comprehended the whole of Bengal.

Sandip Babu would consult me about every little thing touching the Cause. At first I felt very awkward and would hang back, but that soon wore off. Whatever I suggested seemed to astonish him. He would go into raptures and say:

'Men can only think. You women have a way of understanding without thinking. Woman was created out of God's own fancy. Man, He had to hammer into shape.'

Letters used to come to Sandip Babu from all parts of the country which were submitted to me for my opinion. Occasionally he disagreed with me. But I would not argue with him. Then after a day or two – as if a new light had suddenly dawned upon him – he would send for me and say: 'It was my mistake. Your suggestion was the correct one.' He would often confess to me that wherever he had taken steps contrary to my advice he had gone wrong. Thus I gradually came to be convinced that behind whatever was taking place was Sandip Babu, and behind Sandip Babu was the plain common sense of a woman. The glory of a great responsibility filled my being.

My husband had no place in our counsels. Sandip Babu treated him as a younger brother, of whom personally one may be very fond and yet have no use for his business advice. He would tenderly and smilingly talk about my husband's childlike innocence, saying that his curious doctrine and perversities of mind had a flavour of humour which made them all the more lovable. It was seemingly this very affection for Nikhil which led Sandip Babu to forbear from troubling him with the burden of the country.

Nature has many anodynes in her pharmacy, which she secretly administers when vital relations are being insidiously severed, so that none may know of the operation, till at last one awakes to know what a great rent has been made. When the knife was busy with my life's most intimate tie, my mind was so clouded with fumes of intoxicating gas that I was not in the least aware of what a cruel thing was happening. Possibly this is woman's nature. When her passion is roused she loses her sensibility for all that is outside it. When, like the river, we women keep to our banks, we give nourishment with all that we have: when we overflow them we destroy with all that we are.

Sandip's Story

11

I can see that something has gone wrong. I got an inkling of it the other day.

Ever since my arrival, Nikhil's sitting-room had become a thing amphibious – half women's apartment, half men's: Bimala had access to it from the zenana, it was not barred to me from the outer side. If we had only gone slow, and made use of our privileges with some restraint, we might not have fallen foul of other people. But we went ahead so vehemently that we could not think of the consequences.

Whenever Bee comes into Nikhil's room, I somehow get to know of it from mine. There are the tinkle of bangles and other little sounds; the door is perhaps shut with a shade of unnecessary vehemence; the bookcase is a trifle stiff and creaks if jerked open. When I enter I find Bee, with her back to the door, ever so busy selecting a book from the shelves. And as I offer to assist her in this difficult task she starts and protests; and then we naturally get on to other topics.

The other day, on an inauspicious[1] Thursday afternoon, I sallied forth from my room at the call of these same sounds. There was a man on guard in the passage. I walked on without so much as glancing at him, but as I approached the door he put himself in my way saying: 'Not that way, sir.'

'Not that way! Why?'

'The Rani Mother is there.'

'Oh, very well. Tell your Rani Mother that Sandip Babu wants to see her.'

'That cannot be, sir. It is against orders.'

I felt highly indignant. 'I order you!' I said in a raised voice. 'Go and announce me.'

The fellow was somewhat taken aback at my attitude. In the meantime I had neared the door. I was on the point of reaching it, when he followed after me and took me by the arm saying: 'No, sir, you must not.'

1. According to the Hindu calendar.

What! To be touched by a flunkey! I snatched away my arm and gave the man a sounding blow. At this moment Bee came out of the room to find the man about to insult me.

I shall never forget the picture of her wrath! That Bee is beautiful is a discovery of my own. Most of our people would see nothing in her. Her tall, slim figure these boors would call 'lanky'. But it is just this lithesomeness of hers that I admire – like an up-leaping fountain of life, coming direct out of the depths of the Creator's heart. Her complexion is dark, but it is the lustrous darkness of a sword-blade, keen and scintillating.

'Nanku!' she commanded, as she stood in the doorway, pointing with her finger, 'leave us.'

'Do not be angry with him,' said I. 'If it is against orders, it is I who should retire.'

Bee's voice was still trembling as she replied: 'You must not go. Come in.'

It was not a request, but again a command! I followed her in, and taking a chair fanned myself with a fan which was on the table. Bee scribbled something with a pencil on a sheet of paper and, summoning a servant, handed it to him saying: 'Take this to the Maharaja.'

'Forgive me,' I resumed. 'I was unable to control myself, and hit that man of yours.'

'You served him right,' said Bee.

'But it was not the poor fellow's fault, after all. He was only obeying his orders.'

Here Nikhil came in, and as he did so I left my seat with a rapid movement and went and stood near the window with my back to the room.

'Nanku, the guard, has insulted Sandip Babu,' said Bee to Nikhil.

Nikhil seemed to be so genuinely surprised that I had to turn round and stare at him. Even an outrageously good man fails in keeping up his pride of truthfulness before his wife – if she be the proper kind of woman.

'He insolently stood in the way when Sandip Babu was coming in here,' continued Bee. 'He said he had orders . . .'

'Whose orders?' asked Nikhil.

'How am I to know?' exclaimed Bee impatiently, her eyes brimming over with mortification.

Nikhil sent for the man and questioned him. 'It was not my fault,' Nanku repeated sullenly. 'I had my orders.'

'Who gave you the order?'

'The Bara Rani Mother.'

We were all silent for a while. After the man had left, Bee said: 'Nanku must go!'

Nikhil remained silent. I could see that his sense of justice would not allow this. There was no end to his qualms. But this time he was up against a tough problem. Bee was not the woman to take things lying down. She would have to get even with her sister-in-law by punishing this fellow. And as Nikhil remained silent, her eyes flashed fire. She knew not how to pour her scorn upon her husband's feebleness of spirit. Nikhil left the room after a while without another word.

The next day Nanku was not to be seen. On inquiry, I learnt that he had been sent off to some other part of the estates, and that his wages had not suffered by such transfer.

I could catch glimpses of the ravages of the storm raging over this, behind the scenes. All I can say is, that Nikhil is a curious creature, quite out of the common.

The upshot was, that after this Bee began to send for me to the sitting-room, for a chat, without any contrivance, or pretence of its being an accident. Thus from bare suggestion we came to broad hint: the implied came to be expressed. The daughter-in-law of a princely house lives in a starry region so remote from the ordinary outsider that there is not even a regular road for his approach. What a triumphal progress of Truth was this which, gradually but persistently, thrust aside veil after veil of obscuring custom, till at length Nature herself was laid bare.

Truth? Of course it was the truth! The attraction of man and woman for each other is fundamental. The whole world of matter, from the speck of dust upwards, is ranged on its side. And yet men would keep it hidden away out of sight, behind a tissue of words; and with home-made sanctions and prohibitions make of it a domestic utensil. Why, it's as absurd

54

as melting down the solar system to make a watch-chain for one's son-in-law![1]

When, in spite of all, reality awakes at the call of what is but naked truth, what a gnashing of teeth and beating of breasts is there! But can one carry on a quarrel with a storm? It never takes the trouble to reply, it only gives a shaking.

I am enjoying the sight of this truth, as it gradually reveals itself. These tremblings of steps, these turnings of the face, are sweet to me: and sweet are the deceptions which deceive not only others, but also Bee herself. When Reality has to meet the unreal, deception is its principal weapon; for its enemies always try to shame Reality by calling it gross, and so it needs must hide itself, or else put on some disguise. The circumstances are such that it dare not frankly avow: 'Yes, I am gross, because I am true. I am flesh. I am passion. I am hunger, unashamed and cruel.'

All is now clear to me. The curtain flaps, and through it I can see the preparations for the catastrophe. The little red ribbon, which peeps through the luxuriant masses of her hair, with its flush of secret longing, it is the lolling tongue of the red storm cloud. I feel the warmth of each turn of her *sari*, each suggestion of her raiment, of which even the wearer may not be fully conscious.

Bee was not conscious, because she was ashamed of the reality; to which men have given a bad name, calling it Satan; and so it has to steal into the garden of paradise in the guise of a snake, and whisper secrets into the ears of man's chosen consort and make her rebellious; then farewell to all ease; and after that comes death!

My poor little Queen Bee is living in a dream. She knows not which way she is treading. It would not be safe to awaken her before the time. It is best for me to pretend to be equally unconscious.

The other day, at dinner, she was gazing at me in a curious sort of way, little realizing what such glances mean! As my eyes met hers, she turned away with a flush. 'You are surprised at my appetite,' I remarked. 'I can hide everything,

1. The son-in-law is the pet of a Hindu household.

except that I am greedy! Anyhow, why trouble to blush for me, since I am shameless?'

This only made her colour more furiously, as she stammered: 'No, no, I was only . . .'

'I know,' I interrupted. 'Women have a weakness for greedy men; for it is this greed of ours which gives them the upper hand. The indulgence which I have always received at their hands has made me all the more shameless. I do not mind your watching the good things disappear, not one bit. I mean to enjoy every one of them.'

The other day I was reading an English book in which sex-problems were treated in an audaciously realistic manner. I had left it lying in the sitting-room. As I went there the next afternoon, for something or other, I found Bee seated with this book in her hand. When she heard my footsteps she hurriedly put it down and placed another book over it – a volume of Mrs Hemans's poems.

'I have never been able to make out,' I began, 'why women are so shy about being caught reading poetry. We men – lawyers, mechanics, or what not – may well feel ashamed. If we must read poetry, it should be at dead of night, within closed doors. But you women are so akin to poesy. The Creator Himself is a lyric poet, and Jayadeva[1] must have practised the divine art seated at His feet.'

Bee made no reply, but only blushed uncomfortably. She made as if she would leave the room. Whereupon I protested: 'No, no, pray read on. I will just take a book I left here, and run away.' With which I took up my book from the table. 'Lucky you did not think of glancing over its pages,' I continued, 'or you would have wanted to chastise me.'

'Indeed! Why?' asked Bee.

'Because it is not poetry,' said I. 'Only blunt things, bluntly put, without any finicking niceness. I wish Nikhil would read it.'

Bee frowned a little as she murmured: 'What makes you wish that?'

'He is a man, you see, one of us. My only quarrel with him

1. A Vaishnava poet (Sanskrit) whose lyrics of the adoration of the Divinity serve as well to express all shades of human passion.

is that he delights in a misty vision of this world. Have you not observed how this trait of his makes him look on *Swadeshi* as if it was some poem of which the metre must be kept correct at every step? We, with the clubs of our prose, are the iconoclasts of metre.'

'What has your book to do with *Swadeshi*?'

'You would know if you only read it. Nikhil wants to go by made-up maxims, in *Swadeshi* as in everything else; so he knocks up against human nature at every turn, and then falls to abusing it. He never will realize that human nature was created long before phrases were, and will survive them too.'

Bee was silent for a while and then gravely said: 'Is it not a part of human nature to try and rise superior to itself?'

I smiled inwardly. 'These are not your words', I thought to myself. 'You have learnt them from Nikhil. *You* are a healthy human being. Your flesh and blood have responded to the call of reality. You are burning in every vein with life-fire – do I not know it? How long should they keep you cool with the wet towel of moral precepts?'

'The weak are in the majority,' I said aloud. 'They are continually poisoning the ears of men by repeating these shibboleths. Nature has denied them strength – it is thus that they try to enfeeble others.'

'We women are weak,' replied Bimala. 'So I suppose we must join in the conspiracy of the weak.'

'Women weak!' I exclaimed with a laugh. 'Men belaud you as delicate and fragile, so as to delude you into thinking yourselves weak. But it is you women who are strong. Men make a great outward show of their so-called freedom, but those who know their inner minds are aware of their bondage. They have manufactured scriptures with their own hands to bind themselves; with their very idealism they have made golden fetters of women to wind round their body and mind. If men had not that extraordinary faculty of entangling themselves in meshes of their own contriving, nothing could have kept them bound. But as for you women, you have desired to conceive reality with body and soul. You have given birth to reality. You have suckled reality at your breasts.'

Bee was well read for a woman, and would not easily give in to my arguments. 'If that were true,' she objected, 'men would not have found women attractive.'

'Women realize the danger,' I replied. 'They know that men love delusions, so they give them full measure by borrowing their own phrases. They know that man, the drunkard, values intoxication more than food, and so they try to pass themselves off as an intoxicant. As a matter of fact, but for the sake of man, woman has no need for any make-believe.'

'Why, then, are you troubling to destroy the illusion?'

'For freedom. I want the country to be free. I want human relations to be free.'

111

I was aware that it is unsafe suddenly to awake a sleepwalker. But I am so impetuous by nature, a halting gait does not suit me. I knew I was overbold that day. I knew that the first shock of such ideas is apt to be almost intolerable. But with women it is always audacity that wins.

Just as we were getting on nicely, who should walk in but Nikhil's old tutor Chandranath Babu. The world would have been not half a bad place to live in but for these schoolmasters, who make one want to quit in disgust. The Nikhil type wants to keep the world always a school. This incarnation of a school turned up that afternoon at the psychological moment.

We all remain schoolboys in some corner of our hearts, and I, even I, felt somewhat pulled up. As for poor Bee, she at once took her place solemnly, like the topmost girl of the class on the front bench. All of a sudden she seemed to remember that she had to face her examination.

Some people are so like eternal pointsmen lying in wait by the line, to shunt one's train of thought from one rail to another.

Chandranath Babu had no sooner come in than he cast about for some excuse to retire, mumbling: 'I beg your pardon, I . . .'

Before he could finish, Bee went up to him and made a profound obeisance, saying: 'Pray do not leave us, sir. Will you not take a seat?' She looked like a drowning person clutching at him for support – the little coward!

But possibly I was mistaken. It is quite likely that there was a touch of womanly wile in it. She wanted, perhaps, to raise her value in my eyes. She might have been pointedly saying to me: 'Please don't imagine for a moment that I am entirely overcome by you. My respect for Chandranath Babu is even greater.'

Well, indulge in your respect by all means! Schoolmasters thrive on it. But not being one of them, I have no use for that empty compliment.

Chandranath Babu began to talk about *Swadeshi*. I thought I would let him go on with his monologues. There is nothing like letting an old man talk himself out. It makes him feel that he is winding up the world, forgetting all the while how far away the real world is from his wagging tongue.

But even my worst enemy would not accuse me of patience. And when Chandranath Babu went on to say: 'If we expect to gather fruit where we have sown no seed, then we . . .' I had to interrupt him.

'Who wants fruit?' I cried. 'We go by the Author of the *Gita* who says that we are concerned only with the doing, not with the fruit of our deeds.'

'What is it then that you *do* want?' asked Chandranath Babu.

'Thorns!' I exclaimed, 'which cost nothing to plant.'

'Thorns do not obstruct others only,' he replied. 'They have a way of hurting one's own feet.'

'That is all right for a copy-book,' I retorted. 'But the real thing is that we have this burning at heart. Now we have only to cultivate thorns for others' soles; afterwards when they hurt us we shall find leisure to repent. But why be frightened even of that? When at last we have to die it will be time enough to get cold. While we are on fire let us seethe and boil.'

Chandranath Babu smiled. 'Seethe by all means,' he said, 'but do not mistake it for work, or heroism. Nations which have got on in the world have done so by action, not by ebullition. Those who have always lain in dread of work, when with a start they awake to their sorry plight, they look to short-cuts and scamping for their deliverance.'

I was girding up my loins to deliver a crushing reply, when Nikhil came back. Chandranath Babu rose, and looking towards Bee, said: 'Let me go now, my little mother, I have some work to attend to.'

As he left, I showed Nikhil the book in my hand. 'I was telling Queen Bee about this book,' I said.

Ninety-nine per cent of people have to be deluded with lies, but it is easier to delude this perpetual pupil of the schoolmaster with the truth. He is best cheated openly. So, in playing with him, the simplest course was to lay my cards on the table.

Nikhil read the title on the cover, but said nothing. 'These writers,' I continued, 'are busy with their brooms, sweeping away the dust of epithets with which men have covered up this world of ours. So, as I was saying, I wish you would read it.'

'I have read it,' said Nikhil.

'Well, what do you say?'

'It is all very well for those who really care to think, but poison for those who shirk thought.'

'What do you mean?'

'Those who preach "Equal Rights of Property" should not be thieves. For, if they are, they would be preaching lies. When passion is in the ascendant, this kind of book is not rightly understood.'

'Passion,' I replied, 'is the street lamp which guides us. To call it untrue is as hopeless as to expect to see better by plucking out our natural eyes.'

Nikhil was visibly growing excited. 'I accept the truth of passion,' he said, 'only when I recognize the truth of restraint. By pressing what we want to see right into our eyes we only injure them: we do not see. So does the violence of passion, which would leave no space between the mind and its object, defeat its purpose.'

'It is simply your intellectual foppery,' I replied, 'which makes you indulge in moral delicacy, ignoring the savage side of truth. This merely helps you to mystify things, and so you fail to do your work with any degree of strength.'

'The intrusion of strength,' said Nikhil impatiently, 'where strength is out of place, does not help you in your work . . . But why are we arguing about these things? Vain arguments only brush off the fresh bloom of truth.'

I wanted Bee to join in the discussion, but she had not said a word up to now. Could I have given her too rude a shock, leaving her assailed with doubts and wanting to learn her lesson afresh from the schoolmaster? Still, a thorough shaking-up is essential. One must begin by realizing that things supposed to be unshakeable can be shaken.

'I am glad I had this talk with you,' I said to Nikhil, 'for I was on the point of lending this book to Queen Bee to read.'

'What harm?' said Nikhil. 'If I could read the book, why not Bimala too? All I want to say is, that in Europe people look at everything from the viewpoint of science. But man is neither mere physiology, nor biology, nor psychology, nor even sociology. For God's sake don't forget that. Man is infinitely more than the natural science of himself. You laugh at me, calling me the schoolmaster's pupil, but that is what you are, not I. You want to find the truth of man from your science teachers, and not from your own inner being.'

'But why all this excitement?' I mocked.

'Because I see you are bent on insulting man and making him petty.'

'Where on earth do you see all that?'

'In the air, in my outraged feelings. You would go on wounding the great, the unselfish, the beautiful in man.'

'What mad idea is this of yours?'

Nikhil suddenly stood up. 'I tell you plainly, Sandip,' he said, 'man may be wounded unto death, but he will not die. This is the reason why I am ready to suffer all, knowing all, with eyes open.'

With these words he hurriedly left the room.

I was staring blankly at his retreating figure, when the sound of a book, falling from the table, made me turn to find Bee following him with quick, nervous steps, making a detour to avoid passing too near me.

A curious creature, that Nikhil! He feels the danger threatening his home, and yet why does he not turn me out?

61

I know, he is waiting for Bimal to give him the cue. If Bimal tells him that their mating has been a misfit, he will bow his head and admit that it may have been a blunder! He has not the strength of mind to understand that to acknowledge a mistake is the greatest of all mistakes. He is a typical example of how ideas make for weakness. I have not seen another like him – so whimsical a product of nature! He would hardly do as a character in a novel or drama, to say nothing of real life.

And Bee? I am afraid her dream-life is over from today. She has at length understood the nature of the current which is bearing her along. Now she must either advance or retreat, open-eyed. The chances are she will now advance a step, and then retreat a step. But that does not disturb me. When one is on fire, this rushing to and fro makes the blaze all the fiercer. The fright she has got will only fan her passion.

Perhaps I had better not say much to her, but simply select some modern books for her to read. Let her gradually come to the conviction that to acknowledge and respect passion as the supreme reality, is to be modern – not to be ashamed of it, not to glorify restraint. If she finds shelter in some such word as 'modern', she will find strength.

Be that as it may, I must see this out to the end of the Fifth Act. I cannot, unfortunately, boast of being merely a spectator, seated in the royal box, applauding now and again. There is a wrench at my heart, a pang in every nerve. When I have put out the light and am in my bed, little touches, little glances, little words flit about and fill the darkness. When I get up in the morning, I thrill with lively anticipations, my blood seems to course through me to the strains of music . . .

There was a double photo-frame on the table with Bee's photograph by the side of Nikhil's. I had taken out hers. Yesterday I showed Bee the empty side and said: 'Theft becomes necessary only because of miserliness, so its sin must be divided between the miser and the thief. Do you not think so?'

'It was not a good one,' observed Bee simply, with a little smile.

'What is to be done?' said I. 'A portrait cannot be better than a portrait. I must be content with it, such as it is.'

Bee took up a book and began to turn over the pages. 'If you are annoyed,' I went on, 'I must make a shift to fill up the vacancy.'

Today I have filled it up. This photograph of mine was taken in my early youth. My face was then fresher, and so was my mind. Then I still cherished some illusions about this world and the next. Faith deceives men, but it has one great merit: it imparts a radiance to the features.

My portrait now reposes next to Nikhil's, for are not the two of us old friends?

Chapter Four
*

Nikhil's Story

III

I WAS never self-conscious. But nowadays I often try to take an outside view – to see myself as Bimal sees me. What a dismally solemn picture it makes, my habit of taking things too seriously!

Better, surely, to laugh away the world than flood it with tears. That is, in fact, how the world gets on. We relish our food and rest, only because we can dismiss, as so many empty shadows, the sorrows scattered everywhere, both in the home and in the outer world. If we took them as true, even for a moment, where would be our appetite, our sleep?

But I cannot dismiss myself as one of these shadows, and so the load of my sorrow lies eternally heavy on the heart of my world.

Why not stand out aloof in the highway of the universe, and feel yourself to be part of the all? In the midst of the immense, age-long concourse of humanity, what is Bimal to you? Your wife? What is a wife? A bubble of a name blown big with your own breath, so carefully guarded night and day, yet ready to burst at any pin-prick from outside.

My wife – and so, forsooth, my very own! If she says: 'No, I am myself' – am I to reply: 'How can that be? Are you not mine?'

'My wife' – Does that amount to an argument, much less the truth? Can one imprison a whole personality within that name?

My wife! – Have I not cherished in this little world all that

64

is purest and sweetest in my life, never for a moment letting it down from my bosom to the dust? What incense of worship, what music of passion, what flowers of my spring and of my autumn, have I not offered up at its shrine? If, like a toy paper-boat, she be swept along into the muddy waters of the gutter – would I not also . . . ?

There it is again, my incorrigible solemnity! Why 'muddy'? What 'gutter'? Names, called in a fit of jealousy, do not change the facts of the world. If Bimal is not mine, she is not; and no fuming, or fretting, or arguing will serve to prove that she is. If my heart is breaking – let it break! That will not make the world bankrupt – nor even me; for man is so much greater than the things he loses in this life. The very ocean of tears has its other shore, else none would have ever wept.

But then there is Society to be considered . . . which let Society consider! If I weep it is for myself, not for Society. If Bimal should say she is not mine, what care I where my Society wife may be?

Suffering there must be; but I must save myself, by any means in my power, from one form of self-torture: I must never think that my life loses its value because of any neglect it may suffer. The full value of my life does not all go to buy my narrow domestic world; its great commerce does not stand or fall with some petty success or failure in the bartering of my personal joys and sorrows.

The time has come when I must divest Bimala of all the ideal decorations with which I decked her. It was owing to my own weakness that I indulged in such idolatry. I was too greedy. I created an angel of Bimala, in order to exaggerate my own enjoyment. But Bimala is what she is. It is preposterous to expect that she should assume the rôle of an angel for my pleasure. The Creator is under no obligation to supply me with angels, just because I have an avidity for imaginary perfection.

I must acknowledge that I have merely been an accident in Bimala's life. Her nature, perhaps, can only find true union with one like Sandip. At the same time, I must not, in false modesty, accept my rejection as my desert. Sandip certainly has attractive qualities, which had their sway also upon myself; but yet, I feel sure, he is not a greater man than I. If the wreath of victory falls to his lot today, and I am over-looked, then the dispenser of the wreath will be called to judgement.

I say this in no spirit of boasting. Sheer necessity has driven me to the pass, that to secure myself from utter desolation I must recognize all the value that I truly possess. Therefore, through the terrible experience of suffering let there come upon me the joy of deliverance — deliverance from self-distrust.

I have come to distinguish what is really in me from what I foolishly imagined to be there. The profit and loss account has been settled, and that which remains is myself — not a crippled self, dressed in rags and tatters, not a sick self to be nursed on invalid diet, but a spirit which has gone through the worst, and has survived.

My master passed through my room a moment ago and said with his hand on my shoulder: 'Get away to bed, Nikhil, the night is far advanced.'

The fact is, it has become so difficult for me to go to bed till late — till Bimal is fast asleep. In the day-time we meet, and even converse, but what am I to say when we are alone together, in the silence of the night? — so ashamed do I feel in mind and body.

'How is it, sir, you have not yet retired?' I asked in my turn. My master smiled a little, as he left me, saying: 'My sleeping days are over. I have now attained the waking age.'

I had written thus far, and was about to rise to go off bedwards when, through the window before me, I saw the heavy pall of July cloud suddenly part a little, and a big star shine through. It seemed to say to me: 'Dreamland ties are made, and dreamland ties are broken, but I am here for ever — the everlasting lamp of the bridal night.'

All at once my heart was full with the thought that my Eternal Love was steadfastly waiting for me through the ages, behind the veil of material things. Through many a life, in many a mirror, have I seen her image — broken mirrors, crooked mirrors, dusty mirrors. Whenever I have sought to make the mirror my very own, and shut it up within my box, I have lost sight of the image. But what of that. What have I to do with the mirror, or even the image?

My beloved, your smile shall never fade, and every dawn there shall appear fresh for me the vermilion mark on your forehead!

'What childish cajolery of self-deception,' mocks some devil from his dark corner – 'silly prattle to make children quiet!'

That may be. But millions and millions of children, with their million cries, have to be kept quiet. Can it be that all this multitude is quieted with only a lie? No, my Eternal Love cannot deceive me, for she is true!

She is true; that is why I have seen her and shall see her so often, even in my mistakes, even through the thickest mist of tears. I have seen her and lost her in the crowd of life's market-place, and found her again; and I shall find her once more when I have escaped through the loophole of death.

Ah, cruel one, play with me no longer! If I have failed to track you by the marks of your footsteps on the way, by the scent of your tresses lingering in the air, make me not weep for that for ever. The unveiled star tells me not to fear. That which is eternal must always be there.

Now let me go and see my Bimala. She must have spread her tired limbs on the bed, limp after her struggles, and be asleep. I will leave a kiss on her forehead without waking her – that shall be the flower-offering of my worship. I believe I could forget everything after death – all my mistakes, all my sufferings – but some vibration of the memory of that kiss would remain; for the wreath which is being woven out of the kisses of many a successive birth is to crown the Eternal Beloved.

As the gong of the watch rang out, sounding the hour of two, my sister-in-law came into the room. 'Whatever are you doing, brother dear?'[1] she cried. 'For pity's sake go to bed and stop worrying so. I cannot bear to look on that awful

1. When a relationship is established by marriage, or by mutual understanding arising out of special friendship or affection, the persons so related call each other in terms of such relationship, and not by name.

shadow of pain on your face.' Tears welled up in her eyes and overflowed as she entreated me thus.

I could not utter a word, but took the dust of her feet, as I went off to bed.

Bimala's Story

VII

At first I suspected nothing, feared nothing; I simply felt dedicated to my country. What a stupendous joy there was in this unquestioning surrender. Verily had I realized how, in thoroughness of self-destruction, man can find supreme bliss.

For aught I know, this frenzy of mine might have come to a gradual, natural end. But Sandip Babu would not have it so, he would insist on revealing himself. The tone of his voice became as intimate as a touch, every look flung itself on its knees in beggary. And, through it all, there burned a passion which in its violence made as though it would tear me up by the roots, and drag me along by the hair.

I will not shirk the truth. This cataclysmal desire drew me by day and by night. It seemed desperately alluring – this making havoc of myself. What a shame it seemed, how terrible, and yet how sweet! Then there was my overpowering curiosity, to which there seemed no limit. He of whom I knew but little, who never could assuredly be mine, whose youth flared so vigorously in a hundred points of flame – oh, the mystery of his seething passions, so immense, so tumultuous!

I began with a feeling of worship, but that soon passed away. I ceased even to respect Sandip; on the contrary, I began to look down upon him. Nevertheless this flesh-and-blood lute of mine, fashioned with my feeling and fancy, found in him a master-player. What though I shrank from his touch, and even came to loathe the lute itself; its music was conjured up all the same.

I must confess there was something in me which . . . what shall I say? . . . which makes me wish I could have died!

Chandranath Babu, when he finds leisure, comes to me. He

has the power to lift my mind up to an eminence from where I can see in a moment the boundary of my life extended on all sides and so realize that the lines, which I took from my bounds, were merely imaginary.

But what is the use of it all? Do I really desire emancipation? Let suffering come to our house; let the best in me shrivel up and become black; but let this infatuation not leave me – such seems to be my prayer.

When, before my marriage, I used to see a brother-in-law of mine, now dead, mad with drink – beating his wife in his frenzy, and then sobbing and howling in maudlin repentance, vowing never to touch liquor again, and yet, the very same evening, sitting down to drink and drink – it would fill me with disgust. But my intoxication today is still more fearful. The stuff has not to be procured or poured out: it springs within my veins, and I know not how to resist it.

Must this continue to the end of my days? Now and again I start and look upon myself, and think my life to be a nightmare which will vanish all of a sudden with all its untruth. It has become so frightfully incongruous. It has no connection with its past. What it is, how it could have come to this pass, I cannot understand.

One day my sister-in-law remarked with a cutting laugh: 'What a wonderfully hospitable Chota Rani we have! Her guest absolutely will not budge. In our time there used to be guests, too; but they had not such lavish looking after – we were so absurdly taken up with our husbands. Poor brother Nikhil is paying the penalty of being born too modern. He should have come as a guest if he wanted to stay on. Now it looks as if it were time for him to quit . . . O you little demon, do your glances never fall, by chance, on his agonized face?'

This sarcasm did not touch me; for I knew that these women had it not in them to understand the nature of the cause of my devotion. I was then wrapped in the protecting armour of the exaltation of sacrifice, through which such shafts were powerless to reach and shame me.

Chapter Four

For some time all talk of the country's cause has been dropped. Our conversation nowadays has become full of modern sex-problems, and various other matters, with a sprinkling of poetry, both old Vaishnava and modern English, accompanied by a running undertone of melody, low down in the bass, such as I have never in my life heard before, which seems to me to sound the true manly note, the note of power.

The day had come when all cover was gone. There was no longer even the pretence of a reason why Sandip Babu should linger on, or why I should have confidential talks with him every now and then. I felt thoroughly vexed with myself, with my sister-in-law, with the ways of the world, and I vowed I would never again go to the outer apartments, not if I were to die for it.

For two whole days I did not stir out. Then, for the first time, I discovered how far I had travelled. My life felt utterly tasteless. Whatever I touched I wanted to thrust away. I felt myself waiting – from the crown of my head to the tips of my toes – waiting for something, somebody; my blood kept tingling with some expectation.

I tried busying myself with extra work. The bedroom floor was clean enough but I insisted on its being scrubbed over again under my eyes. Things were arranged in the cabinets in one kind of order; I pulled them all out and rearranged them in a different way. I found no time that afternoon even to do up my hair; I hurriedly tied it into a loose knot, and went and worried everybody, fussing about the store-room. The stores seemed short, and pilfering must have been going on of late, but I could not muster up the courage to take any particular person to task – for might not the thought have crossed somebody's mind: 'Where were your eyes all these days!'

In short, I behaved that day as one possessed. The next day I tried to do some reading. What I read I have no idea, but after a spell of absentmindedness I found I had wandered away, book in hand, along the passage leading towards the

70

outer apartments, and was standing by a window looking out upon the verandah running along the row of rooms on the opposite side of the quadrangle. One of these rooms, I felt, had crossed over to another shore, and the ferry had ceased to ply. I felt like the ghost of myself of two days ago, doomed to remain where I was, and yet not really there, blankly looking out for ever.

As I stood there, I saw Sandip come out of his room into the verandah, a newspaper in his hand. I could see that he looked extraordinarily disturbed. The courtyard, the railings, in front, seemed to rouse his wrath. He flung away his newspaper with a gesture which seemed to want to rend the space before him.

I felt I could no longer keep my vow. I was about to move on towards the sitting-room, when I found my sister-in-law behind me. 'O Lord, this beats everything!' she ejaculated, as she glided away. I could not proceed to the outer apartments.

The next morning when my maid came calling, 'Rani Mother, it is getting late for giving out the stores,' I flung the keys to her, saying, 'Tell Harimati to see to it,' and went on with some embroidery of English pattern on which I was engaged, seated near the window.

Then came a servant with a letter. 'From Sandip Babu,' said he. What unbounded boldness! What must the messenger have thought? There was a tremor within my breast as I opened the envelope. There was no address on the letter, only the words: *An urgent matter – touching the Cause. Sandip.*

I flung aside the embroidery. I was up on my feet in a moment, giving a touch or two to my hair by the mirror. I kept the *sari* I had on, changing only my jacket – for one of my jackets had its associations.

I had to pass through one of the verandahs, where my sister-in-law used to sit in the morning slicing betel-nut. I refused to feel awkward. 'Whither away, Chota Rani?' she cried.

'To the sitting-room outside.'

'So early! A matinée, eh?'

And, as I passed on without further reply, she hummed after me a flippant song.

IX

When I was about to enter the sitting-room, I saw Sandip immersed in an illustrated catalogue of British Academy pictures, with his back to the door. He has a great notion of himself as an expert in matters of Art.

One day my husband said to him: 'If the artists ever want a teacher, they need never lack for one so long as you are there.' It had not been my husband's habit to speak cuttingly, but latterly there has been a change and he never spares Sandip.

'What makes you suppose that artists need no teachers?' Sandip retorted.

'Art is a creation,' my husband replied. 'So we should humbly be content to receive our lessons about Art from the work of the artist.'

Sandip laughed at this modesty, saying: 'You think that meekness is a kind of capital which increases your wealth the more you use it. It is my conviction that those who lack pride only float about like water reeds which have no roots in the soil.'

My mind used to be full of contradictions when they talked thus. On the one hand I was eager that my husband should win in argument and that Sandip's pride should be shamed. Yet, on the other, it was Sandip's unabashed pride which attracted me so. It shone like a precious diamond, which knows no diffidence, and sparkles in the face of the sun itself.

I entered the room. I knew Sandip could hear my footsteps as I went forward, but he pretended not to, and kept his eyes on the book.

I dreaded his Art talks, for I could not overcome my delicacy about the pictures he talked of, and the things he said, and had much ado in putting on an air of overdone insensibility to hide my qualms. So, I was almost on the point of retracing my steps, when, with a deep sigh, Sandip raised his eyes, and affected to be startled at the sight of me. 'Ah, you have come!' he said.

In his words, in his tone, in his eyes, there was a world of suppressed reproach, as if the claims he had acquired over me made my absence, even for these two or three days, a grievous wrong. I knew this attitude was an insult to me, but, alas, I had not the power to resent it.

I made no reply, but though I was looking another way, I could not help feeling that Sandip's plaintive gaze had planted itself right on my face, and would take no denial. I did so wish he would say something, so that I could shelter myself behind his words. I cannot tell how long this went on, but at last I could stand it no longer. 'What is this matter,' I asked, 'you are wanting to tell me about?'

Sandip again affected surprise as he said: 'Must there always be some matter? Is friendship by itself a crime? Oh, Queen Bee, to think that you should make so light of the greatest thing on earth! Is the heart's worship to be shut out like a stray cur?'

There was again that tremor within me. I could feel the crisis coming, too importunate to be put off. Joy and fear struggled for the mastery. Would my shoulders, I wondered, be broad enough to stand its shock, or would it not leave me overthrown, with my face in the dust?

I was trembling all over. Steadying myself with an effort I repeated: 'You summoned me for something touching the Cause, so I have left my household duties to attend to it.'

'That is just what I was trying to explain,' he said, with a dry laugh. 'Do you not know that I come to worship? Have I not told you that, in you, I visualize the *Shakti* of our country? The Geography of a country is not the whole truth. No one can give up his life for a map! When I see you before me, then only do I realize how lovely my country is. When you have anointed me with your own hands, then shall I know I have the sanction of my country; and if, with that in my heart, I fall fighting, it shall not be on the dust of some map-made land, but on a lovingly spread skirt – do you know what kind of skirt? – like that of the earthen-red *sari* you wore the other day, with a broad blood-red border. Can I ever forget it? Such are the visions which give vigour to life, and joy to death!'

Sandip's eyes took fire as he went on, but whether it was the fire of worship, or of passion, I could not tell. I was reminded of the day on which I first heard him speak, when

I could not be sure whether he was a person, or just a living flame.

I had not the power to utter a word. You cannot take shelter behind the walls of decorum when in a moment the fire leaps up and, with the flash of its sword and the roar of its laughter, destroys all the miser's stores. I was in terror lest he should forget himself and take me by the hand. For he shook like a quivering tongue of fire; his eyes showered scorching sparks on me.

'Are you for ever determined,' he cried after a pause, 'to make gods of your petty household duties – you who have it in you to send us to life or to death? Is this power of yours to be kept veiled in a zenana? Cast away all false shame, I pray you; snap your fingers at the whispering around. Take your plunge today into the freedom of the outer world.'

When, in Sandip's appeals, his worship of the country gets to be subtly interwoven with his worship of me, then does my blood dance, indeed, and the barriers of my hesitation totter. His talks about Art and Sex, his distinctions between Real and Unreal, had but clogged my attempts at response with some revolting nastiness. This, however, now burst again into a glow before which my repugnance faded away. I felt that my resplendent womanhood made me indeed a goddess. Why should not its glory flash from my forehead with visible brilliance? Why does not my voice find a word, some audible cry, which would be like a sacred spell to my country for its fire initiation?

All of a sudden my maid Khema rushed into the room, dishevelled. 'Give me my wages and let me go,' she screamed. 'Never in all my life have I been so . . .' The rest of her speech was drowned in sobs.

'What is the matter?'

Thako, the Bara Rani's maid, it appeared, had for no rhyme or reason reviled her in unmeasured terms. She was in such a state, it was no manner of use trying to pacify her by saying I would look into the matter afterwards.

The slime of domestic life that lay beneath the lotus bank of womanhood came to the surface. Rather than allow Sandip a prolonged vision of it, I had to hurry back within.

X

My sister-in-law was absorbed in her betel-nuts, the suspicion of a smile playing about her lips, as if nothing untoward
had happened. She was still humming the same song.

'Why has your Thako been calling poor Khema names?' I
burst out.

'Indeed? The wretch! I will have her broomed out of the
house. What a shame to spoil your morning out like this! As
for Khema, where are the hussy's manners to go and disturb
you when you are engaged? Anyhow, Chota Rani, don't you
worry yourself with these domestic squabbles. Leave them to
me, and return to your friend.'

How suddenly the wind in the sails of our mind veers
round! This going to meet Sandip outside seemed, in the
light of the zenana code, such an extraordinarily out-of-the-
way thing to do that I went off to my own room, at a loss for
a reply. I knew this was my sister-in-law's doing and that she
had egged her maid on to contrive this scene. But I had
brought myself to such an unstable poise that I dared not
have my fling.

Why, it was only the other day that I found I could not
keep up to the last the unbending hauteur with which I had
demanded from my husband the dismissal of the man Nanku.
I felt suddenly abashed when the Bara Rani came up and
said: 'It is really all my fault, brother dear. We are old-
fashioned folk, and I did not quite like the ways of your
Sandip Babu, so I only told the guard . . . but how was I to
know that our Chota Rani would take this as an insult? – I
thought it would be the other way about! Just my incorrigible
silliness!'

The thing which seems so glorious when viewed from the
heights of the country's cause, looks so muddy when seen
from the bottom. One begins by getting angry, and then feels
disgusted.

I shut myself into my room, sitting by the window, thinking
how easy life would be if only one could keep in harmony
with one's surroundings. How simply the senior Rani sits in
her verandah with her betel-nuts and how inaccessible to me

has become my natural seat beside my daily duties! Where will it all.end, I asked myself? Shall I ever recover, as from a delirium, and forget it all; or am I to be dragged to depths from which there can be no escape in this life? How on earth did I manage to let my good fortune escape me, and spoil my life so? Every wall of this bedroom of mine, which I first entered nine years ago as a bride, stares at me in dismay.

When my husband came home, after his M.A. examination, he brought for me this orchid belonging to some far-away land beyond the seas. From beneath these few little leaves sprang such a cascade of blossoms, it looked as if they were pouring forth from some overturned urn of Beauty. We decided, together, to hang it here, over this window. It flowered only that once, but we have always been in hope of its doing so once more. Curiously enough I have kept on watering it these days, from force of habit, and it is still green.

It is now four years since I framed a photograph of my husband in ivory and put it in the niche over there. If I happen to look that way I have to lower my eyes. Up to last week I used regularly to put there the flowers of my worship, every morning after my bath. My husband has often chided me over this.

'It shames me to see you place me on a height to which I do not belong,' he said one day.

'What nonsense!'

'I am not only ashamed, but also jealous!'

'Just hear him! Jealous of whom, pray?'

'Of that false me. It only shows that I am too petty for you, that you want some extraordinary man who can overpower you with his superiority, and so you needs must take refuge in making for yourself another "me".'

'This kind of talk only makes me angry,' said I.

'What is the use of being angry with me?' he replied. 'Blame your fate which allowed you no choice, but made you take me blindfold. This keeps you trying to retrieve its blunder by making me out a paragon.'

I felt so hurt at the bare idea that tears started to my eyes that day. And whenever I think of that now, I cannot raise my eyes to the niche.

For now there is another photograph in my jewel case. The other day, when arranging the sitting-room, I brought away that double photo frame, the one in which Sandip's portrait was next to my husband's. To this portrait I have no flowers of worship to offer, but it remains hidden away under my gems. It has all the greater fascination because kept secret. I look at it now and then with doors closed. At night I turn up the lamp, and sit with it in my hand, gazing and gazing. And every night I think of burning it in the flame of the lamp, to be done with it for ever; but every night I heave a sigh and smother it again in my pearls and diamonds.

Ah, wretched woman! What a wealth of love was twined round each one of those jewels! Oh, why am I not dead?

Sandip had impressed it on me that hesitation is not in the nature of woman. For her, neither right nor left has any existence – she only moves forward. When the women of our country wake up, he repeatedly insisted, their voice will be unmistakably confident in its utterance of the cry: 'I *want.*'

'I want!' Sandip went on one day – this was the primal word at the root of all creation. It had no maxim to guide it, but it became fire and wrought itself into suns and stars. Its partiality is terrible. Because it had a desire for man, it ruthlessly sacrificed millions of beasts for millions of years to achieve that desire. That terrible word 'I want' has taken flesh in woman, and therefore men, who are cowards, try with all their might to keep back this primeval flood with their earthen dykes. They are afraid lest, laughing and dancing as it goes, it should wash away all the hedges and props of their pumpkin field. Men, in every age, flatter themselves that they have secured this force within the bounds of their convenience, but it gathers and grows. Now it is calm and deep like a lake, but gradually its pressure will increase, the dykes will give way, and the force which has so long been dumb will rush forward with the roar: 'I want!'

These words of Sandip echo in my heart-beats like a war-drum. They shame into silence all my conflicts with myself. What do I care what people may think of me? Of what value are that orchid and that niche in my bedroom? What power have they to belittle me, to put me to shame? The primal fire of creation burns in me.

I felt a strong desire to snatch down the orchid and fling it out of the window, to denude the niche of its picture, to lay bare and naked the unashamed spirit of destruction that raged within me. My arm was raised to do it, but a sudden pang passed through my breast, tears started to my eyes. I threw myself down and sobbed: 'What is the end of all this, what is the end?'

Sandip's Story

IV

When I read these pages of the story of my life I seriously question myself: Is this Sandip? Am I made of words? Am I merely a book with a covering of flesh and blood?

The earth is not a dead thing like the moon. She breathes. Her rivers and oceans send up vapours in which she is clothed. She is covered with a mantle of her own dust which flies about the air. The onlooker, gazing upon the earth from the outside, can see only the light reflected from this vapour and this dust. The tracks of the mighty continents are not distinctly visible.

The man, who is alive as this earth is, is likewise always enveloped in the mist of the ideas which he is breathing out. His real land and water remain hidden, and he appears to be made of only lights and shadows.

It seems to me, in this story of my life, that, like a living plant, I am displaying the picture of an ideal world. But I am not merely what I want, what I think – I am also what I do not love, what I do *not* wish to be. My creation had begun before I was born. I had no choice in regard to my surroundings and so must make the best of such material as comes to my hand.

My theory of life makes me certain that the Great is cruel. To be just is for ordinary men – it is reserved for the great to be unjust. The surface of the earth was even. The volcano butted it with its fiery horn and found its own eminence – its justice was not towards its obstacle, but towards itself. Successful injustice and genuine cruelty have been the only forces by which individual or nation has become millionaire or monarch.

That is why I preach the great discipline of Injustice. I say to everyone: Deliverance is based upon injustice. Injustice is the fire which must keep on burning something in order to save itself from becoming ashes. Whenever an individual or nation becomes incapable of perpetrating injustice it is swept into the dust-bin of the world.

As yet this is only my idea – it is not completely myself. There are rifts in the armour through which something peeps out which is extremely soft and sensitive. Because, as I say, the best part of myself was created before I came to this stage of existence.

From time to time I try my followers in their lesson of cruelty. One day we went on a picnic. A goat was grazing by. I asked them: 'Who is there among you that can cut off a leg of that goat, alive, with this knife, and bring it to me?' While they all hesitated, I went myself and did it. One of them fainted at the sight. But when they saw me unmoved they took the dust of my feet, saying that I was above all human weaknesses. That is to say, they saw that day the vaporous envelope which was my idea, but failed to perceive the inner me, which by a curious freak of fate has been created tender and merciful.

In the present chapter of my life, which is growing in interest every day round Bimala and Nikhil, there is also much that remains hidden underneath. This malady of ideas which afflicts me is shaping my life within: nevertheless a great part of my life remains outside its influence; and so there is set up a discrepancy between my outward life and its inner design which I try my best to keep concealed even from myself; otherwise it may wreck not only my plans, but my very life.

Life is indefinite – a bundle of contradictions. We men, with our ideas, strive to give it a particular shape by melting it into a particular mould – into the definiteness of success. All the world-conquerors, from Alexander down to the

American millionaires, mould themselves into a sword or a mint, and thus find that distinct image of themselves which is the source of their success.

The chief controversy between Nikhil and myself arises from this: that though I say 'know thyself', and Nikhil also says 'know thyself', his interpretation makes this 'knowing' tantamount to 'not knowing'.

'Winning your kind of success,' Nikhil once objected, 'is success gained at the cost of the soul: but the soul is greater than success.'

I simply said in answer: 'Your words are too vague.'

'That I cannot help,' Nikhil replied. 'A machine is distinct enough, but not so life. If to gain distinctness you try to know life as a machine, then such mere distinctness cannot stand for truth. The soul is not as distinct as success, and so you only lose your soul if you seek it in your success.'

'Where, then, is this wonderful soul?'

'Where it knows itself in the infinite and transcends its success.'

'But how does all this apply to our work for the country?'

'It is the same thing. Where our country makes itself the final object, it gains success at the cost of the soul. Where it recognizes the Greatest as greater than all, there it may miss success, but gains its soul.'

'Is there any example of this in history?'

'Man is so great that he can despise not only the success, but also the example. Possibly example is lacking, just as there is no example of the flower in the seed. But there is the urgence of the flower in the seed all the same.'

It is not that I do not at all understand Nikhil's point of view; that is rather where my danger lies. I was born in India and the poison of its spirituality runs in my blood. However loudly I may proclaim the madness of walking in the path of self-abnegation, I cannot avoid it altogether.

This is exactly how such curious anomalies happen nowadays in our country. We must have our religion and also our nationalism; our *Bhagavadgita* and also our *Bande Mataram*. The result is that both of them suffer. It is like performing with an English military band, side by side with our Indian festive pipes. I must make it the purpose of my life to put an end to this hideous confusion.

I want the western military style to prevail, not the Indian. We shall then not be ashamed of the flag of our passion, which mother Nature has sent with us as our standard into the battlefield of life. Passion is beautiful and pure – pure as the lily that comes out of the slimy soil. It rises superior to its defilement and needs no Pears' soap to wash it clean.

v

A question has been worrying me the last few days. Why am I allowing my life to become entangled with Bimala's? Am I a drifting log to be caught up at any and every obstacle?

Not that I have any false shame at Bimala becoming an object of my desire. It is only too clear how she wants me, and so I look on her as quite legitimately mine. The fruit hangs on the branch by the stem, but that is no reason why the claim of the stem should be eternal. Ripe fruit cannot for ever swear by its slackening stem-hold. All its sweetness has been accumulated for me; to surrender itself to my hand is the reason of its existence, its very nature, its true morality. So I must pluck it, for it becomes me not to make it futile.

But what is teasing me is that I am getting entangled. Am I not born to rule? – to bestride my proper steed, the crowd, and drive it as I will; the reins in my hand, the destination known only to me, and for it the thorns, the mire, on the road? This steed now awaits me at the door, pawing and champing its bit, its neighing filling the skies. But where am I, and what am I about, letting day after day of golden opportunity slip by?

I used to think I was like a storm – that the torn flowers with which I strewed my path would not impede my progress. But I am only wandering round and round a flower like a bee – not a storm. So, as I was saying, the colouring of ideas which man gives himself is only superficial. The inner man remains as ordinary as ever. If someone, who could see right

81

into me, were to write my biography, he would make me out to be no different from that lout of a Panchu, or even from Nikhil!

Last night I was turning over the pages of my old diary ... I had just graduated, and my brain was bursting with philosophy. Even so early I had vowed not to harbour any illusions, whether of my own or others' imagining, but to build my life on a solid basis of reality. But what has since been its actual story? Where is its solidity? It has rather been a network, where, though the thread be continuous, more space is taken up by the holes. Fight as I may, these will not own defeat. Just as I was congratulating myself on steadily following the thread, here I am badly caught in a hole! For I have become susceptible to compunctions.

'I want it; it is here; let me take it' – This is a clear-cut, straightforward policy. Those who can pursue its course with vigour needs must win through in the end. But the gods would not have it that such journey should be easy, so they have deputed the siren Sympathy to distract the wayfarer, to dim his vision with her tearful mist.

I can see that poor Bimala is struggling like a snared deer. What a piteous alarm there is in her eyes! How she is torn with straining at her bonds! This sight, of course, should gladden the heart of a true hunter. And so do I rejoice; but, then, I am also touched; and therefore I dally, and standing on the brink I am hesitating to pull the noose fast.

There have been moments, I know, when I could have bounded up to her, clasped her hands and folded her to my breast, unresisting. Had I done so, she would not have said one word. She was aware that some crisis was impending, which in a moment would change the meaning of the whole world. Standing before that cavern of the incalculable but yet expected, her face went pale and her eyes glowed with a fearful ecstasy. Within that moment, when it arrives, an eternity will take shape, which our destiny awaits, holding its breath.

But I have let this moment slip by. I did not, with uncompromising strength, press the almost certain into the absolutely assured. I now see clearly that some hidden elements in my nature have openly ranged themselves as obstacles in my path.

That is exactly how Ravana, whom I look upon as the real hero of the *Ramayana*, met with his doom. He kept Sita in his Asoka garden, awaiting her pleasure, instead of taking her straight into his harem. This weak spot in his otherwise grand character made the whole of the abduction episode futile. Another such touch of compunction made him disregard, and be lenient to, his traitorous brother Bibhisan, only to get himself killed for his pains.

Thus does the tragic in life come by its own. In the beginning it lies, a little thing, in some dark under-vault, and ends by overthrowing the whole superstructure. The real tragedy is, that man does not know himself for what he really is.

VI

Then again there is Nikhil. Crank though he be, laugh at him as I may, I cannot get rid of the idea that he is my friend. At first I gave no thought to his point of view, but of late it has begun to shame and hurt me. Therefore I have been trying to talk and argue with him in the same enthusiastic way as of old, but it does not ring true. It is even leading me at times into such a length of unnaturalness as to pretend to agree with him. But such hypocrisy is not in my nature, nor in that of Nikhil either. This, at least, is something we have in common. That is why, nowadays, I would rather not come across him, and have taken to fighting shy of his presence.

All these are signs of weakness. No sooner is the possibility of a wrong admitted than it becomes actual, and clutches you by the throat, however you may then try to shake off all belief in it. What I should like to be able to tell Nikhil frankly is, that happenings such as these must be looked in the face – as great Realities – and that which is the Truth should not be allowed to stand between true friends.

There is no denying that I have really weakened. It was not this weakness which won over Bimala; she burnt her wings in the blaze of the full strength of my unhesitating manliness.

Whenever smoke obscures its lustre she also becomes confused, and draws back. Then comes a thorough revulsion of feeling, and she fain would take back the garland she has put round my neck, but cannot; and so she only closes her eyes, to shut it out of sight.

But all the same I must not swerve from the path I have chalked out. It would never do to abandon the cause of the country, especially at the present time. I shall simply make Bimala one with my country. The turbulent west wind which has swept away the country's veil of conscience, will sweep away the veil of the wife from Bimala's face, and in that uncovering there will be no shame. The ship will rock as it bears the crowd across the ocean, flying the pennant of *Bande Mataram*, and it will serve as the cradle to my power, as well as to my love.

Bimala will see such a majestic vision of deliverance, that her bonds will slip from about her, without shame, without her even being aware of it. Fascinated by the beauty of this terrible wrecking power, she will not hesitate a moment to be cruel. I have seen in Bimala's nature the cruelty which is the inherent force of existence – the cruelty which with its unrelenting might keeps the world beautiful.

If only women could be set free from the artificial fetters put round them by men, we could see on earth the living image of Kali, the shameless, pitiless goddess. I am a worshipper of Kali, and one day I shall truly worship her, setting Bimala on her altar of Destruction. For this let me get ready.

The way of retreat is absolutely closed for both of us. We shall despoil each other: get to hate each other: but never more be free.

Chapter Five

☀

Nikhil's Story

IV

EVERYTHING is rippling and waving with the flood of August. The young shoots of rice have the sheen of an infant's limbs. The water has invaded the garden next to our house. The morning light, like the love of the blue sky, is lavished upon the earth ... Why cannot I sing? The water of the distant river is shimmering with light; the leaves are glistening; the rice-fields, with their fitful shivers, break into gleams of gold; and in this symphony of Autumn, only I remain voiceless. The sunshine of the world strikes my heart, but is not reflected back.

When I realize the lack of expressiveness in myself, I know why I am deprived. Who could bear my company day and night without a break? Bimala is full of the energy of life, and so she has never become stale to me for a moment, in all these nine years of our wedded life.

My life has only its dumb depths; but no murmuring rush. I can only receive: not impart movement. And therefore my company is like fasting. I recognize clearly today that Bimala has been languishing because of a famine of companionship.

Then whom shall I blame? Like Vidyapati I can only lament:

> *It is August, the sky breaks into a passionate rain;*
> *Alas, empty is my house.*

My house, I now see, was built to remain empty, because its doors cannot open. But I never knew till now that its divinity had been sitting outside. I had fondly believed that

85

she had accepted my sacrifice, and granted in return her boon. But, alas, my house has all along been empty.

Every year, about this time, it was our practice to go in a house-boat over the broads of Samalda. I used to tell Bimala that a song must come back to its refrain over and over again. The original refrain of every song is in Nature, where the rain-laden wind passes over the rippling stream, where the green earth, drawing its shadow-veil over its face, keeps its ear close to the speaking water. There, at the beginning of time, a man and a woman first met – not within walls. And therefore we two must come back to Nature, at least once a year, to tune our love anew to the first pure note of the meeting of hearts.

The first two anniversaries of our married life I spent in Calcutta, where I went through my examinations. But from the next year onwards, for seven years without a break, we have celebrated our union among the blossoming water-lilies. Now begins the next octave of my life.

It was difficult for me to ignore the fact that the same month of August had come round again this year. Does Bimala remember it, I wonder? – she has given me no reminder. Everything is mute about me.

> *It is August, the sky breaks into a passionate rain;*
> *And empty is my house.*

The house which becomes empty through the parting of lovers, still has music left in the heart of its emptiness. But the house that is empty because hearts are asunder, is awful in its silence. Even the cry of pain is out of place there.

This cry of pain must be silenced in me. So long as I continue to suffer, Bimala will never have true freedom. I *must* free her completely, otherwise I shall never gain *my* freedom from untruth . . .

I think I have come to the verge of understanding one thing. Man has so fanned the flame of the loves of men and women, as to make it overpass its rightful domain, and now, even in the name of humanity itself, he cannot bring it back under control. Man's worship has idolized his passion. But there must be no more human sacrifices at its shrine . . .

I went into my bedroom this morning, to fetch a book. It is long since I have been there in the day-time. A pang passed through me as I looked round it today, in the morning light. On the clothes rack was hanging a *sari* of Bimala's, crinkled ready for wear. On the dressing-table were her perfumes, her comb, her hair-pins, and with them, still, her vermilion box! Underneath were her tiny gold-embroidered slippers.

Once, in the old days, when Bimala had not yet overcome her objections to shoes, I had got these out from Lucknow, to tempt her. The first time she was ready to drop for very shame, to go in them even from the room to the verandah. Since then she has worn out many shoes, but has treasured up this pair. When first showing her the slippers, I chaffed her over a curious practice of hers; 'I have caught you taking the dust of my feet, thinking me asleep! These are the offerings of my worship to ward the dust off the feet of my wakeful divinity.' 'You must not say such things,' she protested, 'or I will never wear your shoes!'

This bedroom of mine – it has a subtle atmosphere which goes straight to my heart. I was never aware, as I am today, how my thirsting heart has been sending out its roots to cling round each and every familiar object. The severing of the main root, I see, is not enough to set life free. Even these little slippers serve to hold one back.

My wandering eyes fall on the niche. My portrait there is looking the same as ever, in spite of the flowers scattered round it having been withered black! Of all the things in the room their greeting strikes me as sincere. They are still here simply because it was not felt worth while even to remove them. Never mind; let me welcome truth, albeit in such sere and sorry garb, and look forward to the time when I shall be able to do so unmoved, as does my photograph.

As I stood there, Bimal came in from behind. I hastily turned my eyes from the niche to the shelves as I muttered: 'I came to get Amiel's Journal.' What need had I to volunteer an explanation? I felt like a wrong-doer, a trespasser, prying into a secret not meant for me. I could not look Bimal in the face, but hurried away.

V

I had just made the discovery that it was useless to keep up a pretence of reading in my room outside, and also that it was equally beyond me to busy myself attending to anything at all – so that all the days of my future bid fair to congeal into one solid mass and settle heavily on my breast for good – when Panchu, the tenant of a neighbouring *zamindar*, came up to me with a basketful of cocoa-nuts and greeted me with a profound obeisance.

'Well, Panchu,' said I. 'What is all this for?'

I had got to know Panchu through my master. He was extremely poor, nor was I in a position to do anything for him; so I supposed this present was intended to procure a tip to help the poor fellow to make both ends meet. I took some money from my purse and held it out towards him, but with folded hands he protested: 'I cannot take that, sir!'

'Why, what is the matter?'

'Let me make a clean breast of it, sir. Once, when I was hard pressed, I stole some cocoa-nuts from the garden here. I am getting old, and may die any day, so I have come to pay them back.'

Amiel's Journal could not have done me any good that day. But these words of Panchu lightened my heart. There are more things in life than the union or separation of man and woman. The great world stretches far beyond, and one can truly measure one's joys and sorrows when standing in its midst.

Panchu was devoted to my master. I know well enough how he manages to eke out a livelihood. He is up before dawn every day, and with a basket of *pan* leaves, twists of tobacco, coloured cotton yarn, little combs, looking-glasses, and other trinkets beloved of the village women, he wades through the knee-deep water of the marsh and goes over to the *Namasudra* quarters. There he barters his goods for rice, which fetches him a little more than their price in money. If he can get back soon enough he goes out again, after a hurried meal, to the sweetmeat seller's, where he assists in beating sugar for wafers. As soon as he comes home he sits at his shell-bangle making, plodding on often till midnight. All this cruel toil does not earn, for himself and his family, a bare two meals a day during much more than half the year. His method of eating is to begin with a good filling draught of water, and his staple food is the cheapest kind of seedy banana. And yet the family has to go with only one meal a day for the rest of the year.

At one time I had an idea of making him a charity allowance, 'But,' said my master, 'your gift may destroy the man, it cannot destroy the hardship of his lot. Mother Bengal has not only this one Panchu. If the milk in her breasts has run dry, that cannot be supplied from the outside.'

These are thoughts which give one pause, and I decided to devote myself to working it out. That very day I said to Bimal: 'Let us dedicate our lives to removing the root of this sorrow in our country.'

'You are my Prince Siddharta,[1] I see,' she replied with a smile. 'But do not let the torrent of your feelings end by sweeping me away also!'

'Siddharta took his vows alone. I want ours to be a joint arrangement.'

The idea passed away in talk. The fact is, Bimala is at heart what is called a 'lady'. Though her own people are not well off, she was born a Rani. She has no doubts in her mind that there is a lower unit of measure for the trials and troubles of the 'lower classes'. Want is, of course, a permanent feature of their lives, but does not necessarily mean 'want' to them. Their very smallness protects them, as the banks protect the pool; by widening bounds only the slime is exposed.

The real fact is that Bimala has only come into my home, not into my life. I had magnified her so, leaving her such a large place, that when I lost her, my whole way of life became narrow and confined. I had thrust aside all other objects into a corner to make room for Bimala – taken up as I was with decorating her and dressing her and educating her and moving round her day and night; forgetting how great is humanity and how nobly precious is man's life. When the

1. The name by which Buddha was known when a Prince, before renouncing the world.

actualities of everyday things get the better of the man, then is Truth lost sight of and freedom missed. So painfully important did Bimala make the mere actualities, that the truth remained concealed from me. That is why I find no gap in my misery, and spread this minute point of my emptiness over all the world. And so, for hours on this Autumn morning, the refrain has been humming in my ears:

It is the month of August, and the sky breaks into a passionate
rain;
    Alas, my house is empty.

Bimala's Story

XI

The change which had, in a moment, come over the mind of Bengal was tremendous. It was as if the Ganges had touched the ashes of the sixty thousand sons of Sagar[1] which no fire could enkindle, no other water knead again into living clay. The ashes of lifeless Bengal suddenly spoke up: 'Here am I.'

I have read somewhere that in ancient Greece a sculptor had the good fortune to impart life to the image made by his own hand. Even in that miracle, however, there was the process of form preceding life. But where was the unity in this heap of barren ashes? Had they been hard like stone, we might have had hopes of some form emerging, even as Ahalya, though turned to stone, at last won back her humanity. But these scattered ashes must have dropped to the dust through gaps in the Creator's fingers, to be blown hither and thither by the wind. They had become heaped up, but were never before united. Yet in this day which had come to Bengal, even this collection of looseness had taken shape, and proclaimed in a thundering voice, at our very door: 'Here I am.'

How could we help thinking that it was all supernatural?

1. The condition of the curse which had reduced them to ashes was such that they could only be restored to life if the stream of the Ganges was brought down to them.

This moment of our history seemed to have dropped into our hand like a jewel from the crown of some drunken god. It had no resemblance to our past; and so we were led to hope that all our wants and miseries would disappear by the spell of some magic charm, that for us there was no longer any boundary line between the possible and the impossible. Everything seemed to be saying to us: 'It is coming; it has come!'

Thus we came to cherish the belief that our history needed no steed, but that like heaven's chariot it would move with its own inherent power – At least no wages would have to be paid to the charioteer; only his wine cup would have to be filled again and again. And then in some impossible paradise the goal of our hopes would be reached.

My husband was not altogether unmoved, but through all our excitement it was the strain of sadness in him which deepened and deepened. He seemed to have a vision of something beyond the surging present.

I remember one day, in the course of the arguments he continually had with Sandip, he said: 'Good fortune comes to our gate and announces itself, only to prove that we have not the power to receive it – that we have not kept things ready to be able to invite it into our house.'

'No,' was Sandip's answer. 'You talk like an atheist because you do not believe in our gods. To us it has been made quite visible that the Goddess has come with her boon, yet you distrust the obvious signs of her presence.'

'It is because I strongly believe in my God,' said my husband, 'that I feel so certain that our preparations for his worship are lacking. God has power to give the boon, but we must have power to accept it.'

This kind of talk from my husband would only annoy me. I could not keep from joining in: 'You think this excitement is only a fire of drunkenness, but does not drunkenness, up to a point, give strength?'

'Yes,' my husband replied. 'It may give strength, but not weapons.'

'But strength is the gift of God,' I went on. 'Weapons can be supplied by mere mechanics.'

My husband smiled. 'The mechanics will claim their wages before they deliver their supplies,' he said.

Sandip swelled his chest as he retorted: 'Don't you trouble about that. Their wages shall be paid.'

'I shall bespeak the festive music when the payment has been made, not before,' my husband answered.

'You needn't imagine that we are depending on your bounty for the music,' said Sandip scornfully. 'Our festival is above all money payments.'

And in his thick voice he began to sing:

> *'My lover of the unpriced love, spurning payments,*
> *Plays upon the simple pipe, bought for nothing,*
> *Drawing my heart away.'*

Then with a smile he turned to me and said: 'If I sing, Queen Bee, it is only to prove that when music comes into one's life, the lack of a good voice is no matter. When we sing merely on the strength of our tunefulness, the song is belittled. Now that a full flood of music has swept over our country, let Nikhil practise his scales, while we rouse the land with our cracked voices:

> *'My house cries to me: Why go out to lose your all?*
> *My life says: All that you have, fling to the winds!*
> *If we must lose our all, let us lose it: what is it worth after*
> *   all?*
> *If I must court ruin, let me do it smilingly:*
> *For my quest is the death-draught of immortality.*

'The truth is, Nikhil, that we have all lost our hearts. None can hold us any longer within the bounds of the easily possible, in our forward rush to the hopelessly impossible.

> *'Those who would draw us back,*
> *They know not the fearful joy of recklessness.*
> *They know not that we have had our call*
> *From the end of the crooked path.*
> *All that is good and straight and trim —*
> *Let it topple over in the dust.'*

I thought that my husband was going to continue the discussion, but he rose silently from his seat and left us.

The thing that was agitating me within was merely a variation of the stormy passion outside, which swept the country from one end to the other. The car of the wielder of my destiny was fast approaching, and the sound of its wheels reverberated in my being. I had a constant feeling that something extraordinary might happen any moment, for which, however, the responsibility would not be mine. Was I not removed from the plane in which right and wrong, and the feelings of others, have to be considered? Had I ever wanted this – had I ever been waiting or hoping for any such thing? Look at my whole life and tell me then, if I was in any way accountable.

Through all my past I had been consistent in my devotion – but when at length it came to receiving the boon, a different god appeared! And just as the awakened country, with its *Bande Mataram*, thrills in salutation to the unrealized future before it, so do all my veins and nerves send forth shocks of welcome to the unthought-of, the unknown, the importunate Stranger.

One night I left my bed and slipped out of my room on to the open terrace. Beyond our garden wall are fields of ripening rice. Through the gaps in the village groves to the North, glimpses of the river are seen. The whole scene slept in the darkness like the vague embryo of some future creation.

In that future I saw my country, a woman like myself, standing expectant. She has been drawn forth from her home corner by the sudden call of some Unknown. She has had no time to pause or ponder, or to light herself a torch, as she rushes forward into the darkness ahead. I know well how her very soul responds to the distant flute-strains which call her; how her breast rises and falls; how she feels she nears it, nay it is already hers, so that it matters not even if she run blindfold. She is no mother. There is no call to her of children in their hunger, no home to be lighted of an evening, no household work to be done. So; she hies to her tryst, for this is the land of the Vaishnava Poets. She has left home, forgotten domestic duties; she has nothing but an unfathomable yearning which hurries her on – by what road, to what goal, she recks not.

I, also, am possessed of just such a yearning. I likewise have lost my home and also lost my way. Both the end and the means have become equally shadowy to me. There remain only the yearning and the hurrying on. Ah! wretched wanderer through the night, when the dawn reddens you will see no trace of a way to return. But why return? Death will serve as well. If the Dark which sounded the flute should lead to destruction, why trouble about the hereafter? When I am merged in its blackness, neither I, nor good and bad, nor laughter, nor tears, shall be any more!

XII

In Bengal the machinery of time being thus suddenly run at full pressure, things which were difficult became easy, one following soon after another. Nothing could be held back any more, even in our corner of the country. In the beginning our district was backward, for my husband was unwilling to put any compulsion on the villagers. 'Those who make sacrifices for their country's sake are indeed her servants,' he would say, 'but those who compel others to make them in her name are her enemies. They would cut freedom at the root, to gain it at the top.'

But when Sandip came and settled here, and his followers began to move about the country, speaking in towns and market-places, waves of excitement came rolling up to us as well. A band of young fellows of the locality attached themselves to him, some even who had been known as a disgrace to the village. But the glow of their genuine enthusiasm lighted them up, within as well as without. It became quite clear that when the pure breezes of a great joy and hope sweep through the land, all dirt and decay are cleansed away. It is hard, indeed, for men to be frank and straight and healthy, when their country is in the throes of dejection.

Then were all eyes turned on my husband, from whose estates alone foreign sugar and salt and cloths had not been banished. Even the estate officers began to feel awkward and ashamed over it. And yet, some time ago, when my husband began to import country-made articles into our village, he had been secretly and openly twitted for his folly, by old and young alike. When *Swadeshi* had not yet become a boast, we had despised it with all our hearts.

My husband still sharpens his Indian-made pencils with his Indian-made knife, does his writing with reed pens, drinks his water out of a bell-metal vessel, and works at night in the light of an old-fashioned castor-oil lamp. But this dull, milk-and-water *Swadeshi* of his never appealed to us. Rather, we had always felt ashamed of the inelegant, unfashionable furniture of his reception-rooms, especially when he had the magistrate, or any other European, as his guest.

My husband used to make light of my protests. 'Why allow such trifles to upset you?' he would say with a smile.

'They will think us barbarians, or at all events wanting in refinement.'

'If they do, I will pay them back by thinking that their refinement does not go deeper than their white skins.'

My husband had an ordinary brass pot on his writing-table which he used as a flower-vase. It has often happened that, when I had news of some European guest, I would steal into his room and put in its place a crystal vase of European make. 'Look here, Bimala,' he objected at length, 'that brass pot is as unconscious of itself as those blossoms are; but this thing protests its purpose so loudly, it is only fit for artificial flowers.'

The Bara Rani, alone, pandered to my husband's whims. Once she comes panting to say: 'Oh, brother, have you heard? Such lovely Indian soaps have come out! My days of luxury are gone by; still, if they contain no animal fat, I should like to try some.'

This sort of thing makes my husband beam all over, and the house is deluged with Indian scents and soaps. Soaps indeed! They are more like lumps of caustic soda. And do I not know that what my sister-in-law uses on herself are the European soaps of old, while these are made over to the maids for washing clothes?

Another time it is: 'Oh, brother dear, do get me some of these new Indian pen-holders.'

Her 'brother' bubbles up as usual, and the Bara Rani's room becomes littered with all kinds of awful sticks that go by the name of *Swadeshi* pen-holders. Not that it makes any difference to her, for reading and writing are out of her line. Still, in her writing-case, lies the selfsame ivory pen-holder, the only one ever handled.

The fact is, all this was intended as a hit at me, because I would not keep my husband company in his vagaries. It was no good trying to show up my sister-in-law's insincerity; my husband's face would set so hard, if I barely touched on it. One only gets into trouble, trying to save such people from being imposed upon!

The Bara Rani loves sewing. One day I could not help blurting out: 'What a humbug you are, sister! When your "brother" is present, your mouth waters at the very mention of *Swadeshi* scissors, but it is the English-made article every time when you work.'

'What harm?' she replied. 'Do you not see what pleasure it gives him? We have grown up together in this house, since he was a boy. I simply cannot bear, as you can, the sight of the smile leaving his face. Poor dear, he has no amusement except this playing at shop-keeping. You are his only dissipation, and you will yet be his ruin!'

'Whatever you may say, it is not right to be double-faced,' I retorted.

My sister-in-law laughed out in my face. 'Oh, our artless little Chota Rani! – straight as a schoolmaster's rod, eh? But a woman is not built that way. She is soft and supple, so that she may bend without being crooked.'

I could not forget those words: 'You are his dissipation, and will be his ruin!' Today I feel – if a man needs must have some intoxicant, let it not be a woman.

XIII

Suksar, within our estates, is one of the biggest trade centres in the district. On one side of a stretch of water there is held a daily bazar; on the other, a weekly market. During the rains when this piece of water gets connected with the river, and boats can come through, great quantities of cotton yarns, and woollen stuffs for the coming winter, are brought in for sale.

At the height of our enthusiasm, Sandip laid it down that all foreign articles, together with the demon of foreign influence, must be driven out of our territory.

'Of course!' said I, girding myself up for a fight.

'I have had words with Nikhil about it,' said Sandip. 'He tells me, he does not mind speechifying, but he will not have coercion.'

'I will see to that,' I said, with a proud sense of power. I knew how deep was my husband's love for me. Had I been in my senses I should have allowed myself to be torn to pieces rather than assert my claim to that, at such a time. But Sandip had to be impressed with the full strength of my *Shakti*.

Sandip had brought home to me, in his irresistible way, how the cosmic Energy was revealed for each individual in the shape of some special affinity. Vaishnava Philosophy, he said, speaks of the *Shakti* of Delight that dwells in the heart of creation, ever attracting the heart of her Eternal Lover. Men have a perpetual longing to bring out this *Shakti* from the hidden depths of their own nature, and those of us who succeed in doing so at once clearly understand the meaning of the music coming to us from the Dark. He broke out singing:

> *'My flute, that was busy with its song,*
> *Is silent now when we stand face to face.*
> *My call went seeking you from sky to sky*
> > *When you lay hidden;*
> *But now all my cry finds its smile*
> > *In the face of my beloved.'*

Listening to his allegories, I had forgotten that I was plain and simple Bimala. I was *Shakti*; also an embodiment of

97

Universal joy. Nothing could fetter me, nothing was impossible for me; whatever I touched would gain new life. The world around me was a fresh creation of mine; for behold, before my heart's response had touched it, there had not been this wealth of gold in the Autumn sky! And this hero, this true servant of the country, this devotee of mine – this flaming intelligence, this burning energy, this shining genius – him also was I creating from moment to moment. Have I not seen how my presence pours fresh life into him time after time?

The other day Sandip begged me to receive a young lad, Amulya, an ardent disciple of his. In a moment I could see a new light flash out from the boy's eyes, and knew that he, too, had a vision of *Shakti* manifest, that my creative force had begun its work in his blood. 'What sorcery is this of yours!' exclaimed Sandip next day. 'Amulya is a boy no longer, the wick of his life is all ablaze. Who can hide your fire under your home-roof? Every one of them must be touched up by it, sooner or later, and when every lamp is alight what a grand carnival of a *Dewali* we shall have in the country!'

Blinded with the brilliance of my own glory I had decided to grant my devotee this boon. I was overweeningly confident that none could baulk me of what I really wanted. When I returned to my room after my talk with Sandip, I loosed my hair and tied it up over again. Miss Gilby had taught me a way of brushing it up from the neck and piling it in a knot over my head. This style was a favourite one with my husband. 'It is a pity,' he once said, 'that Providence should have chosen poor me, instead of poet Kalidas, for revealing all the wonders of a woman's neck. The poet would probably have likened it to a flower-stem; but I feel it to be a torch, holding aloft the black flame of your hair.' With which he . . . but why, oh why, do I go back to all that?

I sent for my husband. In the old days I could contrive a hundred and one excuses, good or bad, to get him to come to me. Now that all this had stopped for days I had lost the art of contriving.

Nikhil's Story

VI

Panchu's wife has just died of a lingering consumption. Panchu must undergo a purification ceremony to cleanse himself of sin and to propitiate his community. The community has calculated and informed him that it will cost one hundred and twenty-three rupees.

'How absurd!' I cried, highly indignant. 'Don't submit to this, Panchu. What can they do to you?'

Raising to me his patient eyes like those of a tired-out beast of burden, he said: 'There is my eldest girl, sir, she will have to be married. And my poor wife's last rites have to be put through.'

'Even if the sin were yours, Panchu,' I mused aloud, 'you have surely suffered enough for it already.'

'That is so, sir,' he naïvely assented. 'I had to sell part of my land and mortgage the rest to meet the doctor's bills. But there is no escape from the offerings I have to make the Brahmins.'

What was the use of arguing? When will come the time, I wondered, for the purification of the Brahmins themselves who can accept such offerings?

After his wife's illness and funeral, Panchu, who had been tottering on the brink of starvation, went altogether beyond his depth. In a desperate attempt to gain consolation of some sort he took to sitting at the feet of a wandering ascetic, and succeeded in acquiring philosophy enough to forget that his children went hungry. He kept himself steeped for a time in the idea that the world is vanity, and if of pleasure it has none, pain also is a delusion. Then, at last, one night he left his little ones in their tumble-down hovel, and started off wandering on his own account.

I knew nothing of this at the time, for just then a veritable ocean-churning by gods and demons was going on in my mind. Nor did my master tell me that he had taken Panchu's deserted children under his own roof and was caring for them, though alone in the house, with his school to attend to the whole day.

After a month Panchu came back, his ascetic fervour considerably worn off. His eldest boy and girl nestled up to him, crying: 'Where have you been all this time, father?' His youngest boy filled his lap; his second girl leant over his back with her arms around his neck; and they all wept together. 'O sir!' sobbed Panchu, at length, to my master. 'I have not the power to give these little ones enough to eat – I am not free to run away from them. What has been my sin that I should be scourged so, bound hand and foot?'

In the meantime the thread of Panchu's little trade connections had snapped and he found he could not resume them. He clung on to the shelter of my master's roof, which had first received him on his return, and said not a word of going back home. 'Look here, Panchu,' my master was at last driven to say. 'If you don't take care of your cottage, it will tumble down altogether. I will lend you some money with which you can do a bit of peddling and return it me little by little.'

Panchu was not excessively pleased – was there then no such thing as charity on earth? And when my master asked him to write out a receipt for the money, he felt that this favour, demanding a return, was hardly worth having. My master, however, did not care to make an outward gift which would leave an inward obligation. To destroy self-respect is to destroy caste, was his idea.

After signing the note, Panchu's obeisance to my master fell off considerably in its reverence – the dust-taking was left out. It made my master smile; he asked nothing better than that courtesy should stoop less low. 'Respect given and taken truly balances the account between man and man,' was the way he put it, 'but veneration is overpayment.'

Panchu began to buy cloth at the market and peddle it about the village. He did not get much of cash payment, it is true, but what he could realize in kind, in the way of rice, jute, and other field produce, went towards settlement of his account. In two months' time he was able to pay back an instalment of my master's debt, and with it there was a corresponding reduction in the depth of his bow. He must have begun to feel that he had been revering as a saint a mere man, who had not even risen superior to the lure of lucre.

While Panchu was thus engaged, the full shock of the *Swadeshi* flood fell on him.

VII

It was vacation time, and many youths of our village and its neighbourhood had come home from their schools and colleges. They attached themselves to Sandip's leadership with enthusiasm, and some, in their excess of zeal, gave up their studies altogether. Many of the boys had been free pupils of my school here, and some held college scholarships from me in Calcutta. They came up in a body, and demanded that I should banish foreign goods from my Suksar market.

I told them I could not do it.

They were sarcastic: 'Why, Maharaja, will the loss be too much for you?'

I took no notice of the insult in their tone, and was about to reply that the loss would fall on the poor traders and their customers, not on me, when my master, who was present, interposed.

'Yes, the loss will be his – not yours, that is clear enough,' he said.

'But for one's country . . .'

'The country does not mean the soil, but the men on it,' interrupted my master again. 'Have you yet wasted so much as a glance on what was happening to them? But now you would dictate what salt they shall eat, what clothes they shall wear. Why should they put up with such tyranny, and why should we let them?'

'But we have taken to Indian salt and sugar and cloth ourselves.'

'You may do as you please to work off your irritation, to keep up your fanaticism. You are well off, you need not mind the cost. The poor do not want to stand in your way, but you insist on their submitting to your compulsion. As it is, every moment of theirs is a life-and-death struggle for a bare living;

you cannot even imagine the difference a few pice means to them – so little have you in common. You have spent your whole past in a superior compartment, and now you come down to use them as tools for the wreaking of your wrath. I call it cowardly.'

They were all old pupils of my master, so they did not venture to be disrespectful, though they were quivering with indignation. They turned to me. 'Will you then be the only one, Maharaja, to put obstacles in the way of what the country would achieve?'

'Who am I, that I should dare do such a thing? Would I not rather lay down my life to help it?'

The M.A. student smiled a crooked smile, as he asked: 'May we enquire what you are actually doing to help?'

'I have imported Indian mill-made yarn and kept it for sale in my Suksar market, and also sent bales of it to markets belonging to neighbouring *zamindars*.'

'But we have been to your market, Maharaja,' the same student exclaimed, 'and found nobody buying this yarn.'

'That is neither my fault nor the fault of my market. It only shows the whole country has not taken your vow.'

'That is not all,' my master went on. 'It shows that what you have pledged yourselves to do is only to pester others. You want dealers, who have not taken your vow, to buy that yarn; weavers, who have not taken your vow, to make it up; then their wares eventually to be foisted on to consumers who, also, have not taken your vow. The method? Your clamour, and the *zamindars*' oppression. The result: all right-eousness yours, all privations theirs!'

'And may we venture to ask, further, what your share of the privation has been?' pursued a science student.

'You want to know, do you?' replied my master. 'It is Nikhil himself who has to buy up that Indian mill yarn; he has had to start a weaving school to get it woven; and to judge by his past brilliant business exploits, by the time his cotton fabrics leave the loom their cost will be that of cloth-of-gold; so they will only find a use, perhaps, as curtains for his drawing-room, even though their flimsiness may fail to screen him. When you get tired of your vow, you will laugh the loudest at their artistic effect. And if their workmanship is ever truly appreciated at all, it will be by foreigners.'

I have known my master all my life, but have never seen him so agitated. I could see that the pain had been silently accumulating in his heart for some time, because of his surpassing love for me, and that his habitual self-possession had become secretly undermined to the breaking point.

'You are our elders,' said the medical student. 'It is unseemly that we should bandy words with you. But tell us, pray, finally, are you determined not to oust foreign articles from your market?'

'I will not,' I said, 'because they are not mine.'

'Because that will cause you a loss!' smiled the M.A. student.

'Because he, whose is the loss, is the best judge,' retorted my master.

With a shout of *Bande Mataram* they left us.

Chapter Six

✻

Nikhil's Story

VIII

A FEW days later, my master brought Panchu round to me. His *zamindar*, it appeared, had fined him a hundred rupees, and was threatening him with ejectment.

'For what fault?' I enquired.

'Because,' I was told, 'he has been found selling foreign cloths. He begged and prayed Harish Kundu, his *zamindar*, to let him sell off his stock, bought with borrowed money, promising faithfully never to do it again; but the *zamindar* would not hear of it, and insisted on his burning the foreign stuff there and then, if he wanted to be let off. Panchu in his desperation blurted out defiantly: 'I can't afford it! You are rich; why not buy it up and burn it?' This only made Harish Kundu red in the face as he shouted: 'The scoundrel must be taught manners, give him a shoe-beating!' So poor Panchu got insulted as well as fined.'

'What happened to the cloth?'

'The whole bale was burnt.'

'Who else was there?'

'Any number of people, who all kept shouting *Bande Mataram*. Sandip was also there. He took up some of the ashes, crying: "Brothers! This is the first funeral pyre lighted by your village in celebration of the last rites of foreign commerce. These are sacred ashes. Smear yourselves with them in token of your *Swadeshi* vow."'

'Panchu,' said I, turning to him, 'you must lodge a complaint.'

'No one will bear me witness,' he replied.

'None bear witness? – Sandip! Sandip!'

Sandip came out of his room at my call. 'What is the matter?' he asked.

'Won't you bear witness to the burning of this man's cloth?'

Sandip smiled. 'Of course I shall be a witness in the case,' he said. 'But I shall be on the opposite side.'

'What do you mean,' I exclaimed, 'by being a witness on this or that side? Will you not bear witness to the truth?'

'Is the thing which happens the only truth?'

'What other truths can there be?'

'The things that ought to happen! The truth we must build up will require a great deal of untruth in the process. Those who have made their way in the world have created truth, not blindly followed it.'

'And so –'

'And so I will bear what you people are pleased to call false witness, as they have done who have created empires, built up social systems, founded religious organizations. Those who would rule do not dread untruths; the shackles of truth are reserved for those who will fall under their sway. Have you not read history? Do you not know that in the immense cauldrons, where vast political developments are simmering, untruths are the main ingredients?'

'Political cookery on a large scale is doubtless going on, but –'

'Oh, I know! You, of course, will never do any of the cooking. You prefer to be one of those down whose throats the hotchpotch which is being cooked will be crammed. They will partition Bengal and say it is for your benefit. They will seal the doors of education and call it raising the standard. But you will always remain good boys, snivelling in your corners. We bad men, however, must see whether we cannot erect a defensive fortification of untruth.'

'It is no use arguing about these things, Nikhil,' my master interposed. 'How can they who do not feel the truth within them, realize that to bring it out from its obscurity into the light is man's highest aim – not to keep on heaping material outside?'

Sandip laughed. 'Right, sir!' said he. 'Quite a correct speech for a schoolmaster. That is the kind of stuff I have read in books; but in the real world I have seen that man's chief business is the accumulation of outside material. Those who are masters in the art, advertise the biggest lies in their business, enter false accounts in their political ledgers with their broadest-pointed pens, launch their newspapers daily laden with untruths, and send preachers abroad to disseminate falsehood like flies carrying pestilential germs. I am a humble follower of these great ones. When I was attached to the Congress party I never hesitated to dilute ten per cent of truth with ninety per cent of untruth. And now, merely because I have ceased to belong to that party, I have not forgotten the basic fact that man's goal is not truth but success.'

'True success,' corrected my master.

'Maybe,' replied Sandip, 'but the fruit of true success ripens only by cultivating the field of untruth, after tearing up the soil and pounding it into dust. Truth grows up by itself like weeds and thorns, and only worms can expect to get fruit from it!' With this he flung out of the room.

My master smiled as he looked towards me. 'Do you know, Nikhil,' he said, 'I believe Sandip is not irreligious – his religion is of the obverse side of truth, like the dark moon, which is still a moon, for all that its light has gone over to the wrong side.'

'That is why,' I assented, 'I have always had an affection for him, though we have never been able to agree. I cannot contemn him, even now; though he has hurt me sorely, and may yet hurt me more.'

'I have begun to realize that,' said my master. 'I have long wondered how you could go on putting up with him. I have, at times, even suspected you of weakness. I now see that though you two do not rhyme, your rhythm is the same.'

'Fate seems bent on writing *Paradise Lost* in blank verse, in my case, and so has no use for a rhyming friend!' I remarked, pursuing his conceit.

'But what of Panchu?' resumed my master.

'You say Harish Kundu wants to eject him from his ancestral

holding. Supposing I buy it up and then keep him on as my tenant?'

'And his fine?'

'How can the *zamindar* realize that if he becomes my tenant?'

'His burnt bale of cloth?'

'I will procure him another. I should like to see anyone interfering with a tenant of mine, for trading as he pleases!'

'I am afraid, sir,' interposed Panchu despondently, 'while you big folk are doing the fighting, the police and the law vultures will merrily gather round, and the crowd will enjoy the fun, but when it comes to getting killed, it will be the turn of only poor me!'

'Why, what harm can come to you?'

'They will burn down my house, sir, children and all!'

'Very well, I will take charge of your children,' said my master. 'You may go on with any trade you like. They shan't touch you.'

That very day I bought up Panchu's holding and entered into formal possession. Then the trouble began.

Panchu had inherited the holding of his grandfather as his sole surviving heir. Everybody knew this. But at this juncture an aunt turned up from somewhere, with her boxes and bundles, her rosary, and a widowed niece. She ensconced herself in Panchu's home and laid claim to a life interest in all he had.

Panchu was dumbfounded. 'My aunt died long ago,' he protested.

In reply he was told that he was thinking of his uncle's first wife, but that the former had lost no time in taking to himself a second.

'But my uncle died before my aunt,' exclaimed Panchu, still more mystified. 'Where was the time for him to marry again?'

This was not denied. But Panchu was reminded that it had never been asserted that the second wife had come after the death of the first, but the former had been married by his uncle during the latter's lifetime. Not relishing the idea of living with a co-wife she had remained in her father's house till her husband's death, after which she had got religion and retired to holy Brindaban, whence she was now coming. These facts were well known to the officers of Harish Kundu, as well as to some of his tenants. And if the *zamindar*'s summons should be peremptory enough, even some of those who had partaken of the marriage feast would be forthcoming!

IX

One afternoon, when I happened to be specially busy, word came to my office room that Bimala had sent for me. I was startled.

'Who did you say had sent for me?' I asked the messenger.

'The Rani Mother.'

'The Bara Rani?'

'No, sir, the Chota Rani Mother.'

The Chota Rani! It seemed a century since I had been sent for by her. I kept them all waiting there, and went off into the inner apartments. When I stepped into our room I had another shock of surprise to find Bimala there with a distinct suggestion of being dressed up. The room, which from persistent neglect had latterly acquired an air of having grown absent-minded, had regained something of its old order this afternoon. I stood there silently, looking enquiringly at Bimala.

She flushed a little and the fingers of her right hand toyed for a time with the bangles on her left arm. Then she abruptly broke the silence. 'Look here! Is it right that ours should be the only market in all Bengal which allows foreign goods?'

'What, then, would be the right thing to do?' I asked.

'Order them to be cleared out!'

'But the goods are not mine.'

'Is not the market yours?'

'It is much more theirs who use it for trade.'

'Let them trade in Indian goods, then.'

'Nothing would please me better. But suppose they do not?'

'Nonsense! How dare they be so insolent? Are you not . . .'

'I am very busy this afternoon and cannot stop to argue it out. But I must refuse to tyrannize.'

'It would not be tyranny for selfish gain, but for the sake of the country.'

'To tyrannize for the country is to tyrannize over the country. But that I am afraid you will never understand.' With this I came away.

All of a sudden the world shone out for me with a fresh clearness. I seemed to feel it in my blood, that the Earth had lost the weight of its earthiness, and its daily task of sustaining life no longer appeared a burden, as with a wonderful access of power it whirled through space telling its beads of days and nights. What endless work, and withal what illimitable energy of freedom! None shall check it, oh, none can ever check it! From the depths of my being an uprush of joy, like a waterspout, sprang high to storm the skies.

I repeatedly asked myself the meaning of this outburst of feeling. At first there was no intelligible answer. Then it became clear that the bond against which I had been fretting inwardly, night and day, had broken. To my surprise I discovered that my mind was freed from all mistiness. I could see everything relating to Bimala as if vividly pictured on a camera screen. It was palpable that she had specially dressed herself up to coax that order out of me. Till that moment, I had never viewed Bimala's adornment as a thing apart from herself. But today the elaborate manner in which she had done up her hair, in the English fashion, made it appear a mere decoration. That which before had the mystery of her personality about it, and was priceless to me, was now out to sell itself cheap.

As I came away from that broken cage of a bedroom, out into the golden sunlight of the open, there was the avenue of bauhinias, along the gravelled path in front of my verandah, suffusing the sky with a rosy flush. A group of starlings beneath the trees were noisily chattering away. In the distance an empty bullock cart, with its nose on the ground, held up its tail aloft – one of its unharnessed bullocks grazing, the other resting on the grass, its eyes dropping for very comfort, while a crow on its back was pecking away at the insects on its body.

I seemed to have come closer to the heartbeats of the great

earth in all the simplicity of its daily life; its warm breath fell on me with the perfume of the bauhinia blossoms; and an anthem, inexpressibly sweet, seemed to peal forth from this world, where I, in my freedom, live in the freedom of all else.

We, men, are knights whose quest is that freedom to which our ideals call us. She who makes for us the banner under which we fare forth is the true Woman for us. We must tear away the disguise of her who weaves our net of enchantment at home, and know her for what she is. We must beware of clothing her in the witchery of our own longings and imaginings, and thus allow her to distract us from our true quest.

Today I feel that I shall win through. I have come to the gateway of the simple; I am now content to see things as they are. I have gained freedom myself; I shall allow freedom to others. In my work will be my salvation.

I know that, time and again, my heart will ache, but now that I understand its pain in all its truth, I can disregard it. Now that I know it concerns only me, what after all can be its value? The suffering which belongs to all mankind shall be my crown.

Save me, Truth! Never again let me hanker after the false paradise of Illusion. If I must walk alone, let me at least tread your path. Let the drum-beats of Truth lead me to Victory.

Sandip's Story

VII

Bimala sent for me that day, but for a time she could not utter a word; her eyes kept brimming up to the verge of overflowing. I could see at once that she had been unsuccessful with Nikhil. She had been so proudly confident that she would have her own way – but I had never shared her confidence. Woman knows man well enough where he is weak, but she is quite unable to fathom him where he is strong. The fact is that man is as much a mystery to woman as woman is to man. If that were not so, the separation of the sexes would only have been a waste of Nature's energy.

Ah pride, pride! The trouble was, not that the necessary thing had failed of accomplishment, but that the entreaty, which had cost her such a struggle to make, should have been refused. What a wealth of colour and movement, suggestion and deception, group themselves round this 'me' and 'mine' in woman. That is just where her beauty lies – she is ever so much more personal than man. When man was being made, the Creator was a schoolmaster – His bag full of commandments and principles; but when He came to woman, He resigned His headmastership and turned artist, with only His brush and paint-box.

When Bimala stood silently there, flushed and tearful in her broken pride, like a storm-cloud, laden with rain and charged with lightning, lowering over the horizon, she looked so absolutely sweet that I had to go right up to her and take her by the hand. It was trembling, but she did not snatch it away. 'Bee,' said I, 'we two are colleagues, for our aims are one. Let us sit down and talk it over.'

I led her, unresisting, to a seat. But strange! at that very point the rush of my impetuosity suffered an unaccountable check – just as the current of the mighty Padma, roaring on in its irresistible course, all of a sudden gets turned away from the bank it is crumbling by some trifling obstacle beneath the surface. When I pressed Bimala's hand my nerves rang music, like tuned-up strings; but the symphony stopped short at the first movement.

What stood in the way? Nothing singly; it was a tangle of a multitude of things – nothing definitely palpable, but only that unaccountable sense of obstruction. Anyhow, this much has become plain to me, that I cannot swear to what I really am. It is because I am such a mystery to my own mind that my attraction for myself is so strong! If once the whole of myself should become known to me, I would then fling it all away – and reach beatitude!

As she sat down, Bimala went ashy pale. She, too, must have realized what a crisis had come and gone, leaving her unscathed. The comet had passed by, but the brush of its

111

burning tail had overcome her. To help her to recover herself I said: 'Obstacles there will be, but let us fight them through, and not be down-hearted. Is not that best, Queen?'

Bimala cleared her throat with a little cough, but simply to murmur: 'Yes.'

'Let us sketch out our plan of action,' I continued, as I drew a piece of paper and a pencil from my pocket.

I began to make a list of the workers who had joined us from Calcutta and to assign their duties to each. Bimala interrupted me before I was through, saying wearily: 'Leave it now; I will join you again this evening'; and then she hurried out of the room. It was evident she was not in a state to attend to anything. She must be alone with herself for a while – perhaps lie down on her bed and have a good cry!

When she left me, my intoxication began to deepen, as the cloud colours grow richer after the sun is down. I felt I had let the moment of moments slip by. What an awful coward I had been! She must have left me in sheer disgust at my qualms – and she was right!

While I was tingling all over with these reflections, a servant came in and announced Amulya, one of our boys. I felt like sending him away for the time, but he stepped in before I could make up my mind. Then we fell to discussing the news of the fights which were raging in different quarters over cloth and sugar and salt; and the air was soon clear of all fumes of intoxication. I felt as if awakened from a dream. I leapt to my feet feeling quite ready for the fray – *Bande Mataram!*

The news was various. Most of the traders who were tenants of Harish Kundu had come over to us. Many of Nikhil's officials were also secretly on our side, pulling the wires in our interest. The Marwari shopkeepers were offering to pay a penalty, if only allowed to clear their present stocks. Only some Mahomedan traders were still obdurate.

One of them was taking home some German-made shawls for his family. These were confiscated and burnt by one of our village boys. This had given rise to trouble. We offered to buy him Indian woollen stuffs in their place. But where were cheap Indian woollens to be had? We could not very well indulge him in Cashmere shawls! He came and complained to Nikhil, who advised him to go to law. Of course Nikhil's men saw to it that the trial should come to nothing, even his law-agent being on our side!

The point is, if we have to replace burnt foreign clothes with Indian cloth every time, and on the top of that fight through a law-suit, where is the money to come from? And the beauty of it is that this destruction of foreign goods is increasing their demand and sending up the foreigner's profits – very like what happened to the fortunate shopkeeper whose chandeliers the nabob delighted in smashing, tickled by the tinkle of the breaking glass.

The next problem is – since there is no such thing as cheap and gaudy Indian woollen stuff, should we be rigorous in our boycott of foreign flannels and merinos, or make an exception in their favour?

'Look here!' said I at length on the first point, 'we are not going to keep on making presents of Indian stuff to those who have got their foreign purchases confiscated. The penalty is intended to fall on them, not on us. If they go to law, we must retaliate by burning down their granaries! – What startles you, Amulya? It is not the prospect of a grand illumination that delights me! You must remember, this is War. If you are afraid of causing suffering, go in for love-making, you will never do for this work!'

The second problem I solved by deciding to allow no compromise with foreign articles, in any circumstance whatever. In the good old days, when these gaily coloured foreign shawls were unknown, our peasantry used to manage well enough with plain cotton quilts – they must learn to do so again. They may not look as gorgeous, but this is not the time to think of looks.

Most of the boatmen had been won over to refuse to carry foreign goods, but the chief of them, Mirjan, was still insubordinate.

'Could you not get his boat sunk?' I asked our manager here.

'Nothing easier, sir,' he replied. 'But what if afterwards I am held responsible?'

'Why be so clumsy as to leave any loophole for responsibility? However, if there must be any, my shoulders will be there to bear it.'

Mirjan's boat was tied near the landing-place after its freight had been taken over to the market-place. There was no one on it, for the manager had arranged for some entertainment to which all had been invited. After dusk the boat, loaded with rubbish, was holed and set adrift. It sank in mid-stream.

Mirjan understood the whole thing. He came to me in tears to beg for mercy. 'I was wrong, sir –' he began.

'What makes you realize that all of a sudden?' I sneered.

He made no direct reply. 'The boat was worth two thousand rupees,' he said. 'I now see my mistake, and if excused this time I will never . . .' with which he threw himself at my feet.

I asked him to come ten days later. If only we could pay him that two thousand rupees at once, we could buy him up body and soul. This is just the sort of man who could render us immense service, if won over. We shall never be able to make any headway unless we can lay our hands on plenty of money.

As soon as Bimala came into the sitting-room, in the evening, I said as I rose up to receive her: 'Queen! Everything is ready, success is at hand, but we must have money.'

'Money? How much money?'

'Not so very much, but by hook or by crook we must have it!'

'But how much?'

'A mere fifty thousand rupees will do for the present.'

Bimala blenched inwardly at the figure, but tried not to show it. How could she again admit defeat?

'Queen!' said I, 'you only can make the impossible possible. Indeed you have already done so. Oh, that I could show you the extent of your achievement – then you would know it. But the time for that is not now. Now we want money!'

'You shall have it,' she said.

I could see that the thought of selling her jewels had occurred to her. So I said: 'Your jewels must remain in reserve. One can never tell when they may be wanted.' And

then, as Bimala stared blankly at me in silence, I went on:
'This money must come from your husband's treasury.'

Bimala was still more taken aback. After a long pause she
said: 'But how am I to get his money?'

'Is not his money yours as well?'

'Ah, no!' she said, her wounded pride hurt afresh.

'If not,' I cried, 'neither is it his, but his country's, whom
he has deprived of it, in her time of need!'

'But how am I to get it?' she repeated.

'Get it you shall and must. You know best how. You must
get it for Her to whom it rightfully belongs. *Bande Mataram!*
These are the magic words which will open the door of his
iron safe, break through the walls of his strong-room, and
confound the hearts of those who are disloyal to its call. Say
Bande Mataram, Bee!'

'*Bande Mataram!*'

115

Chapter Seven

*

Sandip's Story

VIII

WE are men, we are kings, we must have our tribute. Ever since we have come upon the Earth we have been plundering her; and the more we claimed, the more she submitted. From primeval days have we men been plucking fruits, cutting down trees, digging up the soil, killing beast, bird and fish. From the bottom of the sea, from underneath the ground, from the very jaws of death, it has all been grabbing and grabbing and grabbing – no strong-box in Nature's store-room has been respected or left unrifled.

The one delight of this Earth is to fulfil the claims of those who are men. She has been made fertile and beautiful and complete through her endless sacrifices to them. But for this, she would be lost in the wilderness, not knowing herself, the doors of her heart shut, her diamonds and pearls never seeing the light.

Likewise, by sheer force of our claims, we men have opened up all the latent possibilities of women. In the process of surrendering themselves to us, they have ever gained their true greatness. Because they had to bring all the diamonds of their happiness and the pearls of their sorrow into our royal treasury, they have found their true wealth. So for men to accept is truly to give: for women to give is truly to gain.

The demand I have just made from Bimala, however, is indeed a large one! At first I felt scruples; for is it not the habit of man's mind to be in purposeless conflict with itself? I thought I had imposed too hard a task. My first impulse was

116

to call her back, and tell her I would rather not make her life wretched by dragging her into all these troubles. I forgot, for the moment, that it was the mission of man to be aggressive, to make woman's existence fruitful by stirring up disquiet in the depth of her passivity, to make the whole world blessed by churning up the immeasurable abyss of suffering! This is why man's hands are so strong, his grip so firm.

Bimala had been longing with all her heart that I, Sandip, should demand of her some great sacrifice – should call her to her death. How else could she be happy? Had she not waited all these weary years only for an opportunity to weep out her heart – so satiated was she with the monotony of her placid happiness? And therefore, at the very sight of me, her heart's horizon darkened with the rain clouds of her impending days of anguish. If I pity her and save her from her sorrows, what then was the purpose of my being born a man?

The real reason of my qualms is that my demand happens to be for money. That savours of beggary, for money is man's, not woman's. That is why I had to make it a big figure. A thousand or two would have the air of petty theft. Fifty thousand has all the expanse of romantic brigandage.

Ah, but riches should really have been mine! So many of my desires have had to halt, again and again, on the road to accomplishment simply for want of money. This does not become me! Had my fate been merely unjust, it could be forgiven – but its bad taste is unpardonable. It is not simply a hardship that a man like me should be at his wit's end to pay his house rent, or should have to carefully count out the coins for an Intermediate Class railway ticket – it is vulgar!

It is equally clear that Nikhil's paternal estates are a superfluity to him. For him it would not have been at all unbecoming to be poor. He would have cheerfully pulled in the double harness of indigent mediocrity with that precious master of his.

I should love to have, just for once, the chance to fling about fifty thousand rupees in the service of my country and to the satisfaction of myself. I am a nabob born, and it is a great dream of mine to get rid of this disguise of poverty, though it be for a day only, and to see myself in my true character.

117

I have grave misgivings, however, as to Bimala ever getting that fifty thousand rupees within her reach, and it will probably be only a thousand or two which will actually come to hand. Be it so. The wise man is content with half a loaf, or any fraction for that matter, rather than no bread.

I must return to these personal reflections of mine later. News comes that I am wanted at once. Something has gone wrong . . .

It seems that the police have got a clue to the man who sank Mirjan's boat for us. He was an old offender. They are on his trail, but he should be too practised a hand to be caught blabbing. However, one never knows. Nikhil's back is up, and his manager may not be able to have things his own way.

'If I get into trouble, sir,' said the manager when I saw him, 'I shall have to drag you in!'

'Where is the noose with which you can catch me?' I asked.

'I have a letter of yours, and several of Amulya Babu's.'

I could not see that the letter marked 'urgent' to which I had been hurried into writing a reply was wanted urgently for this purpose only! I am getting to learn quite a number of things.

The point now is, that the police must be bribed and hush-money paid to Mirjan for his boat. It is also becoming evident that much of the cost of this patriotic venture of ours will find its way as profit into the pockets of Nikhil's manager. However, I must shut my eyes to that for the present, for is he not shouting *Bande Mataram* as lustily as I am?

This kind of work has always to be carried on with leaky vessels which let as much through as they fetch in. We all have a hidden fund of moral judgement stored away within us, and so I was about to wax indignant with the manager, and enter in my diary a tirade against the unreliability of our countrymen. But, if there be a god, I must acknowledge with gratitude to him that he has given me a clear-seeing mind, which allows nothing inside or outside it to remain vague. I may delude others, but never myself. So I was unable to continue angry.

Whatever is true is neither good nor bad, but simply true, and that is Science. A lake is only the remnant of water which has not been sucked into the ground. Underneath the cult of *Bande Mataram*, as indeed at the bottom of all mundane affairs, there is a region of slime, whose absorbing power must be reckoned with. The manager will take what he wants; I also have my own wants. These lesser wants form a part of the wants of the great Cause – the horse must be fed and the wheels must be oiled if the best progress is to be made.

The long and short of it is that money we must have, and that soon. We must take whatever comes the readiest, for we cannot afford to wait. I know that the immediate often swallows up the ultimate; that the five thousand rupees of today may nip in the bud the fifty thousand rupees of tomorrow. But I must accept the penalty. Have I not often twitted Nikhil that they who walk in the paths of restraint have never known what sacrifice is? It is we greedy folk who have to sacrifice our greed at every step!

Of the cardinal sins of man, Desire is for men who are men – but Delusion, which is only for cowards, hampers them. Because delusion keeps them wrapped up in past and future, but is the very deuce for confounding their footsteps in the present. Those who are always straining their ears for the call of the remote, to the neglect of the call of the imminent, are like Sakuntala[1] absorbed in the memories of her lover. The guest comes unheeded, and the curse descends, depriving them of the very object of their desire.

The other day I pressed Bimala's hand, and that touch still stirs her mind, as it vibrates in mine. Its thrill must not be deadened by repetition, for then what is now music will descend to mere argument. There is at present no room in her mind for the question 'why?' So I must not deprive Bimala, who is one of those creatures for whom illusion is necessary, of her full supply of it.

As for me, I have so much else to do that I shall have to be content for the present with the foam of the wine cup of passion. O man of desire! Curb your greed, and practise your hand on the harp of illusion till you can bring out all the

1. Sakuntala, after the king, her lover, went back to his kingdom, promising to send for her, was so lost in thoughts of him, that she failed to hear the call of her hermit guest, who thereupon cursed her, saying that the object of her love would forget all about her.

delicate nuances of suggestion. This is not the time to drain the cup to the dregs.

IX

Our work proceeds apace. But though we have shouted ourselves hoarse, proclaiming the Mussulmans to be our brethren, we have come to realize that we shall never be able to bring them wholly round to our side. So they must be suppressed altogether and made to understand that we are the masters. They are now showing their teeth, but one day they shall dance like tame bears to the tune we play.

'If the idea of a United India is a true one,' objects Nikhil, 'Mussulmans are a necessary part of it.'

'Quite so,' said I, 'but we must know their place and keep them there, otherwise they will constantly be giving trouble.'

'So you want to make trouble to prevent trouble?'

'What, then, is your plan?'

'There is only one well-known way of avoiding quarrels,' said Nikhil meaningly.

I know that, like tales written by good people, Nikhil's discourse always ends in a moral. The strange part of it is that with all his familiarity with moral precepts, he still believes in them! He is an incorrigible schoolboy. His only merit is his sincerity. The mischief with people like him is that they will not admit the finality even of death, but keep their eyes always fixed on a hereafter.

I have long been nursing a plan which, if only I could carry it out, would set fire to the whole country. True patriotism will never be roused in our countrymen unless they can visualize the motherland. We must make a goddess of her. My colleagues saw the point at once. 'Let us devise an appropriate image!' they exclaimed. 'It will not do if you devise it,' I admonished them. 'We must get one of the current images accepted as representing the country – the worship of the people must flow towards it along the deep-cut grooves of custom.'

But Nikhil's needs must argue even about this. 'We must

not seek the help of illusions,' he said to me some time ago, 'for what we believe to be the true cause.'

'Illusions are necessary for lesser minds,' I said, 'and to this class the greater portion of the world belongs. That is why divinities are set up in every country to keep up the illusions of the people, for men are only too well aware of their weakness.'

'No,' he replied. 'God is necessary to clear away our illusions. The divinities which keep them alive are false gods.'

'What of that? If need be, even false gods must be invoked, rather than let the work suffer. Unfortunately for us, our illusions are alive enough, but we do not know how to make them serve our purpose. Look at the Brahmins. In spite of our treating them as demi-gods, and untiringly taking the dust of their feet, they are a force going to waste.

'There will always be a large class of people, given to grovelling, who can never be made to do anything unless they are bespattered with the dust of somebody's feet, be it on their heads or on their backs! What a pity if after keeping Brahmins saved up in our armoury for all these ages – keen and serviceable – they cannot be utilized to urge on this rabble in the time of our need.'

But it is impossible to drive all this into Nikhil's head. He has such a prejudice in favour of truth – as though there exists such an objective reality! How often have I tried to explain to him that where untruth truly exists, there it is indeed the truth. This was understood in our country in the old days, and so they had the courage to declare that for those of little understanding untruth is the truth. For them, who can truly believe their country to be a goddess, her image will do duty for the truth. With our nature and our traditions we are unable to realize our country as she is, but we can easily bring ourselves to believe in her image. Those who want to do real work must not ignore this fact.

Nikhil only got excited. 'Because you have lost the power of walking in the path of truth's attainment,' he cried, 'you keep waiting for some miraculous boon to drop from the skies! That is why when your service to the country has fallen centuries into arrears all you can think of is, to make of it an image and stretch out your hands in expectation of gratuitous favours.'

'We want to perform the impossible,' I said. 'So our country needs must be made into a god.'

'You mean you have no heart for possible tasks,' replied Nikhil. 'Whatever is already there is to be left undisturbed; yet there must be a supernatural result.'

'Look here, Nikhil,' I said at length, thoroughly exasperated. 'The things you have been saying are good enough as moral lessons. These ideas have served their purpose, as milk for babes, at one stage of man's evolution, but will no longer do, now that man has cut his teeth.

'Do we not see before our very eyes how things, of which we never even dreamt of sowing the seed, are sprouting up on every side? By what power? That of the deity in our country who is becoming manifest. It is for the genius of the age to give that deity its image. Genius does not argue, it creates. I only give form to what the country imagines.

'I will spread it abroad that the goddess has vouchsafed me a dream. I will tell the Brahmins that they have been appointed her priests, and that their downfall has been due to their dereliction of duty in not seeing to the proper performance of her worship. Do you say I shall be uttering lies? No, say I, it is the truth – nay more, the truth which the country has so long been waiting to learn from my lips. If only I could get the opportunity to deliver my message, you would see the stupendous result.'

'What I am afraid of,' said Nikhil, 'is, that my lifetime is limited and the result you speak of is not the final result. It will have after-effects which may not be immediately apparent.'

'I only seek the result,' said I, 'which belongs to today.'

'The result I seek,' answered Nikhil, 'belongs to all time.'

Nikhil may have had his share of Bengal's greatest gift – imagination, but he has allowed it to be overshadowed and nearly killed by an exotic conscientiousness. Just look at the worship of Durga which Bengal has carried to such heights. That is one of her greatest achievements. I can swear that

Durga is a political goddess and was conceived as the image of the *Shakti* of patriotism in the days when Bengal was praying to be delivered from Mussulman domination. What other province of India has succeeded in giving such wonderful visual expression to the ideal of its quest?

Nothing betrayed Nikhil's loss of the divine gift of imagination more conclusively than his reply to me. 'During the Mussulman domination,' he said, 'the Maratha and the Sikh asked for fruit from the arms which they themselves took up. The Bengali contented himself with placing weapons in the hands of his goddess and muttering incantations to her; and as his country did not really happen to be a goddess the only fruit he got was the lopped-off heads of the goats and buffaloes of the sacrifice. The day that we seek the good of the country along the path of righteousness, He who is greater than our country will grant us true fruition.'

The unfortunate part of it is that Nikhil's words sound so fine when put down on paper. My words, however, are not meant to be scribbled on paper, but to be scored into the heart of the country. The Pandit records his *Treatise on Agriculture* in printer's ink; but the cultivator at the point of his plough impresses his endeavour deep in the soil.

X

When I next saw Bimala I pitched my key high without further ado. 'Have we been able,' I began, 'to believe with all our heart in the god for whose worship we have been born all these millions of years, until he actually made himself visible to us?

'How often have I told you,' I continued, 'that had I not seen you I never would have known all my country as One. I know not yet whether you rightly understand me. The gods are invisible only in their heaven – on earth they show themselves to mortal men.'

Bimala looked at me in a strange kind of way as she gravely replied: 'Indeed I understand you, Sandip.' This was the first time she called me plain Sandip.

'Krishna,' I continued, 'whom Arjuna ordinarily knew only

as the driver of his chariot, had also His universal aspect, of which, too, Arjuna had a vision one day, and that day he saw the Truth. I have seen your Universal Aspect in my country. The Ganges and the Brahmaputra are the chains of gold that wind round and round your neck; in the woodland fringes on the distant banks of the dark waters of the river, I have seen your collyrium-darkened eyelashes; the changeful sheen of your *sari* moves for me in the play of light and shade amongst the swaying shoots of green corn; and the blazing summer heat, which makes the whole sky lie gasping like a red-tongued lion in the desert, is nothing but your cruel radiance.

'Since the goddess has vouchsafed her presence to her votary in such wonderful guise, it is for me to proclaim her worship throughout our land, and then shall the country gain new life. "Your image make we in temple after temple."[1] But this our people have not yet fully realized. So I would call on them in your name and offer for their worship an image from which none shall be able to withhold belief. Oh give me this boon, this power.'

Bimala's eyelids drooped and she became rigid in her seat like a figure of stone. Had I continued she would have gone off into a trance. When I ceased speaking she opened wide her eyes, and murmured with fixed gaze, as though still dazed: 'O Traveller in the path of Destruction! Who is there that can stay your progress? Do I not see that none shall stand in the way of your desires? Kings shall lay their crowns at your feet; the wealthy shall hasten to throw open their treasure for your acceptance; those who have nothing else shall beg to be allowed to offer their lives. O my king, my god! What you have seen in me I know not, but I have seen the immensity of your grandeur in my heart. Who am I, what am I, in its presence? Ah, the awful power of Devastation! Never shall I truly live till it kills me utterly! I can bear it no longer, my heart is breaking!'

Bimala slid down from her seat and fell at my feet, which she clasped, and then she sobbed and sobbed and sobbed.

This is hypnotism indeed – the charm which can subdue the world! No materials, no weapons – but just the delusion

1. A line from Bankim Chatterjee's national song *Bande Mataram*.

of irresistible suggestion. Who says 'Truth shall Triumph'?[1] Delusion shall win in the end. The Bengali understood this when he conceived the image of the ten-handed goddess astride her lion, and spread her worship in the land. Bengal must now create a new image to enchant and conquer the world. *Bande Mataram!*

I gently lifted Bimala back into her chair, and lest reaction should set in, I began again without losing time: 'Queen! The Divine Mother has laid on me the duty of establishing her worship in the land. But, alas, I am poor!'

Bimala was still flushed, her eyes clouded, her accents thick, as she replied: 'You poor? Is not all that each one has yours? What are my caskets full of jewellery for? Drag away from me all my gold and gems for your worship. I have no use for them!'

Once before Bimala had offered up her ornaments. I am not usually in the habit of drawing lines, but I felt I had to draw the line there.[2] I know why I feel this hesitation. It is for man to give ornaments to woman; to take them from her wounds his manliness.

But I must forget myself. Am *I* taking them? They are for the Divine Mother, to be poured in worship at her feet. Oh, but it must be a grand ceremony of worship such as the country has never beheld before. It must be a landmark in our history. It shall be my supreme legacy to the Nation. Ignorant men worship gods. I, Sandip, shall create them.

But all this is a far cry. What about the urgent immediate? At least three thousand is indispensably necessary – five thousand would do roundly and nicely. But how on earth am I to mention money after the high flight we have just taken? And yet time is precious!

1. A quotation from the Upanishads.
2. There is a world of sentiment attached to the ornaments worn by women in Bengal. They are not merely indicative of the love and regard of the giver, but the wearing of them symbolizes all that is held best in wifehood – the constant solicitude for her husband's welfare, the successful performance of the material and spiritual duties of the household entrusted to her care. When the husband dies, and the responsibility for the household changes hands, then are all ornaments cast aside as a sign of the widow's renunciation of worldly concerns. At any other time the giving up of ornaments is always a sign of supreme distress and as such appeals acutely to the sense of chivalry of any Bengali who may happen to witness it.

I crushed all hesitation under foot as I jumped up and made my plunge: 'Queen! Our purse is empty, our work about to stop!'

Bimala winced. I could see she was thinking of that impossible fifty thousand rupees. What a load she must have been carrying within her bosom, struggling under it, perhaps, through sleepless nights! What else had she with which to express her loving worship? Debarred from offering her heart at my feet, she hankers to make this sum of money, so hopelessly large for her, the bearer of her imprisoned feelings. The thought of what she must have gone through gives me a twinge of pain; for she is now wholly mine. The wrench of plucking up the plant by the roots is over. It is now only careful tending and nurture that is needed.

'Queen!' said I, 'that fifty thousand rupees is not particularly wanted just now. I calculate that, for the present, five thousand or even three will serve.'

The relief made her heart rebound. 'I shall fetch you five thousand,' she said in tones which seemed like an outburst of song – the song which Radhika of the Vaishnava lyrics sang:

> *For my lover will I bind in my hair*
> *The flower which has no equal in the three worlds!*

– it is the same tune, the same song: five thousand will I bring! That flower will I bind in my hair!

The narrow restraint of the flute brings out this quality of song. I must not allow the pressure of too much greed to flatten out the reed, for then, as I fear, music will give place to the questions 'Why?' 'What is the use of so much?' 'How am I to get it?' – not a word of which will rhyme with what Radhika sang! So, as I was saying, illusion alone is real – it is the flute itself; while truth is but its empty hollow. Nikhil has of late got a taste of that pure emptiness – one can see it in his face, which pains even me. But it was Nikhil's boast that he wanted the Truth, while mine was that I would never let go illusion from my grasp. Each has been suited to his taste, so why complain?

To keep Bimala's heart in the rarefied air of idealism, I cut short all further discussion over the five thousand rupees. I reverted to the demon-destroying goddess and her worship. When was the ceremony to be held and where? There is a great annual fair at Ruimari, within Nikhil's estates, where hundreds of thousands of pilgrims assemble. That would be a grand place to inaugurate the worship of our goddess!

Bimala waxed intensely enthusiastic. This was not the burning of foreign cloth or the people's granaries, so even Nikhil could have no objection – so thought she. But I smiled inwardly. How little these two persons, who have been together, day and night, for nine whole years, know of each other! They know something perhaps of their home life, but when it comes to outside concerns they are entirely at sea. They had cherished the belief that the harmony of the home with the outside was perfect. Today they realize to their cost that it is too late to repair their neglect of years, and seek to harmonize them now.

What does it matter? Let those who have made the mistake learn their error by knocking against the world. Why need I bother about their plight? For the present I find it wearisome to keep Bimala soaring much longer, like a captive balloon, in regions ethereal. I had better get quite through with the matter in hand.

When Bimala rose to depart and had neared the door I remarked in my most casual manner: 'So, about the money . . .'

Bimala halted and faced back as she said: 'On the expiry of the month, when our personal allowances become due . . .'

'That, I am afraid, would be much too late.'

'When do you want it then?'

'Tomorrow.'

'Tomorrow you shall have it.'

Chapter Eight

✳

Nikhil's Story

X

PARAGRAPHS and letters against me have begun to come out in the local papers; cartoons and lampoons are to follow, I am told. Jets of wit and humour are being splashed about, and the lies thus scattered are convulsing the whole country. They know that the monopoly of mud-throwing is theirs, and the innocent passer-by cannot escape unsoiled.

They are saying that the residents in my estates, from the highest to the lowest, are in favour of *Swadeshi*, but they dare not declare themselves, for fear of me. The few who have been brave enough to defy me have felt the full rigour of my persecution. I am in secret league with the police, and in private communication with the magistrate, and these frantic efforts of mine to add a foreign title of my own earning to the one I have inherited, will not, it is opined, go in vain.

On the other hand, the papers are full of praise for those devoted sons of the motherland, the Kundu and the Chakravarti *zamindars*. If only, say they, the country had a few more of such staunch patriots, the mills of Manchester would have had to sound their own dirge to the tune of *Bande Mataram*.

Then comes a letter in blood-red ink, giving a list of the traitorous *zamindars* whose treasuries have been burnt down because of their failing to support the Cause. Holy Fire, it goes on to say, has been aroused to its sacred function of purifying the country; and other agencies are also at work to see that those who are not true sons of the motherland do cease to encumber her lap. The signature is an obvious *nom-de-plume*.

I could see that this was the doing of our local students. So I sent for some of them and showed them the letter.

The B.A. student gravely informed me that they also had heard that a band of desperate patriots had been formed who would stick at nothing in order to clear away all obstacles to the success of *Swadeshi*.

'If,' said I, 'even one of our countrymen succumbs to these overbearing desperadoes, that will indeed be a defeat for the country!'

'We fail to follow you, Maharaja,' said the history student.

'Our country,' I tried to explain, 'has been brought to death's door through sheer fear – from fear of the gods down to fear of the police; and if you set up, in the name of freedom, the fear of some other bogey, whatever it may be called; if you would raise your victorious standard on the cowardice of the country by means of downright oppression, then no true lover of the country can bow to your decision.'

'Is there any country, sir,' pursued the history student, 'where submission to Government is not due to fear?'

'The freedom that exists in any country,' I replied, 'may be measured by the extent of this reign of fear. Where its threat is confined to those who would hurt or plunder, there the Government may claim to have freed man from the violence of man. But if fear is to regulate how people are to dress, where they shall trade, or what they must eat, then is man's freedom of will utterly ignored, and manhood destroyed at the root.'

'Is not such coercion of the individual will seen in other countries too?' continued the history student.

'Who denies it?' I exclaimed. 'But in every country man has destroyed himself to the extent that he has permitted slavery to flourish.'

'Does it not rather show,' interposed a Master of Arts, 'that trading in slavery is inherent in man – a fundamental fact of his nature?'

'Sandip Babu made the whole thing clear,' said a graduate.

129

'He gave us the example of Harish Kundu, your neighbouring *zamindar*. From his estates you cannot ferret out a single ounce of foreign salt. Why? Because he has always ruled with an iron hand. In the case of those who are slaves by nature, the lack of a strong master is the greatest of all calamities.'

'Why, sir!' chimed in an undergraduate, 'have you not heard of the obstreperous tenant of Chakravarti, the other *zamindar* close by – how the law was set on him till he was reduced to utter destitution? When at last he was left with nothing to eat, he started out to sell his wife's silver ornaments, but no one dared buy them. Then Chakravarti's manager offered him five rupees for the lot. They were worth over thirty, but he had to accept or starve. After taking over the bundle from him the manager coolly said that those five rupees would be credited towards his rent! We felt like having nothing more to do with Chakravarti or his manager after that, but Sandip Babu told us that if we threw over all the live people, we should have only dead bodies from the burning-grounds to carry on the work with! These live men, he pointed out, know what they want and how to get it – they are born rulers. Those who do not know how to desire for themselves, must live in accordance with, or die by virtue of, the desires of such as these. Sandip Babu contrasted them – Kundu and Chakravarti – with you, Maharaja. You, he said, for all your good intentions, will never succeed in planting *Swadeshi* within your territory.'

'It is my desire,' I said, 'to plant something greater than *Swadeshi*. I am not after dead logs but living trees – and these will take time to grow.'

'I am afraid, sir,' sneered the history student, 'that you will get neither log nor tree. Sandip Babu rightly teaches that in order to get, you must snatch. This is taking all of us some time to learn, because it runs counter to what we were taught at school. I have seen with my own eyes that when a rent-collector of Harish Kundu's found one of the tenants with nothing which could be sold up to pay his rent, he was made to sell his young wife! Buyers were not wanting, and the *zamindar*'s demand was satisfied. I tell you, sir, the sight of that man's distress prevented my getting sleep for nights together! But, feel it as I did, this much I realized, that the man who knows how to get the money he is out for, even by selling up his debtor's wife, is a better man than I am. I confess it is beyond me – I am a weakling, my eyes fill with tears. If anybody can save our country it is these Kundus and these Chakravartis and their officials!'

I was shocked beyond words. 'If what you say be true,' I cried, 'I clearly see that it must be the one endeavour of my life to save the country from these same Kundus and Chakravartis and officials. The slavery that has entered into our very bones is breaking out, at this opportunity, as ghastly tyranny. You have been so used to submit to domination through fear, you have come to believe that to make others submit is a kind of religion. My fight shall be against this weakness, this atrocious cruelty!'

These things, which are so simple to ordinary folk, get so twisted in the minds of our B.A.'s and M.A.'s, the only purpose of whose historical quibbles seems to be to torture the truth!

XI

I am worried over Panchu's sham aunt. It will be difficult to disprove her, for though witnesses of a real event may be few or even wanting, innumerable proofs of a thing that has not happened can always be marshalled. The object of this move is, evidently, to get the sale of Panchu's holding to me set aside.

Being unable to find any other way out of it, I was thinking of allowing Panchu to hold a permanent tenure in my estates and building him a cottage on it. But my master would not have it. I should not give in to these nefarious tactics so easily, he objected, and offered to attend to the matter himself.

'You, sir!' I cried, considerably surprised.

'Yes, I,' he repeated.

I could not see, at all clearly, what my master could do to counteract these legal machinations. That evening, at the time he usually came to me, he did not turn up. On my making inquiries, his servant said he had left home with a few things packed in a small trunk, and some bedding, saying he would be back in a few days. I thought he might have sallied forth to hunt for witnesses in Panchu's uncle's village. In that case, however, I was sure that his would be a hopeless quest . . .

During the day I forget myself in my work. As the late autumn afternoon wears on, the colours of the sky become turbid, and so do the feelings of my mind. There are many in this world whose minds dwell in brick-built houses – they can afford to ignore the thing called the outside. But my mind lives under the trees in the open, directly receives upon itself the messages borne by the free winds, and responds from the bottom of its heart to all the musical cadences of light and darkness.

While the day is bright and the world in the pursuit of its numberless tasks crowds around, then it seems as if my life wants nothing else. But when the colours of the sky fade away and the blinds are drawn down over the windows of heaven, then my heart tells me that evening falls just for the purpose of shutting out the world, to mark the time when the darkness must be filled with the One. This is the end to which earth, sky, and waters conspire, and I cannot harden myself against accepting its meaning. So when the gloaming deepens over the world, like the gaze of the dark eyes of the beloved, then my whole being tells me that work alone cannot be the truth of life, that work is not the be-all and the end-all of man, for man is not simply a serf – even though the serfdom be of the True and the Good.

Alas, Nikhil, have you for ever parted company with that self of yours who used to be set free under the starlight, to plunge into the infinite depths of the night's darkness after the day's work was done? How terribly alone is he, who misses companionship in the midst of the multitudinousness of life.

The other day, when the afternoon had reached the meeting-point of day and night, I had no work, nor the mind for work, nor was my master there to keep me company. With

my empty, drifting heart longing to anchor on to something,
I traced my steps towards the inner gardens. I was very fond
of chrysanthemums and had rows of them, of all varieties,
banked up in pots against one of the garden walls. When
they were in flower, it looked like a wave of green breaking
into iridescent foam. It was some time since I had been to
this part of the grounds, and I was beguiled into a cheerful
expectancy at the thought of meeting my chrysanthemums
after our long separation.

As I went in, the full moon had just peeped over the wall,
her slanting rays leaving its foot in deep shadow. It seemed
as if she had come a-tiptoe from behind, and clasped the
darkness over the eyes, smiling mischievously. When I came
near the bank of chrysanthemums, I saw a figure stretched
on the grass in front. My heart gave a sudden thud. The
figure also sat up with a start at my footsteps.

What was to be done next? I was wondering whether it
would do to beat a precipitate retreat. Bimala, also, was
doubtless casting about for some way of escape. But it was
as awkward to go as to stay! Before I could make up my
mind, Bimala rose, pulled the end of her *sari* over her head,
and walked off towards the inner apartments.

This brief pause had been enough to make real to me the
cruel load of Bimala's misery. The plaint of my own life
vanished from me in a moment. I called out: 'Bimala!'

She started and stayed her steps, but did not turn back. I
went round and stood before her. Her face was in the shade,
the moonlight fell on mine. Her eyes were downcast, her
hands clenched.

'Bimala,' said I, 'why should I seek to keep you fast in
this closed cage of mine? Do I not know that thus you cannot
but pine and droop?'

She stood still, without raising her eyes or uttering a
word.

'I know,' I continued, 'that if I insist on keeping you
shackled my whole life will be reduced to nothing but an
iron chain. What pleasure can that be to me?'

She was still silent.

'So,' I concluded, 'I tell you, truly, Bimala, you are free.

133

Whatever I may or may not have been to you, I refuse to be your fetters.' With which I came away towards the outer apartments.

No, no, it was not a generous impulse, nor indifference. I had simply come to understand that never would I be free until I could set free. To try to keep Bimala as a garland round my neck, would have meant keeping a weight hanging over my heart. Have I not been praying with all my strength, that if happiness may not be mine, let it go; if grief needs must be my lot, let it come; but let me not be kept in bondage. To clutch hold of that which is untrue as though it were true, is only to throttle oneself. May I be saved from such self-destruction.

When I entered my room, I found my master waiting there. My agitated feelings were still heaving within me. 'Freedom, sir,' I began unceremoniously, without greeting or inquiry, 'freedom is the biggest thing for man. Nothing can be compared to it – nothing at all!'

Surprised at my outburst, my master looked up at me in silence.

'One can understand nothing from books,' I went on. 'We read in the scriptures that our desires are bonds, fettering us as well as others. But such words, by themselves, are so empty. It is only when we get to the point of letting the bird out of its cage that we can realize how free the bird has set us. Whatever we cage, shackles us with desire whose bonds are stronger than those of iron chains. I tell you, sir, this is just what the world has failed to understand. They all seek to reform something outside themselves. But reform is wanted only in one's own desires, nowhere else, nowhere else!'

'We think,' he said, 'that we are our own masters when we get in our hands the object of our desire – but we are really our own masters only when we are able to cast out our desires from our minds.'

'When we put all this into words, sir,' I went on, 'it sounds like some bald-headed injunction, but when we realize even a little of it we find it to be *amrita* – which the gods have drunk and become immortal. We cannot see Beauty till we let go our hold of it. It was Buddha who conquered the world, not Alexander – this is untrue when stated in dry prose – oh when shall we be able to sing it? When shall all these most intimate truths of the universe overflow the pages of printed books and leap out in a sacred stream like the Ganges from the Gangotrie?'

I was suddenly reminded of my master's absence during the last few days and of my ignorance as to its reason. I felt somewhat foolish as I asked him: 'And where have you been all this while, sir?'

'Staying with Panchu,' he replied.

'Indeed!' I exclaimed. 'Have you been there all these days?'

'Yes. I wanted to come to an understanding with the woman who calls herself his aunt. She could hardly be induced to believe that there could be such an odd character among the gentlefolk as the one who sought their hospitality. When she found I really meant to stay on, she began to feel rather ashamed of herself. "Mother," said I, "you are not going to get rid of me, even if you abuse me! And so long as I stay, Panchu stays also. For you see, do you not, that I cannot stand by and see his motherless little ones sent out into the streets?"

'She listened to my talks in this strain for a couple of days without saying yes or no. This morning I found her tying up her bundles. "We are going back to Brindaban," she said. "Let us have our expenses for the journey." I knew she was not going to Brindaban, and also that the cost of her journey would be substantial. So I have come to you.'

'The required cost shall be paid,' I said.

'The old woman is not a bad sort,' my master went on musingly. 'Panchu was not sure of her caste, and would not let her touch the water-jar, or anything at all of his. So they were continually bickering. When she found I had no objection to her touch, she looked after me devotedly. She is a splendid cook!

'But all remnants of Panchu's respect for me vanished! To the last he had thought that I was at least a simple sort of person. But here was I, risking my caste without a qualm to win over the old woman for my purpose. Had I tried to steal a march on her by tutoring a witness for the trial, that would

135

have been a different matter. Tactics must be met by tactics. But stratagem at the expense of orthodoxy is more than he can tolerate!

'Anyhow, I must stay on a few days at Panchu's even after the woman leaves, for Harish Kundu may be up to any kind of devilry. He has been telling his satellites that he was content to have furnished Panchu with an aunt, but I have gone the length of supplying him with a father. He would like to see, now, how many fathers of his can save him!'

'We may or may not be able to save him,' I said; 'but if we should perish in the attempt to save the country from the thousand-and-one snares – of religion, custom and selfishness – which these people are busy spreading, we shall at least die happy.'

Bimala's Story

XIV

Who could have thought that so much would happen in this one life? I feel as if I have passed through a whole series of births, time has been flying so fast, I did not feel it move at all, till the shock came the other day.

I knew there would be words between us when I made up my mind to ask my husband to banish foreign goods from our market. But it was my firm belief that I had no need to meet argument by argument, for there was magic in the very air about me. Had not so tremendous a man as Sandip fallen helplessly at my feet, like a wave of the mighty sea breaking on the shore? Had I called him? No, it was the summons of that magic spell of mine. And Amulya, poor dear boy, when he first came to me – how the current of his life flushed with colour, like the river at dawn! Truly have I realized how a goddess feels when she looks upon the radiant face of her devotee.

With the confidence begotten of these proofs of my power, I was ready to meet my husband like a lightning-charged cloud. But what was it that happened? Never in all these nine years have I seen such a far-away, distraught look in his eyes – like the desert sky – with no merciful moisture of its own, no colour reflected, even, from what it looked upon. I should have been so relieved if his anger had flashed out! But I could find nothing in him which I could touch. I felt as unreal as a dream – a dream which would leave only the blackness of night when it was over.

In the old days I used to be jealous of my sister-in-law for her beauty. Then I used to feel that Providence had given me no power of my own, that my whole strength lay in the love which my husband had bestowed on me. Now that I had drained to the dregs the cup of power and could not do without its intoxication, I suddenly found it dashed to pieces at my feet, leaving me nothing to live for.

How feverishly I had sat to do my hair that day. Oh, shame, shame on me, the utter shame of it! My sister-in-law, when passing by, had exclaimed: 'Aha, Chota Rani! Your hair seems ready to jump off. Don't let it carry your head with it.'

And then, the other day in the garden, how easy my husband found it to tell me that he set me free! But can freedom – empty freedom – be given and taken so easily as all that? It is like setting a fish free in the sky – for how can I move or live outside the atmosphere of loving care which has always sustained me?

When I came to my room today, I saw only furniture – only the bedstead, only the looking-glass, only the clothes-rack – not the all-pervading heart which used to be there, over all. Instead of it there was freedom, only freedom, mere emptiness! A dried-up watercourse with all its rocks and pebbles laid bare. No feeling, only furniture!

When I had arrived at a state of utter bewilderment, wondering whether anything true was left in my life, and whereabouts it could be, I happened to meet Sandip again. Then life struck against life, and the sparks flew in the same old way. Here was truth – impetuous truth – which rushed in and overflowed all bounds, truth which was a thousand times truer than the Bara Rani with her maid, Thako and her silly songs, and all the rest of them who talked and laughed and wandered about . . .

'Fifty thousand!' Sandip had demanded.

'What is fifty thousand?' cried my intoxicated heart. 'You shall have it!'

How to get it, where to get it, were minor points not worth troubling over. Look at me. Had I not risen, all in one moment, from my nothingness to a height above everything? So shall all things come at my beck and call. I shall get it, get it, get it – there cannot be any doubt.

Thus had I come away from Sandip the other day. Then as I looked about me, where was it – the tree of plenty? Oh, why does this outer world insult the heart so?

And yet get it I must; how, I do not care; for sin there cannot be. Sin taints only the weak; I with my *Shakti* am beyond its reach. Only a commoner can be a thief, the king conquers and takes his rightful spoil . . . I must find out where the treasury is; who takes the money in; who guards it.

I spent half the night standing in the outer verandah peering at the row of office buildings. But how to get that fifty thousand rupees out of the clutches of those iron bars? If by some *mantram* I could have made all those guards fall dead in their places, I would not have hesitated – so pitiless did I feel!

But while a whole gang of robbers seemed dancing a war-dance within the whirling brain of its Rani, the great house of the Rajas slept in peace. The gong of the watch sounded hour after hour, and the sky overhead placidly looked on.

At last I sent for Amulya.

'Money is wanted for the Cause,' I told him. 'Can you not get it out of the treasury?'

'Why not?' said he, with his chest thrown out.

Alas! had I not said 'Why not?' to Sandip just in the same way? The poor lad's confidence could rouse no hopes in my mind.

'How will you do it?' I asked.

The wild plans he began to unfold would hardly bear repetition outside the pages of a penny dreadful.

'No, Amulya,' I said severely, 'you must not be childish.'

'Very well, then,' he said, 'let me bribe those watchmen.'

'Where is the money to come from?'

'I can loot the bazar,' he burst out, without blenching.

'Leave all that alone. I have my ornaments, they will serve.'

'But,' said Amulya, 'it strikes me that the cashier cannot be bribed. Never mind, there is another and simpler way.'

'What is that?'

'Why need you hear it? It is quite simple.'

'Still, I should like to know.'

Amulya fumbled in the pocket of his tunic and pulled out, first a small edition of the *Gita*, which he placed on the table – and then a little pistol, which he showed me, but said nothing further.

Horror! It did not take him a moment to make up his mind to kill our good old cashier![1] To look at his frank, open face one would not have thought him capable of hurting a fly, but how different were the words which came from his mouth. It was clear that the cashier's place in the world meant nothing real to him; it was a mere vacancy, lifeless, feelingless, with only stock phrases from the *Gita* – *Who kills the body kills naught!*

'Whatever do you mean, Amulya?' I exclaimed at length. 'Don't you know that the dear old man has got a wife and children and that he is . . .'

'Where are we to find men who have no wives and children?' he interrupted. 'Look here, Maharani, the thing we call pity is, at bottom, only pity for ourselves. We cannot bear to wound our own tender instincts, and so we do not strike at all – pity indeed! The height of cowardice!'

To hear Sandip's phrases in the mouth of this mere boy staggered me. So delightfully, lovably immature was he – of that age when the good may still be believed in as good, of that age when one really lives and grows. The Mother in me awoke.

1. The cashier is the official who is most in touch with the ladies of a *zamindar*'s household, directly taking their requisitions for household stores and doing their shopping for them, and so he becomes more a member of the family than the others.

For myself there was no longer good or bad – only death, beautiful alluring death. But to hear this stripling calmly talk of murdering an inoffensive old man as the right thing to do, made me shudder all over. The more clearly I saw that there was no sin in his heart, the more horrible appeared to me the sin of his words. I seemed to see the sin of the parents visited on the innocent child.

The sight of his great big eyes shining with faith and enthusiasm touched me to the quick. He was going, in his fascination, straight to the jaws of the python, from which, once in, there was no return. How was he to be saved? Why does not my country become, for once, a real Mother – clasp him to her bosom and cry out: 'Oh, my child, my child, what profits it that you should save me, if so it be that I should fail to save you?'

I know, I know, that all Power on earth waxes great under compact with Satan. But the Mother is there, alone though she be, to contemn and stand against this devil's progress. The Mother cares not for mere success, however great – she wants to give life, to save life. My very soul, today, stretches out its hands in yearning to save this child.

A while ago I suggested robbery to him. Whatever I may now say against it will be put down to a woman's weakness. They only love our weakness when it drags the world in its toils!

'You need do nothing at all, Amulya, I will see to the money,' I told him finally.

When he had almost reached the door, I called him back. 'Amulya,' said I, 'I am your elder sister. Today is not the Brothers' Day[1] according to the calendar, but all the days in the year are really Brothers' Days. My blessing be with you: may God keep you always.'

1. The daughter of the house occupies a place of specially tender affection in a Bengali household (perhaps in Hindu households all over India) because, by dictate of custom, she must be given away in marriage so early. She thus takes corresponding memories with her to her husband's home, where she has to begin as a stranger before she can get into her place. The resulting feeling, of the mistress of her new home for the one she has left, has taken ceremonial form as the Brothers' Day, on which the brothers are invited to the married sisters' houses. Where the sister is the elder, she offers her blessing and receives the brother's reverence, and *vice versa*. Presents, called the offerings of reverence (or blessing), are exchanged.

These unexpected words from my lips took Amulya by surprise. He stood stock-still for a time. Then, coming to himself, he prostrated himself at my feet in acceptance of the relationship and did me reverence. When he rose his eyes were full of tears ... O little brother mine! I am fast going to my death – let me take all your sin away with me. May no taint from me ever tarnish your innocence!

I said to him: 'Let your offering of reverence be that pistol!'

'What do you want with it, sister?'

'I will practise death.'

'Right, sister. Our women, also, must know how to die, to deal death!' with which Amulya handed me the pistol.

The radiance of his youthful countenance seemed to tinge my life with the touch of a new dawn. I put away the pistol within my clothes. May this reverence-offering be the last resource in my extremity ...

The door to the mother's chamber in my woman's heart once opened, I thought it would always remain open. But this pathway to the supreme good was closed when the mistress took the place of the mother and locked it again. The very next day I saw Sandip; and madness, naked and rampant, danced upon my heart.

What was this? Was this, then, my truer self? Never! I had never before known this shameless, this cruel one within me. The snake-charmer had come, pretending to draw this snake from within the fold of my garment – but it was never there, it was his all the time. Some demon has gained possession of me, and what I am doing today is the play of his activity – it has nothing to do with me.

This demon, in the guise of a god, had come with his ruddy torch to call me that day, saying: 'I am your Country. I am your Sandip. I am more to you than anything else of yours. *Bande Mataram!*' And with folded hands I had responded: 'You are my religion. You are my heaven. Whatever else is mine shall be swept away before my love for you. *Bande Mataram!*'

Five thousand is it? Five thousand it shall be! You want it tomorrow? Tomorrow you shall have it! In this desperate orgy, that gift of five thousand shall be as the foam of wine –

and then for the riotous revel! The immovable world shall sway under our feet, fire shall flash from our eyes, a storm shall roar in our ears, what is or is not in front shall become equally dim. And then with tottering footsteps we shall plunge to our death – in a moment all fire will be extinguished, the ashes will be scattered, and nothing will remain behind.

Chapter Nine

※

Bimala's Story

XV

FOR a time I was utterly at a loss to think of any way of getting that money. Then, the other day, in the light of intense excitement, suddenly the whole picture stood out clear before me.

Every year my husband makes a reverence-offering of six thousand rupees to my sister-in-law at the time of the Durga Puja. Every year it is deposited in her account at the bank in Calcutta. This year the offering was made as usual, but it has not yet been sent to the bank, being kept meanwhile in an iron safe, in a corner of the little dressing-room attached to our bedroom.

Every year my husband takes the money to the bank himself. This year he has not yet had an opportunity of going to town. How could I fail to see the hand of Providence in this? The money has been held up because the country wants it – who could have the power to take it away from her to the bank? And how can I have the power to refuse to take the money? The goddess revelling in destruction holds out her blood-cup crying: 'Give me drink. I am thirsty.' I will give her my own heart's blood with that five thousand rupees. Mother, the loser of that money will scarcely feel the loss, but me you will utterly ruin!

Many a time, in the old days, have I inwardly called the Senior Rani a thief, for I charged her with wheedling money out of my trusting husband. After her husband's death, she often used to make away with things belonging to the estate

143

for her own use. This I used to point out to my husband, but he remained silent. I would get angry and say: 'If you feel generous, make gifts by all means, but why allow yourself to be robbed?' Providence must have smiled, then, at these complaints of mine, for tonight I am on the way to rob my husband's safe of my sister-in-law's money.

My husband's custom was to let his keys remain in his pockets when he took off his clothes for the night, leaving them in the dressing-room. I picked out the key of the safe and opened it. The slight sound it made seemed to wake the whole world! A sudden chill turned my hands and feet icy cold, and I shivered all over.

There was a drawer inside the safe. On opening this I found the money, not in currency notes, but in gold rolled up in paper. I had no time to count out what I wanted. There were twenty rolls, all of which I took and tied up in a corner of my *sari*.

What a weight it was. The burden of the theft crushed my heart to the dust. Perhaps notes would have made it seem less like thieving, but this was all gold.

After I had stolen into my room like a thief, it felt like my own room no longer. All the most precious rights which I had over it vanished at the touch of my theft. I began to mutter to myself, as though telling *mantrams*: *Bande Mataram, Bande Mataram*, my Country, my golden Country, all this gold is for you, for none else!

But in the night the mind is weak. I came back into the bedroom where my husband was asleep, closing my eyes as I passed through, and went off to the open terrace beyond, on which I lay prone, clasping to my breast the end of the *sari* tied over the gold. And each one of the rolls gave me a shock of pain.

The silent night stood there with forefinger upraised. I could not think of my house as separate from my country: I had robbed my house, I had robbed my country. For this sin my house had ceased to be mine, my country also was estranged from me. Had I died begging for my country, even unsuccessfully, that would have been worship, acceptable to the gods. But theft is never worship – how then can I offer this gold? Ah me! I am doomed to death myself, must I desecrate my country with my impious touch?

The way to put the money back is closed to me. I have not the strength to return to the room, take again that key, open once more that safe – I should swoon on the threshold of my husband's door. The only road left now is the road in front. Neither have I the strength deliberately to sit down and count the coins. Let them remain behind their coverings: I cannot calculate.

There was no mist in the winter sky. The stars were shining brightly. If, thought I to myself, as I lay out there, I had to steal these stars one by one, like golden coins, for my country – these stars so carefully stored up in the bosom of the darkness – then the sky would be blinded, the night widowed for ever, and my theft would rob the whole world. But was not also this very thing I had done a robbing of the whole world – not only of money, but of trust, of righteousness?

I spent the night lying on the terrace. When at last it was morning, and I was sure that my husband had risen and left the room, then only with my shawl pulled over my head, could I retrace my steps towards the bedroom.

My sister-in-law was about, with her brass pot, watering her plants. When she saw me passing in the distance she cried: 'Have you heard the news, Chota Rani?'

I stopped in silence, all in a tremor. It seemed to me that the rolls of sovereigns were bulging through the shawl. I feared they would burst and scatter in a ringing shower, exposing to all the servants of the house the thief who had made herself destitute by robbing her own wealth.

'Your band of robbers,' she went on, 'have sent an anonymous message threatening to loot the treasury.'

I remained as silent as a thief.

'I was advising Brother Nikhil to seek your protection,' she continued banteringly. 'Call off your minions, Robber Queen! We will offer sacrifices to your *Bande Mataram* if you will but save us. What doings there are these days! – but for the Lord's sake, spare our house at least from burglary.'

I hastened into my room without reply. I had put my foot

145

on quicksand, and could not now withdraw it. Struggling would only send me down deeper.

If only the time would arrive when I could hand over the money to Sandip! I could bear it no longer, its weight was breaking through my very ribs.

It was still early when I got word that Sandip was awaiting me. Today I had no thought of adornment. Wrapped as I was in my shawl, I went off to the outer apartments.

As I entered the sitting-room I saw Sandip and Amulya there, together. All my dignity, all my honour, seemed to run tingling through my body from head to foot and vanish into the ground. I should have to lay bare a woman's uttermost shame in sight of this boy! Could they have been discussing my deed in their meeting place? Had any vestige of a veil of decency been left for me?

We women shall never understand men. When they are bent on making a road for some achievement, they think nothing of breaking the heart of the world into pieces to pave it for the progress of their chariot. When they are mad with the intoxication of creating, they rejoice in destroying the creation of the Creator. This heart-breaking shame of mine will not attract even a glance from their eyes. They have no feeling for life itself – all their eagerness is for their object. What am I to them but a meadow flower in the path of a torrent in flood?

What good will this extinction of me be to Sandip? Only five thousand rupees? Was not I good for something more than only five thousand rupees? Yes, indeed! Did I not learn that from Sandip himself, and was I not able in the light of this knowledge to despise all else in my world? I was the giver of light, of life, of *Shakti*, of immortality – in that belief, in that joy, I had burst all my bounds and come into the open. Had anyone then fulfilled for me that joy, I should have lived in my death. I should have lost nothing in the loss of my all.

Do they want to tell me now that all this was false? The psalm of my praise which was sung so devotedly, did it bring me down from my heaven, not to make heaven of earth, but only to level heaven itself with the dust?

XVI

'The money, Queen?' said Sandip with his keen glance full on my face.

Amulya also fixed his gaze on me. Though not my own mother's child, yet the dear lad is brother to me; for mother is mother all the world over. With his guileless face, his gentle eyes, his innocent youth, he looked at me. And I, a woman – of his mother's sex – how could I hand him poison, just because he asked for it?

'The money, Queen!' Sandip's insolent demand rang in my ears. For very shame and vexation I felt I wanted to fling that gold at Sandip's head. I could hardly undo the knot of my *sari*, my fingers trembled so. At last the paper rolls dropped on the table.

Sandip's face grew black . . . He must have thought that the rolls were of silver . . . What contempt was in his looks. What utter disgust at incapacity. It was almost as if he could have struck me! He must have suspected that I had come to parley with him, to offer to compound his claim for five thousand rupees with a few hundreds. There was a moment when I thought he would snatch up the rolls and throw them out of the window, declaring that he was no beggar, but a king claiming tribute.

'Is that all?' asked Amulya with such pity welling up in his voice that I wanted to sob out aloud. I kept my heart tightly pressed down, and merely nodded my head.

Sandip was speechless. He neither touched the rolls, nor uttered a sound.

My humiliation went straight to the boy's heart. With a sudden, feigned enthusiasm he exclaimed: 'It's plenty. It will do splendidly. You have saved us.' With which he tore open the covering of one of the rolls.

The sovereigns shone out. And in a moment the black covering seemed to be lifted from Sandip's countenance also. His delight beamed forth from his features. Unable to control his sudden revulsion of feeling, he sprang up from his seat towards me. What he intended I know not. I flashed a lightning glance towards Amulya – the colour had left the boy's face as at the stroke of a whip. Then with all my strength I thrust Sandip from me. As he reeled back his head struck the edge of the marble table and he dropped on the floor. There he lay awhile, motionless. Exhausted with my effort, I sank back on my seat.

Amulya's face lightened with a joyful radiance. He did not even turn towards Sandip, but came straight up, took the dust of my feet, and then remained there, sitting on the floor in front of me. O my little brother, my child! This reverence of yours is the last touch of heaven left in my empty world! I could contain myself no longer, and my tears flowed fast. I covered my eyes with the end of my *sari*, which I pressed to my face with both my hands, and sobbed and sobbed. And every time that I felt on my feet his tender touch trying to comfort me my tears broke out afresh.

After a little, when I had recovered myself and taken my hands from my face, I saw Sandip back at the table, gathering up the sovereigns in his handkerchief, as if nothing had happened. Amulya rose to his seat, from his place near my feet, his wet eyes shining.

Sandip coolly looked up at my face as he remarked: 'It is six thousand.'

'What do we want with so much, Sandip Babu?' cried Amulya. 'Three thousand five hundred is all we need for our work.'

'Our wants are not for this one place only,' Sandip replied. 'We shall want all we can get.'

'That may be,' said Amulya. 'But in future I undertake to get you all you want. Out of this, Sandip Babu, please return the extra two thousand five hundred to the Maharani.'

Sandip glanced enquiringly at me.

'No, no,' I exclaimed. 'I shall never touch that money again. Do with it as you will.'

'Can man ever give as woman can?' said Sandip, looking towards Amulya.

'They are goddesses!' agreed Amulya with enthusiasm.

'We men can at best give of our power,' continued Sandip. 'But women give themselves. Out of their own life they give birth, out of their own life they give sustenance. Such gifts

are the only true gifts.' Then turning to me, 'Queen!' said he,
'if what you have given us had been only money I would not
have touched it. But you have given that which is more to
you than life itself!'

There must be two different persons inside men. One of
these in me can understand that Sandip is trying to delude
me; the other is content to be deluded. Sandip has power, but
no strength of righteousness. The weapon of his which rouses
up life smites it again to death. He has the unfailing quiver
of the gods, but the shafts in them are of the demons.

Sandip's handkerchief was not large enough to hold all the
coins. 'Queen,' he asked, 'can you give me another?'

When I gave him mine, he reverently touched his forehead
with it, and then suddenly kneeling on the floor he made me
an obeisance. 'Goddess!' he said, 'it was to offer my reverence
that I had approached you, but you repulsed me, and rolled
me in the dust. Be it so, I accept your repulse as your boon to
me, I raise it to my head in salutation!' with which he pointed
to the place where he had been hurt.

Had I then misunderstood him? Could it be that his
outstretched hands had really been directed towards my feet?
Yet, surely, even Amulya had seen the passion that flamed
out of his eyes, his face. But Sandip is such an adept in
setting music to his chant of praise that I cannot argue; I lose
my power of seeing truth; my sight is clouded over like an
opium-eater's eyes. And so, after all, he gave me back twice
as much in return for the blow I had dealt him – the wound
on his head ended by making me bleed at heart. When I had
received Sandip's obeisance my theft seemed to gain a
dignity, and the gold glittering on the table to smile away all
fear of disgrace, all stings of conscience.

Like me Amulya also was won back. His devotion to
Sandip, which had suffered a momentary check, blazed up
anew. The flower-vase of his mind filled once more with
offerings for the worship of Sandip and me. His simple faith
shone out of his eyes with the pure light of the morning star
at dawn.

After I had offered worship and received worship my sin
became radiant. And as Amulya looked on my face he raised

149

his folded hands in salutation and cried *Bande Mataram!* I cannot expect to have this adoration surrounding me for ever; and yet this has come to be the only means of keeping alive my self-respect.

I can no longer enter my bedroom. The bedstead seems to thrust out a forbidding hand, the iron safe frowns at me. I want to get away from this continual insult to myself which is rankling within me. I want to keep running to Sandip to hear him sing my praises. There is just this one little altar of worship which has kept its head above the all-pervading depths of my dishonour, and so I want to cleave to it night and day; for on whichever side I step away from it, there is only emptiness.

Praise, praise, I want unceasing praise. I cannot live if my wine-cup be left empty for a single moment. So, as the very price of my life, I want Sandip of all the world, today.

XVII

When my husband nowadays comes in for his meals I feel I cannot sit before him; and yet it is such a shame not to be near him that I feel I cannot do that either. So I seat myself where we cannot look at each other's face. That was how I was sitting the other day when the Bara Rani came and joined us.

'It is all very well for you, brother,' said she, 'to laugh away these threatening letters. But they do frighten me so. Have you sent off that money you gave me to the Calcutta bank?'

'No, I have not yet had the time to get it away,' my husband replied.

'You are so careless, brother dear, you had better look out . . .'

'But it is in the iron safe right inside the inner dressing-room,' said my husband with a reassuring smile.

'What if they get in there? You can never tell!'

'If they go so far, they might as well carry you off too!'

'Don't you fear, no one will come for poor me. The real attraction is in your room! But joking apart, don't run the risk of keeping money in the room like that.'

'They will be taking along the Government revenue to Calcutta in a few days now; I will send this money to the bank under the same escort.'

'Very well. But see you don't forget all about it, you are so absent-minded.'

'Even if that money gets lost, while in my room, the loss cannot be yours, Sister Rani.'

'Now, now, brother, you will make me very angry if you talk in that way. Was I making any difference between yours and mine? What if your money is lost, does not that hurt me? If Providence has thought fit to take away my all, it has not left me insensible to the value of the most devoted brother known since the days of Lakshman.[1]

'Well, Junior Rani, are you turned into a wooden doll? You have not spoken a word yet. Do you know, brother, our Junior Rani thinks I try to flatter you. If things came to that pass I should not hesitate to do so, but I know my dear old brother does not need it!'

Thus the Senior Rani chattered on, not forgetting now and then to draw her brother's attention to this or that special delicacy amongst the dishes that were being served. My head was all the time in a whirl. The crisis was fast coming. Something must be done about replacing that money. And as I kept asking myself what could be done, and how it was to be done, the unceasing patter of my sister-in-law's words seemed more and more intolerable.

What made it all the worse was, that nothing could escape my sister-in-law's keen eyes. Every now and then she was casting side glances towards me. What she could read in my face I do not know, but to me it seemed that everything was written there only too plainly.

Then I did an infinitely rash thing. Affecting an easy, amused laugh I said: 'All the Senior Rani's suspicions, I see, are reserved for me — her fears of thieves and robbers are only a feint.'

The Senior Rani smiled mischievously. 'You are right, sister mine. A woman's theft is the most fatal of all thefts. But

1. Of the *Ramayana*. The story of his devotion to his elder brother Rama and his brother's wife Sita, has become a byword.

how can you elude my watchfulness? Am I a man, that you should hoodwink me?'

'If you fear me so,' I retorted, 'let me keep in your hands all I have, as security. If I cause you loss, you can then repay yourself.'

'Just listen to her, our simple little Junior Rani!' she laughed back, turning to my husband. 'Does she not know that there are losses which no security can make good, either in this world or in the next?'

My husband did not join in our exchange of words. When he had finished, he went off to the outer apartments, for nowadays he does not take his mid-day rest in our room.

All my more valuable jewels were in deposit in the treasury in charge of the cashier. Still what I kept with me must have been worth thirty or forty thousand. I took my jewel-box to the Bara Rani's room and opened it out before her, saying: 'I leave these with you, sister. They will keep you quite safe from all worry.'

The Bara Rani made a gesture of mock despair. 'You positively astound me, Chota Rani!' she said. 'Do you really suppose I spend sleepless nights for fear of being robbed by you?'

'What harm if you did have a wholesome fear of me? Does anybody know anybody else in this world?'

'You want to teach me a lesson by trusting me? No, no! I am bothered enough to know what to do with my own jewels, without keeping watch over yours. Take them away, there's a dear, so many prying servants are about.'

I went straight from my sister-in-law's room to the sitting-room outside, and sent for Amulya. With him Sandip came along too. I was in a great hurry, and said to Sandip: 'If you don't mind, I want to have a word or two with Amulya. Would you . . .'

Sandip smiled a wry smile. 'So Amulya and I are separate in your eyes? If you have set about to wean him from me, I must confess I have no power to retain him.'

I made no reply, but stood waiting.

'Be it so,' Sandip went on. 'Finish your special talk with Amulya. But then you must give me a special talk all to myself too, or it will mean a defeat for me. I can stand everything, but not defeat. My share must always be the lion's share. This has been my constant quarrel with Providence. I will defeat the Dispenser of my fate, but not take defeat at his hands.' With a crushing look at Amulya, Sandip walked out of the room.

'Amulya, my own little brother, you must do one thing for me,' I said.

'I will stake my life for whatever duty you may lay on me, sister.'

I brought out my jewel-box from the folds of my shawl and placed it before him. 'Sell or pawn these,' I said, 'and get me six thousand rupees as fast as ever you can.'

'No, no, Sister Rani,' said Amulya, touched to the quick. 'Let these jewels be. I will get you six thousand all the same.'

'Oh, don't be silly,' I said impatiently. 'There is no time for any nonsense. Take this box. Get away to Calcutta by the night train. And bring me the money by the day after tomorrow positively.'

Amulya took a diamond necklace out of the box, held it up to the light and put it back gloomily.

'I know,' I told him, 'that you will never get the proper price for these diamonds, so I am giving you jewels worth about thirty thousand. I don't care if they all go, but I must have that six thousand without fail.'

'Do you know, Sister Rani,' said Amulya, 'I have had a quarrel with Sandip Babu over that six thousand rupees he took from you? I cannot tell you how ashamed I felt. But Sandip Babu would have it that we must give up even our shame for the country. That may be so. But this is somehow different. I do not fear to die for the country, to kill for the country – that much *Shakti* has been given me. But I cannot forget the shame of having taken money from you. There Sandip Babu is ahead of me. He has no regrets or compunctions. He says we must get rid of the idea that the money belongs to the one in whose box it happens to be – if we cannot, where is the magic of *Bande Mataram*?'

Amulya gathered enthusiasm as he talked on. He always warms up when he has me for a listener. 'The *Gita* tells us,'

153

he continued, 'that no one can kill the soul. Killing is a mere word. So also is the taking away of money. Whose is the money? No one has created it. No one can take it away with him when he departs this life, for it is no part of his soul. Today it is mine, tomorrow my son's, the next day his creditor's. Since, in fact, money belongs to no one, why should any blame attach to our patriots if, instead of leaving it for some worthless son, they take it for their own use?'

When I hear Sandip's words uttered by this boy, I tremble all over. Let those who are snake-charmers play with snakes; if harm comes to them, they are prepared for it. But these boys are so innocent, all the world is ready with its blessing to protect them. They play with a snake not knowing its nature, and when we see them smilingly, trustfully, putting their hands within reach of its fangs, then we understand how terribly dangerous the snake is. Sandip is right when he suspects that though I, for myself, may be ready to die at his hands, this boy I shall wean from him and save.

'So the money is wanted for the use of your patriots?' I questioned with a smile.

'Of course it is!' said Amulya proudly. 'Are they not our kings? Poverty takes away from their regal power. Do you know, we always insist on Sandip Babu travelling First Class? He never shirks kingly honours – he accepts them not for himself, but for the glory of us all. The greatest weapon of those who rule the world, Sandip Babu has told us, is the hypnotism of their display. To take the vow of poverty would be for them not merely a penance – it would mean suicide.'

At this point Sandip noiselessly entered the room. I threw my shawl over the jewel-case with a rapid movement.

'The special-talk business not yet over?' he asked with a sneer in his tone.

'Yes, we've quite finished,' said Amulya apologetically. 'It was nothing much.'

'No, Amulya,' I said, 'we have not quite finished.'

'So exit Sandip for the second time, I suppose?' said Sandip.

'If you please.'

'And as to Sandip's re-entry . . .'

'Not today. I have no time.'

'I see!' said Sandip as his eyes flashed. 'No time to waste, only for special talks!'

Jealousy! Where the strong man shows weakness, there the weaker sex cannot help beating her drums of victory. So I repeated firmly: 'I really have no time.'

Sandip went away looking black. Amulya was greatly perturbed. 'Sister Rani,' he pleaded, 'Sandip Babu is annoyed.'

'He has neither cause nor right to be annoyed,' I said with some vehemence. 'Let me caution you about one thing, Amulya. Say nothing to Sandip Babu about the sale of my jewels – on your life.'

'No, I will not.'

'Then you had better not delay any more. You must get away by tonight's train.'

Amulya and I left the room together. As we came out on the verandah Sandip was standing there. I could see he was waiting to waylay Amulya. To prevent that I had to engage him. 'What is it you wanted to tell me, Sandip Babu?' I asked.

'I have nothing special to say – mere small talk. And since you have not the time . . .'

'I can give you just a little.'

By this time Amulya had left. As we entered the room Sandip asked: 'What was that box Amulya carried away?'

The box had not escaped his eyes. I remained firm. 'If I could have told you, it would have been made over to him in your presence!'

'So you think Amulya will not tell me?'

'No, he will not.'

Sandip could not conceal his anger any longer. 'You think you will gain the mastery over me?' he blazed out. 'That shall never be. Amulya, there, would die a happy death if I deigned to trample him under foot. I will never, so long as I live, allow you to bring him to your feet!'

Oh, the weak! the weak! At last Sandip has realized that he is weak before me! That is why there is this sudden outburst of anger. He has understood that he cannot meet the power that I wield, with mere strength. With a glance I can crumble his strongest fortifications. So he must needs resort to bluster. I simply smiled in contemptuous silence. At last have I come to a level above him. I must never lose this vantage ground; never descend lower again. Amidst all my degradation this bit of dignity must remain to me!

'I know,' said Sandip, after a pause, 'it was your jewel-case.'

'You may guess as you please,' said I, 'but you will get nothing out of me.'

'So you trust Amulya more than you trust me? Do you know that the boy is the shadow of my shadow, the echo of my echo — that he is nothing if I am not at his side?'

'Where he is not your echo, he is himself, Amulya. And that is where I trust him more than I can trust your echo!'

'You must not forget that you are under a promise to render up all your ornaments to me for the worship of the Divine Mother. In fact your offering has already been made.'

'Whatever ornaments the gods leave to me will be offered up to the gods. But how can I offer those which have been stolen away from me?'

'Look here, it is no use your trying to give me the slip in that fashion. Now is the time for grim work. Let that work be finished, then you can make a display of your woman's wiles to your heart's content — and I will help you in your game.'

The moment I had stolen my husband's money and paid it to Sandip, the music that was in our relations stopped. Not only did I destroy all my own value by making myself cheap, but Sandip's powers, too, lost scope for their full play. You cannot employ your marksmanship against a thing which is right in your grasp. So Sandip has lost his aspect of the hero; a tone of low quarrelsomeness has come into his words.

Sandip kept his brilliant eyes fixed full on my face till they seemed to blaze with all the thirst of the mid-day sky. Once or twice he fidgeted with his feet, as though to leave his seat, as if to spring right on me. My whole body seemed to swim, my veins throbbed, the hot blood surged up to my ears; I felt that if I remained there, I should never get up at all. With a

156

supreme effort I tore myself off the chair, and hastened towards the door.

From Sandip's dry throat there came a muffled cry: 'Whither would you flee, Queen?' The next moment he left his seat with a bound to seize hold of me. At the sound of footsteps outside the door, however, he rapidly retreated and fell back into his chair. I checked my steps near the bookshelf, where I stood staring at the names of the books.

As my husband entered the room, Sandip exclaimed: 'I say, Nikhil, don't you keep Browning among your books here? I was just telling Queen Bee of our college club. Do you remember that contest of ours over the translation of those lines from Browning? You don't?

> She should never have looked at me
> If she meant I should not love her!
> There are plenty . . . men, you call such,
> I suppose . . . she may discover
> All her soul to, if she pleases,
> And yet leave much as she found them:
> But I'm not so, and she knew it
> When she fixed me, glancing round them.

'I managed to get together the words to render it into Bengali, somehow, but the result was hardly likely to be a "joy forever" to the people of Bengal. I really did think at one time that I was on the verge of becoming a poet, but Providence was kind enough to save me from that disaster. Do you remember old Dakshina? If he had not become a Salt Inspector, he would have been a poet. I remember his rendering to this day . . .

'No, Queen Bee, it is no use rummaging those bookshelves. Nikhil has ceased to read poetry since his marriage – perhaps he has no further need for it. But I suppose "the fever fit of poesy", as the Sanskrit has it, is about to attack me again.'

'I have come to give you a warning, Sandip,' said my husband.

'About the fever fit of poesy?'

My husband took no notice of this attempt at humour. 'For some time,' he continued, 'Mahomedan preachers have been

157

about stirring up the local Mussulmans. They are all wild with you, and may attack you any moment.'

'Are you come to advise flight?'

'I have come to give you information, not to offer advice.'

'Had these estates been mine, such a warning would have been necessary for the preachers, not for me. If, instead of trying to frighten me, you give them a taste of your intimidation, that would be worthier both of you and me. Do you know that your weakness is weakening your neighbouring *zamindars* also?'

'I did not offer you my advice, Sandip. I wish you, too, would refrain from giving me your. Besides, it is useless. And there is another thing I want to tell you. You and your followers have been secretly worrying and oppressing my tenantry. I cannot allow that any longer. So I must ask you to leave my territory.'

'For fear of the Mussulmans, or is there any other fear you have to threaten me with?'

'There are fears the want of which is cowardice. In the name of those fears, I tell you, Sandip, you must go. In five days I shall be starting for Calcutta. I want you to accompany me. You may of course stay in my house there – to that there is no objection.'

'All right, I have still five days' time then. Meanwhile, Queen Bee, let me hum to you my song of parting from your honey-hive. Ah! you poet of modern Bengal! Throw open your doors and let me plunder your words. The theft is really yours, for it is my song which you have made your own – let the name be yours by all means, but the song is mine.' With this Sandip struck up in a deep, husky voice, which threatened to be out of tune, a song in the *Bhairavi* mode:

'In the springtime of your kingdom, my Queen,
  *Meetings and partings chase each other in their endless hide
  and seek,*
  *And flowers blossom in the wake of those that droop and die
  in the shade.*
  In the springtime of your kingdom, my Queen,
  My meeting with you had its own songs,

158

But has not also my leave-taking any gift to offer you?
That gift is my secret hope, which I keep hidden in the
  shadows of your flower garden,
That the rains of July may sweetly temper your fiery June.'

His boldness was immense – boldness which had no veil, but was naked as fire. One finds no time to stop it: it is like trying to resist a thunderbolt: the lightning flashes: it laughs at all resistance.

I left the room. As I was passing along the verandah towards the inner apartments, Amulya suddenly made his appearance and came and stood before me.

'Fear nothing, Sister Rani,' he said. 'I am off tonight and shall not return unsuccessful.'

'Amulya,' said I, looking straight into his earnest, youthful face, 'I fear nothing for myself, but may I never cease to fear for you.'

Amulya turned to go, but before he was out of sight I called him back and asked: 'Have you a mother, Amulya?'

'I have.'

'A sister?'

'No, I am the only child of my mother. My father died when I was quite little.'

'Then go back to your mother, Amulya.'

'But, Sister Rani, I have now both mother and sister.'

'Then, Amulya, before you leave tonight, come and have your dinner here.'

'There won't be time for that. Let me take some food for the journey, consecrated with your touch.'

'What do you specially like, Amulya?'

'If I had been with my mother I should have had lots of *Poush* cakes. Make some for me with your own hands, Sister Rani!'

159

Chapter Ten

※

Nikhil's Story

XII

I LEARNT from my master that Sandip had joined forces with Harish Kundu, and there was to be a grand celebration of the worship of the demon-destroying Goddess. Harish Kundu was extorting the expenses from his tenantry. Pandits Kaviratna and Vidyavagish had been commissioned to compose a hymn with a double meaning.

My master has just had a passage at arms with Sandip over this. 'Evolution is at work amongst the gods as well,' says Sandip. 'The grandson has to remodel the gods created by the grandfather to suit his own taste, or else he is left an atheist. It is my mission to modernize the ancient deities. I am born the saviour of the gods, to emancipate them from the thraldom of the past.'

I have seen from our boyhood what a juggler with ideas is Sandip. He has no interest in discovering truth, but to make a quizzical display of it rejoices his heart. Had he been born in the wilds of Africa he would have spent a glorious time inventing argument after argument to prove that cannibalism is the best means of promoting true communion between man and man. But those who deal in delusion end by deluding themselves, and I fully believe that, each time Sandip creates a new fallacy, he persuades himself that he has found the truth, however contradictory his creations may be to one another.

However, I shall not give a helping hand to establish a liquor distillery in my country. The young men, who are ready to offer their services for their country's cause, must not fall into this habit of getting intoxicated. The people who want to exact work by drugging methods set more value on the excitement than on the minds they intoxicate.

I had to tell Sandip, in Bimala's presence, that he must go. Perhaps both will impute to me the wrong motive. But I must free myself also from all fear of being misunderstood. Let even Bimala misunderstand me . . .

A number of Mahomedan preachers are being sent over from Dacca. The Mussulmans in my territory had come to have almost as much of an aversion to the killing of cows as the Hindus. But now cases of cow-killing are cropping up here and there. I had the news first from some of my Mussulman tenants with expressions of their disapproval. Here was a situation which I could see would be difficult to meet. At the bottom was a pretence of fanaticism, which would cease to be a pretence if obstructed. That is just where the ingenuity of the move came in!

I sent for some of my principal Hindu tenants and tried to get them to see the matter in its proper light. 'We can be staunch in our own convictions,' I said, 'but we have no control over those of others. For all that many of us are Vaishnavas, those of us who are Shaktas go on with their animal sacrifices just the same. That cannot be helped. We must, in the same way, let the Mussulmans do as they think best. So please refrain from all disturbance.'

'Maharaja,' they replied, 'these outrages have been unknown for so long.'

'That was so,' I said, 'because such was their spontaneous desire. Let us behave in such a way that the same may become true, over again. But a breach of the peace is not the way to bring this about.'

'No, Maharaja,' they insisted, 'those good old days are gone. This will never stop unless you put it down with a strong hand.'

'Oppression,' I replied, 'will not only not prevent cow-killing, it may lead to the killing of men as well.'

One of them had had an English education. He had learnt to repeat the phrases of the day. 'It is not only a question of orthodoxy,' he argued. 'Our country is mainly agricultural, and cows are . . .'

'Buffaloes in this country,' I interrupted, 'likewise give milk and are used for ploughing. And therefore, so long as we dance frantic dances on our temple pavements, smeared with their blood, their severed heads carried on our shoulders, religion will only laugh at us if we quarrel with Mussulmans in her name, and nothing but the quarrel itself will remain true. If the cow alone is to be held sacred from slaughter, and not the buffalo, then that is bigotry, not religion.'

'But are you not aware, sir, of what is behind all this?' pursued the English-knowing tenant. 'This has only become possible because the Mussulman is assured of safety, even if he breaks the law. Have you not heard of the Pachur case?'

'Why is it possible,' I asked, 'to use the Mussulmans thus, as tools against us? Is it not because we have fashioned them into such with our own intolerance? That is how Providence punishes us. Our accumulated sins are being visited on our own heads.'

'Oh, well, if that be so, let them be visited on us. But we shall have our revenge. We have undermined what was the greatest strength of the authorities, their devotion to their own laws. Once they were truly kings, dispensing justice; now they themselves will become law-breakers, and so no better than robbers. This may not go down to history, but we shall carry it in our hearts for all time . . .'

The evil reports about me which are spreading from paper to paper are making me notorious. News comes that my effigy has been burnt at the river-side burning-ground of the Chakravartis, with due ceremony and enthusiasm; and other insults are in contemplation. The trouble was that they had come to ask me to take shares in a Cotton Mill they wanted to start. I had to tell them that I did not so much mind the loss of my own money, but I would not be a party to causing a loss to so many poor shareholders.

'Are we to understand, Maharaja,' said my visitors, 'that the prosperity of the country does not interest you?'

'Industry may lead to the country's prosperity,' I explained, 'but a mere desire for its prosperity will not make for success in industry. Even when our heads were cool, our industries did not flourish. Why should we suppose that they will do so just because we have become frantic?'

'Why not say plainly that you will not risk your money?'

'I will put in my money when I see that it is industry which prompts you. But, because you have lighted a fire, it does not follow that you have the food to cook over it.'

XIII

What is this? Our Chakua sub-treasury looted! A remittance of seven thousand five hundred rupees was due from there to headquarters. The local cashier had changed the cash at the Government Treasury into small currency notes for convenience in carrying, and had kept them ready in bundles. In the middle of the night an armed band had raided the room, and wounded Kasim, the man on guard. The curious part of it was that they had taken only six thousand rupees and left the rest scattered on the floor, though it would have been as easy to carry that away also. Anyhow, the raid of the dacoits was over; now the police raid would begin. Peace was out of the question.

When I went inside, I found the news had travelled before me. 'What a terrible thing, brother,' exclaimed the Bara Rani. 'Whatever shall we do?'

I made light of the matter to reassure her. 'We still have something left,' I said with a smile. 'We shall manage to get along somehow.'

'Don't joke about it, brother dear. Why are they all so angry with you? Can't you humour them? Why put everybody out?'

'I cannot let the country go to rack and ruin, even if that would please everybody.'

'That was a shocking thing they did at the burning-grounds. It's a horrid shame to treat you so. The Chota Rani has got rid of all her fears by dint of the Englishwoman's teaching, but as for me, I had to send for the priest to avert the omen before I could get any peace of mind. For my sake, dear, do get away to Calcutta. I tremble to think what they may do, if you stay on here.'

My sister-in-law's genuine anxiety touched me deeply.

'And, brother,' she went on, 'did I not warn you, it was not well to keep so much money in your room? They might get wind of it any day. It is not the money – but who knows . . .'

To calm her I promised to remove the money to the treasury at once, and then get it away to Calcutta with the first escort going. We went together to my bedroom. The dressing-room door was shut. When I knocked, Bimala called out: 'I am dressing.'

'I wonder at the Chota Rani,' exclaimed my sister-in-law, 'dressing so early in the day! One of their *Bande Mataram* meetings, I suppose. Robber Queen!' she called out in jest to Bimala. 'Are you counting your spoils inside?'

'I will attend to the money a little later,' I said, as I came away to my office room outside.

I found the Police Inspector waiting for me. 'Any trace of the dacoits?' I asked.

'I have my suspicions.'

'On whom?'

'Kasim, the guard.'

'Kasim? But was he not wounded?'

'A mere nothing. A flesh wound on the leg. Probably self-inflicted.'

'But I cannot bring myself to believe it. He is such a trusted servant.'

'You may have trusted him, but that does not prevent his being a thief. Have I not seen men trusted for twenty years together, suddenly developing . . .'

'Even if it were so, I could not send him to gaol. But why should he have left the rest of the money lying about?'

'To put us off the scent. Whatever you may say, Maharaja, he must be an old hand at the game. He mounts guard during his watch, right enough, but I feel sure he has a finger in all the dacoities going on in the neighbourhood.'

With this the Inspector proceeded to recount the various methods by which it was possible to be concerned in a dacoity twenty or thirty miles away, and yet be back in time for duty.

'Have you brought Kasim here?' I asked.

'No,' was the reply, 'he is in the lock-up. The Magistrate is due for the investigation.'

'I want to see him,' I said.

When I went to his cell he fell at my feet, weeping. 'In God's name,' he said, 'I swear I did not do this thing.'

'I do not doubt you, Kasim,' I assured him. 'Fear nothing. They can do nothing to you, if you are innocent.'

Kasim, however, was unable to give a coherent account of the incident. He was obviously exaggerating. Four or five hundred men, big guns, numberless swords, figured in his narrative. It must have been either his disturbed state of mind or a desire to account for his easy defeat. He would have it that this was Harish Kundu's doing; he was even sure he had heard the voice of Ekram, the head retainer of the Kundus.

'Look here, Kasim,' I had to warn him, 'don't you be dragging other people in with your stories. You are not called upon to make out a case against Harish Kundu, or anybody else.'

XIV

On returning home I asked my master to come over. He shook his head gravely. 'I see no good in this,' said he – 'this setting aside of conscience and putting the country in its place. All the sins of the country will now break out, hideous and unashamed.'

'Who do you think could have . . .'

'Don't ask me. But sin is rampant. Send them all away, right away from here.'

'I have given them one more day. They will be leaving the day after tomorrow.'

'And another thing. Take Bimala away to Calcutta. She is getting too narrow a view of the outside world from here, she cannot see men and things in their true proportions. Let her see the world – men and their work – give her a broad vision.'

'That is exactly what I was thinking.'

'Well, don't make any delay about it. I tell you, Nikhil, man's history has to be built by the united effort of all the races in the world, and therefore this selling of conscience for political reasons – this making a fetish of one's country, won't do. I know that Europe does not at heart admit this, but there she has not the right to pose as our teacher. Men who die for the truth become immortal: and, if a whole people can die for the truth, it will also achieve immortality in the history of humanity. Here, in this land of India, amid the mocking laughter of Satan piercing the sky, may the feeling for this truth become real! What a terrible epidemic of sin has been brought into our country from foreign lands . . .'

The whole day passed in the turmoil of investigation. I was tired out when I retired for the night. I left over sending my sister-in-law's money to the treasury till next morning.

I woke up from my sleep at dead of night. The room was dark. I thought I heard a moaning somewhere. Somebody must have been crying. Sounds of sobbing came heavy with tears like fitful gusts of wind in the rainy night. It seemed to me that the cry rose from the heart of my room itself. I was alone. For some days Bimala had her bed in another room adjoining mine. I rose up and when I went out I found her in the balcony lying prone upon her face on the bare floor.

This is something that cannot be written in words. He only knows it who sits in the bosom of the world and receives all its pangs in His own heart. The sky is dumb, the stars are mute, the night is still, and in the midst of it all that one sleepless cry!

We give these sufferings names, bad or good, according to the classifications of the books, but this agony which is welling up from a torn heart, pouring into the fathomless dark, has it any name? When in that midnight, standing under the silent stars, I looked upon that figure, my mind was struck with awe, and I said to myself: 'Who am I to judge her?' O life, O death, O God of the infinite existence, I bow my head in silence to the mystery which is in you.

Once I thought I should turn back. But I could not. I sat down on the ground near Bimala and placed my hand on her head. At the first touch her whole body seemed to stiffen, but the next moment the hardness gave way, and the tears burst out. I gently passed my fingers over her forehead. Suddenly her hands groping for my feet grasped them and drew them to herself, pressing them against her breast with such force that I thought her heart would break.

Bimala's Story

XVIII

Amulya is due to return from Calcutta this morning. I told the servants to let me know as soon as he arrived, but could not keep still. At last I went outside to await him in the sitting-room.

When I sent him off to sell the jewels I must have been thinking only of myself. It never even crossed my mind that so young a boy, trying to sell such valuable jewellery, would at once be suspected. So helpless are we women, we needs must place on others the burden of our danger. When we go to our death we drag down those who are about us.

I had said with pride that I would save Amulya – as if she who was drowning could save others. But instead of saving him, I have sent him to his doom. My little brother, such a sister have I been to you that Death must have smiled on that Brothers' Day when I gave you my blessing – I, who wander distracted with the burden of my own evil-doing.

I feel today that man is at times attacked with evil as with the plague. Some germ finds its way in from somewhere, and then in the space of one night Death stalks in. Why cannot the stricken one be kept far away from the rest of the world? I, at least, have realized how terrible is the contagion – like a fiery torch which burns that it may set the world on fire.

It struck nine. I could not get rid of the idea that Amulya was in trouble, that he had fallen into the clutches of the police. There must be great excitement in the Police Office – whose are the jewels? – where did he get them? And in the end I shall have to furnish the answer, in public, before all the world.

What is that answer to be? Your day has come at last, Bara Rani, you whom I have so long despised. You, in the shape of the public, the world, will have your revenge. O God, save me this time, and I will cast all my pride at my sister-in-law's feet.

I could bear it no longer. I went straight to the Bara Rani. She was in the verandah, spicing her betel leaves, Thako at her side. The sight of Thako made me shrink back for a moment, but I overcame all hesitation, and making a low obeisance I took the dust of my elder sister-in-law's feet.

'Bless my soul, Chota Rani,' she exclaimed, 'what has come upon you? Why this sudden reverence?'

'It is my birthday, sister,' said I. 'I have caused you pain. Give me your blessing today that I may never do so again. My mind is so small.' I repeated my obeisance and left her hurriedly, but she called me back.

'You never before told me that this was your birthday, Chotie darling! Be sure to come and have lunch with me this afternoon. You positively must.'

O God, let it really be my birthday today. Can I not be born over again? Cleanse me, my God, and purify me and give me one more trial!

I went again to the sitting-room to find Sandip there. A feeling of disgust seemed to poison my very blood. The face of his, which I saw in the morning light, had nothing of the magic radiance of genius.

'Will you leave the room,' I blurted out.

Sandip smiled. 'Since Amulya is not here,' he remarked, 'I should think my turn had come for a special talk.'

My fate was coming back upon me. How was I to take away the right I myself had given. 'I would be alone,' I repeated.

'Queen,' he said, 'the presence of another person does not prevent your being alone. Do not mistake me for one of the crowd. I, Sandip, am always alone, even when surrounded by thousands.'

'Please come some other time. This morning I am . . .'

'Waiting for Amulya?'

I turned to leave the room for sheer vexation, when Sandip drew out from the folds of his cloak that jewel-casket of mine and banged it down on the marble table. I was thoroughly startled. 'Has not Amulya gone, then?' I exclaimed.

'Gone where?'

'To Calcutta?'

'No,' chuckled Sandip.

Ah, then my blessing had come true, in spite of all. He was saved. Let God's punishment fall on me, the thief, if only Amulya be safe.

The change in my countenance roused Sandip's scorn. 'So pleased, Queen!' sneered he. 'Are these jewels so very precious? How then did you bring yourself to offer them to the Goddess? Your gift was actually made. Would you now take it back?'

Pride dies hard and raises its fangs to the last. It was clear to me I must show Sandip I did not care a rap about these jewels. 'If they have excited your greed,' I said, 'you may have them.'

'My greed today embraces the wealth of all Bengal,' replied Sandip. 'Is there a greater force than greed? It is the steed of the great ones of the earth, as is the elephant, Airauat, the steed of Indra. So then these jewels are mine?'

As Sandip took up and replaced the casket under his cloak, Amulya rushed in. There were dark rings under his eyes, his lips were dry, his hair tumbled: the freshness of his youth seemed to have withered in a single day. Pangs gripped my heart as I looked on him.

'My box!' he cried, as he went straight up to Sandip without a glance at me. 'Have you taken that jewel-box from my trunk?'

'Your jewel-box?' mocked Sandip.

'It was my trunk!'

Sandip burst out into a laugh. 'Your distinctions between mine and yours are getting rather thin, Amulya,' he cried. 'You will die a religious preacher yet, I see.'

Amulya sank on a chair with his face in his hands. I went up to him and placing my hand on his head asked him: 'What is your trouble, Amulya?'

He stood straight up as he replied: 'I had set my heart, Sister Rani, on returning your jewels to you with my own hand. Sandip Babu knew this, but he forestalled me.'

'What do I care for my jewels?' I said. 'Let them go. No harm is done.'

'Go? Where?' asked the mystified boy.

'The jewels are mine,' said Sandip. 'Insignia bestowed on me by my Queen!'

'No, no, no,' broke out Amulya wildly. 'Never, Sister Rani! I brought them back for you. You shall not give them away to anybody else.'

'I accept your gift, my little brother,' said I. 'But let him, who hankers after them, satisfy his greed.'

Amulya glared at Sandip like a beast of prey, as he growled: 'Look here, Sandip Babu, you know that even hanging has no terrors for me. If you dare take away that box of jewels . . .'

With an attempt at a sarcastic laugh Sandip said: 'You also ought to know by this time, Amulya, that I am not the man to be afraid of you.'

'Queen Bee,' he went on, turning to me, 'I did not come here today to take these jewels, I came to give them to you. You would have done wrong to take my gift at Amulya's hands. In order to prevent it, I had first to make them clearly mine. Now these my jewels are my gift to you. Here they are! Patch up any understanding with this boy you like. I must go. You have been at your special talks all these days together, leaving me out of them. If special happenings now come to pass, don't blame me.

'Amulya,' he continued, 'I have sent on your trunks and things to your lodgings. Don't you be keeping any belongings of yours in my room any longer.' With this parting shot, Sandip flung out of the room.

XIX

'I have had no peace of mind, Amulya,' I said to him, 'ever since I sent you off to sell my jewels.'

'Why, Sister Rani?'

'I was afraid lest you should get into trouble with them, lest they should suspect you for a thief. I would rather go without that six thousand. You must now do another thing for me – go home at once, home to your mother.'

Amulya produced a small bundle and said: 'But, sister, I have got the six thousand.'

'Where from?'

'I tried hard to get gold,' he went on, without replying to my question, 'but could not. So I had to bring it in notes.'

'Tell me truly, Amulya, swear by me, where did you get this money?'

'That I will not tell you.'

Everything seemed to grow dark before my eyes. 'What terrible thing have you done, Amulya?' I cried. 'Is it then . . .'

'I know you will say I got this money wrongly. Very well, I admit it. But I have paid the full price for my wrong-doing. So now the money is mine.'

I no longer had any desire to learn more about it. My very blood-vessels contracted, making my whole body shrink within itself.

'Take it away, Amulya,' I implored. 'Put it back where you got it from.'

'That would be hard indeed!'

'It is not hard, brother dear. It was an evil moment when you first came to me. Even Sandip has not been able to harm you as I have done.'

Sandip's name seemed to stab him.

'Sandip!' he cried. 'It was you alone who made me come to know that man for what he is. Do you know, sister, he has not spent a pice out of those sovereigns he took from you? He shut himself into his room, after he left you, and gloated over the gold, pouring it out in a heap on the floor. "This is not money," he exclaimed, "but the petals of the divine lotus of power; crystallized strains of music from the pipes that play in the paradise of wealth! I cannot find it in my heart to change them, for they seem longing to fulfil their destiny of adorning the neck of Beauty. Amulya, my boy, don't you look at these with your fleshly eye, they are Lakshmi's smile, the gracious radiance of Indra's queen. No, no, I can't give them up to that boor of a manager. I am sure, Amulya, he was telling us lies. The police haven't traced the man who sank that boat. It's the manager who wants to make something out of it. We must get those letters back from him."

'I asked him how we were to do this; he told me to use force or threats. I offered to do so if he would return the gold.

That, he said, we could consider later. I will not trouble you, sister, with all I did to frighten the man into giving up those letters and burn them – it is a long story. That very night I came to Sandip and said: "We are now safe. Let me have the sovereigns to return them tomorrow to my sister, the Maharani." But he cried, "What infatuation is this of yours? Your precious sister's skirt bids fair to hide the whole country from you. Say *Bande Mataram* and exorcize the evil spirit."

'You know, Sister Rani, the power of Sandip's magic. The gold remained with him. And I spent the whole dark night on the bathing-steps of the lake muttering *Bande Mataram*.

'Then when you gave me your jewels to sell, I went again to Sandip. I could see he was angry with me. But he tried not to show it. "If I still have them hoarded up in any box of mine you may take them," said he, as he flung me his keys. They were nowhere to be seen. "Tell me where they are," I said. "I will do so," he replied, "when I find your infatuation has left you. Not now."

'When I found I could not move him, I had to employ other methods. Then I tried to get the sovereigns from him in exchange for my currency notes for six thousand rupees. "You shall have them," he said, and disappeared into his bedroom, leaving me waiting outside. There he broke open my trunk and came straight to you with your casket through some other passage. He would not let me bring it, and now he dares call it his gift. How can I tell how much he has deprived me of? I shall never forgive him.

'But, oh sister, his power over me has been utterly broken. And it is you who have broken it!'

'Brother dear,' said I, 'if that is so, then my life is justified. But more remains to be done, Amulya. It is not enough that the spell has been destroyed. Its stains must be washed away. Don't delay any longer, go at once and put back the money where you took it from. Can you not do it, dear?'

'With your blessing everything is possible, Sister Rani.'

'Remember, it will not be your expiation alone, but mine also. I am a woman; the outside world is closed to me, else I would have gone myself. My hardest punishment is that I must put on you the burden of my sin.'

'Don't say that, sister. The path I was treading was not your path. It attracted me because of its dangers and difficulties. Now that your path calls me, let it be a thousand times more difficult and dangerous, the dust of your feet will help me to win through. Is it then your command that this money be replaced?'

'Not my command, brother mine, but a command from above.'

'Of that I know nothing. It is enough for me that this command from above comes from your lips. And, sister, I thought I had an invitation here. I must not lose that. You must give me your *prasad*[1] before I go. Then, if I can possibly manage it, I will finish my duty in the evening.'

Tears came to my eyes when I tried to smile as I said: 'So be it.'

---

1. Food consecrated by the touch of a revered person.

Chapter Eleven

*

Bimala's Story

XX

WITH Amulya's departure my heart sank within me. On what perilous adventure had I sent this only son of his mother? O God, why need my expiation have such pomp and circumstance? Could I not be allowed to suffer alone without inviting all this multitude to share my punishment? Oh, let not this innocent child fall victim to Your wrath.

I called him back – 'Amulya!'

My voice sounded so feebly, it failed to reach him.

I went up to the door and called again: 'Amulya!'

He had gone.

'Who is there?'

'Rani Mother!'

'Go and tell Amulya Babu that I want him.'

What exactly happened I could not make out – the man, perhaps, was not familiar with Amulya's name – but he returned almost at once followed by Sandip.

'The very moment you sent me away,' he said as he came in, 'I had a presentiment that you would call me back. The attraction of the same moon causes both ebb and flow. I was so sure of being sent for, that I was actually waiting out in the passage. As soon as I caught sight of your man, coming from your room, I said: "Yes, yes, I am coming, I am coming at once!" – before he could utter a word. That up-country lout was surprised, I can tell you! He stared at me, open-mouthed, as if he thought I knew magic.

'All the fights in the world, Queen Bee,' Sandip rambled

on, 'are really fights between hypnotic forces. Spell cast against spell – noiseless weapons which reach even invisible targets. At last I have met in you my match. Your quiver is full, I know, you artful warrior Queen! You are the only one in the world who has been able to turn Sandip out and call Sandip back, at your sweet will. Well, your quarry is at your feet. What will you do with him now? Will you give him the *coup de grâce*, or keep him in your cage? Let me warn you beforehand, Queen, you will find the beast as difficult to kill outright as to keep in bondage. Anyway, why lose time in trying your magic weapons?'

Sandip must have felt the shadow of approaching defeat, and this made him try to gain time by chattering away without waiting for a reply. I believe he knew that I had sent the messenger for Amulya, whose name the man must have mentioned. In spite of that he had deliberately played this trick. He was now trying to avoid giving me any opening to tell him that it was Amulya I wanted, not him. But his stratagem was futile, for I could see his weakness through it. I must not yield up a pin's point of the ground I had gained.

'Sandip Babu,' I said, 'I wonder how you can go on making these endless speeches, without a stop. Do you get them up by heart, beforehand?'

Sandip's face flushed instantly.

'I have heard,' I continued, 'that our professional reciters keep a book full of all kinds of ready-made discourses, which can be fitted into any subject. Have you also a book?'

Sandip ground out his reply through his teeth. 'God has given you women a plentiful supply of coquetry to start with, and on the top of that you have the milliner and the jeweller to help you; but do not think we men are so helpless . . .'

'You had better go back and look up your book, Sandip Babu. You are getting your words all wrong. That's just the trouble with trying to repeat things by rote.'

'You!' shouted Sandip, losing all control over himself. 'You to insult me thus! What is there left of you that I do not know to the very bottom? What . . .' He became speechless.

Sandip, the wielder of magic spells, is reduced to utter

powerlessness, whenever his spell refuses to work. From a king he fell to the level of a boor. Oh, the joy of witnessing his weakness! The harsher he became in his rudeness, the more did this joy well up within me. His snaky coils, with which he used to snare me, are exhausted – I am free. I am saved, saved. Be rude to me, insult me, for that shows you in your truth; but spare me your songs of praise, which were false.

My husband came in at this juncture. Sandip had not the elasticity to recover himself in a moment, as he used to do before. My husband looked at him for a while in surprise. Had this happened some days ago I should have felt ashamed. But today I was pleased – whatever my husband might think. I wanted to have it out to the finish with my weakening adversary.

Finding us both silent and constrained, my husband hesitated a little, and then took a chair. 'Sandip,' he said, 'I have been looking for you, and was told you were here.'

'I *am* here,' said Sandip with some emphasis. 'Queen Bee sent for me early this morning. And I, the humble worker of the hive, left all else to attend her summons.'

'I am going to Calcutta tomorrow. You will come with me.'

'And why, pray? Do you take me for one of your retinue?'

'Oh, very well, take it that you are going to Calcutta, and that I am your follower.'

'I have no business there.'

'All the more reason for going. You have too much business here.'

'I don't propose to stir.'

'Then I propose to shift you.'

'Forcibly?'

'Forcibly.'

'Very well, then, I will make a move. But the world is not divided between Calcutta and your estates. There are other places on the map.'

'From the way you have been going on, one would hardly have thought that there was any other place in the world except my estates.'

Sandip stood up. 'It does happen at times,' he said, 'that a man's whole world is reduced to a single spot. I have realized my universe in this sitting-room of yours, that is why I have been a fixture here.'

Then he turned to me. 'None but you, Queen Bee,' he said, 'will understand my words – perhaps not even you. I salute you. With worship in my heart I leave you. My watchword has changed since you have come across my vision. It is no longer *Bande Mataram* (Hail Mother), but Hail Beloved, Hail Enchantress. The mother protects, the mistress leads to destruction – but sweet is that destruction. You have made the anklet sounds of the dance of death tinkle in my heart. You have changed for me, your devotee, the picture I had of this Bengal of ours – "the soft breeze-cooled land of pure water and sweet fruit".[1] You have no pity, my beloved. You have come to me with your poison cup and I shall drain it, either to die in agony or live triumphing over death.

'Yes,' he continued. 'The mother's day is past. O love, my love, you have made as naught for me the truth and right and heaven itself. All duties have become as shadows: all rules and restraints have snapped their bonds. O love, my love, I could set fire to all the world outside this land on which you have set your dainty feet, and dance in mad revel over the ashes . . . These are mild men. These are good men. They would do good to all – as if this all were a reality! No, no! There is no reality in the world save this one real love of mine. I do you reverence. My devotion to you has made me cruel; my worship of you has lighted the raging flame of destruction within me. I am not righteous. I have no beliefs, I only believe in her whom, above all else in the world, I have been able to realize.'

Wonderful! It was wonderful, indeed. Only a minute ago I had despised this man with all my heart. But what I had thought to be dead ashes now glowed with living fire. The fire in him is true, that is beyond doubt. Oh why has God made man such a mixed creature? Was it only to show his supernatural sleight of hand? Only a few minutes ago I had thought that Sandip, whom I had once taken to be a hero, was only the stage hero of melodrama. But that is not so, not

1. Quotation from the National Song – *Bande Mataram*.

so. Even behind the trappings of the theatre, a true hero may sometimes be lurking.

There is much in Sandip that is coarse, that is sensuous, that is false, much that is overlaid with layer after layer of fleshly covering. Yet – yet it is best to confess that there is a great deal in the depths of him which we do not, cannot understand – much in ourselves too. A wonderful thing is man. What great mysterious purpose he is working out only the Terrible One[1] knows – meanwhile we groan under the brunt of it. Shiva is the Lord of Chaos. He is all Joy. He will destroy our bonds.

I cannot but feel, again and again, that there are two persons in me. One recoils from Sandip in his terrible aspect of Chaos – the other feels that very vision to be sweetly alluring. The sinking ship drags down all who are swimming round it. Sandip is just such a force of destruction. His immense attraction gets hold of one before fear can come to the rescue, and then, in the twinkling of an eye, one is drawn away, irresistibly, from all light, all good, all freedom of the sky, all air that can be breathed – from lifelong accumulations, from everyday cares – right to the bottom of dissolution.

From some realm of calamity has Sandip come as its messenger; and as he stalks the land, muttering unholy incantations, to him flock all the boys and youths. The mother, seated in the lotus-heart of the Country, is wailing her heart out; for they have broken open her store-room, there to hold their drunken revelry. Her vintage of the draught for the immortals they would pour out on the dust; her time-honoured vessels they would smash to pieces. True, I feel with her; but, at the same time, I cannot help being infected with their excitement.

Truth itself has sent us this temptation to test our trustiness in upholding its commandments. Intoxication masquerades in heavenly garb, and dances before the pilgrims saying: 'Fools you are that pursue the fruitless path of renunciation. Its way is long, its time passing slow. So the Wielder of the Thunderbolt has sent me to you. Behold, I the beautiful, the

1. Rudra, the Terrible, a name of Shiva.

178

passionate, I will accept you – in my embrace you shall find
fulfilment.'

After a pause Sandip addressed me again: 'Goddess, the
time has come for me to leave you. It is well. The work of
your nearness has been done. By lingering longer it would
only become undone again, little by little. All is lost, if in our
greed we try to cheapen that which is the greatest thing on
earth. That which is eternal within the moment only becomes
shallow if spread out in time. We were about to spoil our
infinite moment, when it was your uplifted thunderbolt
which came to the rescue. You intervened to save the purity
of your own worship – and in so doing you also saved your
worshipper. In my leave-taking today your worship stands
out the biggest thing. Goddess, I, also, set you free today. My
earthen temple could hold you no longer – every moment it
was on the point of breaking apart. Today I depart to worship
your larger image in a larger temple. I can gain you more
truly only at a distance from yourself. Here I had only your
favour, there I shall be vouchsafed your boon.'

My jewel-casket was lying on the table. I held it up aloft as
I said: 'I charge you to convey these my jewels to the object
of my worship – to whom I have dedicated them through
you.'

My husband remained silent. Sandip left the room.

XXI

I had just sat down to make some cakes for Amulya when the
Bara Rani came upon the scene. 'Oh dear,' she exclaimed,
'has it come to this that you must make cakes for your own
birthday?'

'Is there no one else for whom I could be making them?' I
asked.

'But this is not the day when you should think of feasting
others. It is for us to feast you. I was just thinking of
making something up[1] when I heard the staggering news
which completely upset me. A gang of five or six hundred

1. Any dainties to be offered ceremonially should be made by the lady of the house
herself.

men, they say, has raided one of our treasuries and made off with six thousand rupees. Our house will be looted next, they expect.'

I felt greatly relieved. So it was our own money after all. I wanted to send for Amulya at once and tell him that he need only hand over those notes to my husband and leave the explanations to me.

'You *are* a wonderful creature!' my sister-in-law broke out, at the change in my countenance. 'Have you then really no such thing as fear?'

'I cannot believe it,' I said. 'Why should they loot our house?'

'Not believe it, indeed! Who could have believed that they would attack our treasury, either?'

I made no reply, but bent over my cakes, putting in the cocoa-nut stuffing.

'Well, I'm off,' said the Bara Rani after a prolonged stare at me. 'I must see Brother Nikhil and get something done about sending off my money to Calcutta, before it's too late.'

She was no sooner gone than I left the cakes to take care of themselves and rushed to my dressing-room, shutting myself inside. My husband's tunic with the keys in its pocket was still hanging there – so forgetful was he. I took the key of the iron safe off the ring and kept it by me, hidden in the folds of my dress.

Then there came a knocking at the door. 'I am dressing,' I called out. I could hear the Bara Rani saying: 'Only a minute ago I saw her making cakes and now she is busy dressing up. What next, I wonder! One of their *Bande Mataram* meetings is on, I suppose. I say, Robber Queen,' she called out to me, 'are you taking stock of your loot?'

When they went away I hardly know what made me open the safe. Perhaps there was a lurking hope that it might all be a dream. What if, on pulling out the inside drawer, I should find the rolls of gold there, just as before? . . . Alas, everything was empty as the trust which had been betrayed.

I had to go through the farce of dressing. I had to do my hair up all over again, quite unnecessarily. When I came out

180

my sister-in-law railed at me: 'How many times are you going to dress today?'

'My birthday!' I said.

'Oh, any pretext seems good enough,' she went on. 'Many vain people have I seen in my day, but you beat them all hollow.'

I was about to summon a servant to send after Amulya, when one of the men came up with a little note, which he handed to me. It was from Amulya. 'Sister,' he wrote, you invited me this afternoon, but I thought I should not wait. Let me first execute your bidding and then come for my *prasad*. I may be a little late.'

To whom could he be going to return that money? into what fresh entanglement was the poor boy rushing? O miserable woman, you can only send him off like an arrow, but not recall him if you miss your aim.

I should have declared at once that I was at the bottom of this robbery. But women live on the trust of their surround-ings – this is their whole world. If once it is out that this trust has been secretly betrayed, their place in their world is lost. They have then to stand upon the fragments of the thing they have broken, and its jagged edges keep on wounding them at every turn. To sin is easy enough, but to make up for it is above all difficult for a woman.

For some time past all easy approaches for communion with my husband have been closed to me. How then could I burst on him with this stupendous news? He was very late in coming for his meal today – nearly two o'clock. He was absent-minded and hardly touched any food. I had lost even the right to press him to take a little more. I had to avert my face to wipe away my tears.

I wanted so badly to say to him: 'Do come into our room and rest awhile; you look so tired.' I had just cleared my throat with a little cough, when a servant hurried in to say that the Police Inspector had brought Panchu up to the palace. My husband, with the shadow on his face deepened, left his meal unfinished and went out.

A little later the Bara Rani appeared. 'Why did you not send me word when Brother Nikhil came in?' she complained. 'As he was late I thought I might as well finish my bath in the meantime. However did he manage to get through his meal so soon?'

'Why, did you want him for anything?'

'What is this about both of you going off to Calcutta tomorrow? All I can say is, I am not going to be left here alone. I should get startled out of my life at every sound, with all these dacoits about. Is it quite settled about your going tomorrow?'

'Yes,' said I, though I had only just now heard it; and though, moreover, I was not at all sure that before tomorrow our history might not take such a turn as to make it all one whether we went or stayed. After that, what our home, our life would be like, was utterly beyond my ken – it seemed so misty and phantom-like.

In a very few hours now my unseen fate would become visible. Was there no one who could keep on postponing the flight of these hours, from day to day, and so make them long enough for me to set things right, so far as lay in my power? The time during which the seed lies underground is long – so long indeed that one forgets that there is any danger of its sprouting. But once its shoot shows up above the surface, it grows and grows so fast, there is no time to cover it up, neither with skirt, nor body, nor even life itself.

I will try to think of it no more, but sit quiet— passive and callous – let the crash come when it may. By the day after tomorrow all will be over – publicity, laughter, bewailing, questions, explanations – everything.

But I cannot forget the face of Amulya – beautiful, radiant with devotion. He did not wait, despairing, for the blow of fate to fall, but rushed into the thick of danger. In my misery I do him reverence. He is my boy-god. Under the pretext of his playfulness he took from me the weight of my burden. He would save me by taking the punishment meant for me on his own head. But how am I to bear this terrible mercy of my God?

Oh, my child, my child, I do you reverence. Little brother mine, I do you reverence. Pure are you, beautiful are you, I do you reverence. May you come to my arms, in the next birth, as my own child – that is my prayer.

XXII

Rumour became busy on every side. The police were continually in and out. The servants of the house were in a great flurry.

Khema, my maid, came up to me and said: 'Oh, Rani Mother! for goodness' sake put away my gold necklace and armlets in your iron safe.' To whom was I to explain that the Rani herself had been weaving all this network of trouble, and had got caught in it, too? I had to play the benign protector and take charge of Khema's ornaments and Thako's savings. The milk-woman, in her turn, brought along and kept in my room a box in which were a Benares *sari* and some other of her valued possessions. 'I got these at your wedding,' she told me.

When, tomorrow, my iron safe will be opened in the presence of these — Khema, Thako, the milk-woman and all the rest . . . Let me not think of it! Let me rather try to think what it will be like when this third day of Magh comes round again after a year has passed. Will all the wounds of my home life then be still as fresh as ever? . . .

Amulya writes that he will come later in the evening. I cannot remain alone with my thoughts, doing nothing. So I sit down again to make cakes for him. I have finished making quite a quantity, but still I must go on. Who will eat them? I shall distribute them amongst the servants. I must do so this very night. Tonight is my limit. Tomorrow will not be in my hands.

I went on untiringly, frying cake after cake. Every now and then it seemed to me that there was some noise in the direction of my rooms, upstairs. Could it be that my husband had missed the key of the safe, and the Bara Rani had assembled all the servants to help him to hunt for it? No, I must not pay heed to these sounds. Let me shut the door.

I rose to do so, when Thako came panting in: 'Rani Mother, oh, Rani Mother!'

'Oh get away!' I snapped out, cutting her short. 'Don't come bothering me.'

'The Bara Rani Mother wants you,' she went on. 'Her

183

nephew has brought such a wonderful machine from Calcutta. It talks like a man. Do come and hear it!'

I did not know whether to laugh or to cry. So, of all things, a gramophone needs must come on the scene at such a time, repeating at every winding the nasal twang of its theatrical songs! What a fearsome thing results when a machine apes a man.

The shades of evening began to fall. I knew that Amulya would not delay to announce himself – yet I could not wait. I summoned a servant and said: 'Go and tell Amulya Babu to come straight in here.' The man came back after a while to say that Amulya was not in – he had not come back since he had gone.

'Gone!' The last word struck my ears like a wail in the gathering darkness. Amulya gone! Had he then come like a streak of light from the setting sun, only to be gone for ever? All kinds of possible and impossible dangers flitted through my mind. It was I who had sent him to his death. What if he was fearless? That only showed his own greatness of heart. But after this how was I to go on living all by myself?

I had no memento of Amulya save that pistol – his reverence-offering. It seemed to me that this was a sign given by Providence. This guilt which had contaminated my life at its very root – my God in the form of a child had left with me the means of wiping it away, and then vanished. Oh the loving gift – the saving grace that lay hidden within it!

I opened my box and took out the pistol, lifting it reverently to my forehead. At that moment the gongs clanged out from the temple attached to our house. I prostrated myself in salutation.

In the evening I feasted the whole household with my cakes. 'You have managed a wonderful birthday feast – and all by yourself too!' exclaimed my sister-in-law. 'But you must leave something for us to do.' With this she turned on her gramophone and let loose the shrill treble of the Calcutta actresses all over the place. It seemed like a stable full of neighing fillies.

It got quite late before the feasting was over. I had a sudden longing to end my birthday celebration by taking the dust of my husband's feet. I went up to the bedroom and found him fast asleep. He had had such a worrying, trying day. I raised the edge of the mosquito curtain very very gently, and laid my head near his feet. My hair must have touched him, for he moved his legs in his sleep and pushed my head away.

I then went out and sat in the west verandah. A silk-cotton tree, which had shed all its leaves, stood there in the distance, like a skeleton. Behind it the crescent moon was setting. All of a sudden I had the feeling that the very stars in the sky were afraid of me – that the whole of the night world was looking askance at me. Why? Because I was alone.

There is nothing so strange in creation as the man who is alone. Even he whose near ones have all died, one by one, is not alone – companionship comes for him from behind the screen of death. But he, whose kin are there, yet no longer near, who has dropped out of all the varied companionship of a full home – the starry universe itself seems to bristle to look on him in his darkness.

Where I am, I am not. I am far away from those who are around me. I live and move upon a world-wide chasm of separation, unstable as the dew-drop upon the lotus leaf.

Why do not men change wholly when they change? When I look into my heart, I find everything that was there, still there – only they are topsy-turvy. Things that were well-ordered have become jumbled up. The gems that were strung into a necklace are now rolling in the dust. And so my heart is breaking.

I feel I want to die. Yet in my heart everything still lives – nor even in death can I see the end of it all: rather, in death there seems to be ever so much more of repining. What is to be ended must be ended in this life – there is no other way out.

Oh forgive me just once, only this time, Lord! All that you gave into my hands as the wealth of my life, I have made into my burden. I can neither bear it longer, nor give it up. O Lord, sound once again those flute strains which you played for me, long ago, standing at the rosy edge of my morning sky – and let all my complexities become simple and easy. Nothing save the music of your flute can make whole that

185

which has been broken, and pure that which has been sullied. Create my home anew with your music. No other way can I see.

I threw myself prone on the ground and sobbed aloud. It was for mercy that I prayed – some little mercy from somewhere, some shelter, some sign of forgiveness, some hope that might bring about the end. 'Lord,' I vowed to myself, 'I will lie here, waiting and waiting, touching neither food nor drink, so long as your blessing does not reach me.'

I heard the sound of footsteps. Who says that the gods do not show themselves to mortal men? I did not raise my face to look up, lest the sight of it should break the spell. Come, oh come, come and let your feet touch my head. Come, Lord, and set your foot upon my throbbing heart, and at that moment let me die.

He came and sat near my head. Who? My husband! At the first touch of his presence I felt that I should swoon. And then the pain at my heart burst its way out in an overwhelming flood of tears, tearing through all my obstructing veins and nerves. I strained his feet to my bosom – oh, why could not their impress remain there for ever?

He tenderly stroked my head. I received his blessing. Now I shall be able to take up the penalty of public humiliation which will be mine tomorrow, and offer it, in all sincerity, at the feet of my God.

But what keeps crushing my heart is the thought that the festive flutes which were played at my wedding, nine years ago, welcoming me to this house, will never sound for me again in this life. What rigour of penance is there which can serve to bring me once more, as a bride adorned for her husband, to my place upon that same bridal seat? How many years, how many ages, aeons, must pass before I can find my way back to that day of nine years ago?

God can create new things, but has even He the power to create afresh that which has been destroyed?

Chapter Twelve

Nikhil's Story

XV

TODAY we are going to Calcutta. Our joys and sorrows lie heavy on us if we merely go on accumulating them. Keeping them and accumulating them alike are false. As master of the house I am in an artificial position – in reality I am a wayfarer on the path of life. That is why the true Master of the House gets hurt at every step and at last there comes the supreme hurt of death.

My union with you, my love, was only of the wayside; it was well enough so long as we followed the same road; it will only hamper us if we try to preserve it further. We are now leaving its bonds behind. We are started on our journey beyond, and it will be enough if we can throw each other a glance, or feel the touch of each other's hands in passing. After that? After that there is the larger world-path, the endless current of universal life.

How little can you deprive me of, my love, after all? Whenever I set my ear to it, I can hear the flute which is playing, its fountain of melody gushing forth from the flute-stops of separation. The immortal draught of the goddess is never exhausted. She sometimes breaks the bowl from which we drink it, only to smile at seeing us so disconsolate over the trifling loss. I will not stop to pick up my broken bowl. I will march forward, albeit with unsatisfied heart.

The Bara Rani came and asked me: 'What is the meaning, brother, of all these books being packed up and sent off in box-loads?'

187

'It only means,' I replied, 'that I have not yet been able to get over my fondness for them.'

'I only wish you would keep your fondness for some other things as well! Do you mean you are never coming back home?'

'I shall be coming and going, but shall not immure myself here any more.'

'Oh indeed! Then just come along to my room and see how many things *I* have been unable to shake off *my* fondness for.' With this she took me by the hand and marched me off.

In my sister-in-law's rooms I found numberless boxes and bundles ready packed. She opened one of the boxes and said: 'See, brother, look at all my *pan*-making things. In this bottle I have catechu powder scented with the pollen of screw-pine blossoms. These little tin boxes are all for different kinds of spices. I have not forgotten my playing cards and draught-board either. If you two are over-busy, I shall manage to make other friends there, who will give me a game. Do you remember this comb? It was one of the *Swadeshi* combs you brought for me . . .'

'But what is all this for, Sister Rani? Why have *you* been packing up all these things?'

'Do you think I am not going with you?'

'What an extraordinary idea!'

'Don't you be afraid! I am not going there to flirt with you, nor to quarrel with the Chota Rani! One must die sooner or later, and it is just as well to be on the bank of the holy Ganges before it is too late. It is too horrible to think of being cremated in your wretched burning-ground here, under that stumpy banian tree – that is why I have been refusing to die, and have plagued you all this time.'

At last I could hear the true voice of home. The Bara Rani came into our house as its bride, when I was only six years old. We have played together, through the drowsy afternoons, in a corner of the roof-terrace. I have thrown down to her green *amras* from the tree-top, to be made into deliciously indigestible chutnies by slicing them up with mustard, salt and fragrant herbs. It was my part to gather for her all the forbidden things from the store-room to be used in the marriage celebration of her doll; for, in the penal code of my grandmother, I alone was exempt from punishment. And I used to be appointed her messenger to my brother, whenever she wanted to coax something special out of him, because he could not resist my importunity. I also remember how, when I suffered under the rigorous régime of the doctors of those days – who would not allow anything except warm water and sugared cardamom seeds during feverish attacks – my sister-in-law could not bear my privation and used to bring me delicacies on the sly. What a scolding she got one day when she was caught!

And then, as we grew up, our mutual joys and sorrows took on deeper tones of intimacy. How we quarrelled! Sometimes conflicts of worldly interests roused suspicions and jealousies, making breaches in our love; and when the Chota Rani came in between us, these breaches seemed as if they would never be mended, but it always turned out that the healing forces at bottom proved more powerful than the wounds on the surface.

So has a true relationship grown up between us, from our childhood up till now, and its branching foliage has spread and broadened over every room and verandah and terrace of this great house. When I saw the Bara Rani make ready, with all her belongings, to depart from this house of ours, all the ties that bound us, to their wide-spreading ends, felt the shock.

The reason was clear to me, why she had made up her mind to drift away towards the unknown, cutting asunder all her lifelong bonds of daily habit, and of the house itself, which she had never left for a day since she first entered it at the age of nine. And yet it was this real reason which she could not allow to escape her lips, preferring rather to put forward any other paltry excuse.

She had only this one relationship left in all the world, and the poor, unfortunate, widowed and childless woman had cherished it with all the tenderness hoarded in her heart. How deeply she had felt our proposed separation I never realized so keenly as when I stood amongst her scattered boxes and bundles.

I could see at once that the little differences she used to have with Bimala, about money matters, did not proceed from any sordid worldliness, but because she felt that her claims in regard to this one relationship of her life had been overridden and its ties weakened for her by the coming in between of this other woman from goodness knows where! She had been hurt at every turn and yet had not the right to complain.

And Bimala? She also had felt that the Senior Rani's claim over me was not based merely on our social connection, but went much deeper; and she was jealous of these ties between us, reaching back to our childhood.

Today my heart knocked heavily against the doors of my breast. I sank down upon one of the boxes as I said: 'How I should love, Sister Rani, to go back to the days when we first met in this old house of ours.'

'No, brother dear,' she replied with a sigh, 'I would not live my life again – not as a woman! Let what I have had to bear end with this one birth. I could not bear it over again.'

I said to her: 'The freedom to which we pass through sorrow is greater than the sorrow.'

'That may be so for you men. Freedom is for you. But we women would keep others bound. We would rather be put into bondage ourselves. No, no, brother, you will never get free from our toils. If you needs must spread your wings, you will have to take us with you; we refuse to be left behind. That is why I have gathered together all this weight of luggage. It would never do to allow men to run too light.'

'I can feel the weight of your words,' I said laughing, 'and if we men do not complain of your burdens, it is because women pay us so handsomely for what they make us carry.'

'You carry it,' she said, 'because it is made up of many small things. Whichever one you think of rejecting pleads that it is so light. And so with much lightness we weigh you down . . . When do we start?'

'The train leaves at half past eleven tonight. There will be lots of time.'

'Look here, do be good for once and listen to just one word

of mine. Take a good nap this afternoon. You know you never get any sleep in the train. You look so pulled down, you might go to pieces any moment. Come along, get through your bath first.'

As we went towards my room, Khema, the maid, came up and with an ultra-modest pull at her veil told us, in deprecatingly low tones, that the Police Inspector had arrived with a prisoner and wanted to see the Maharaja.

'Is the Maharaja a thief, or a robber,' the Bara Rani flared up, 'that he should be set upon so by the police? Go and tell the Inspector that the Maharaja is at his bath.'

'Let me just go and see what is the matter,' I pleaded. 'It may be something urgent.'

'No, no,' my sister-in-law insisted. 'Our Chota Rani was making a heap of cakes last night. I'll send some to the Inspector, to keep him quiet till you're ready.' With this she pushed me into my room and shut the door on me.

I had not the power to resist such tyranny – so rare is it in this world. Let the Inspector while away the time eating cakes. What if business is a bit neglected?

The police had been in great form these last few days arresting now this one, now that. Each day some innocent person or other would be brought along to enliven the assembly in my office-room. One more such unfortunate, I supposed, must have been brought in that day. But why should the Inspector alone be regaled with cakes? That would not do at all. I thumped vigorously on the door.

'If you are going mad, be quick and pour some water over your head – that will keep you cool,' said my sister-in-law from the passage.

'Send down cakes for two,' I shouted. 'The person who has been brought in as the thief probably deserves them better. Tell the man to give him a good big helping.'

I hurried through my bath. When I came out, I found Bimal sitting on the floor outside.[1] Could this be my Bimal of old, my proud, sensitive Bimal?

What favour could she be wanting to beg, seated like this

1. Sitting on the bare floor is a sign of mourning, and so, by association of ideas, of an abject attitude of mind.

at my door? As I stopped short, she stood up and said gently with downcast eyes: 'I would have a word with you.'

'Come inside then,' I said.

'But are you going out on any particular business?'

'I was, but let that be. I want to hear . . .'

'No, finish your business first. We will have our talk after you have had your dinner.'

I went off to my sitting-room, to find the Police Inspector's plate quite empty. The person he had brought with him, however, was still busy eating.

'Hullo!' I ejaculated in surprise. 'You, Amulya?'

'It is I, sir,' said Amulya with his mouth full of cake. 'I've had quite a feast. And if you don't mind, I'll take the rest with me.' With this he proceeded to tie up the remaining cakes in his handkerchief.

'What does this mean?' I asked, staring at the Inspector.

The man laughed. 'We are no nearer, sir,' he said, 'to solving the problem of the thief: meanwhile the mystery of the theft deepens.' He then produced something tied up in a rag, which when untied disclosed a bundle of currency notes. 'This, Maharaja,' said the Inspector, 'is your six thousand rupees!'

'Where was it found?'

'In Amulya Babu's hands. He went last evening to the manager of your Chakna sub-office to tell him that the money had been found. The manager seemed to be in a greater state of trepidation at the recovery than he had been at the robbery. He was afraid he would be suspected of having made away with the notes and of now making up a cock-and-bull story for fear of being found out. He asked Amulya to wait, on the pretext of getting him some refreshment, and came straight over to the Police Office. I rode off at once, kept Amulya with me, and have been busy with him the whole morning. He refuses to tell us where he got the money from. I warned him he would be kept under restraint till he did so. In that case, he informed me he would have to lie. Very well, I said, he might do so if he pleased. Then he stated that he had found the money under a bush. I pointed out to him that it was not quite so easy to lie as all that. Under what bush? Where was the place? Why was he there? – All this would have to be stated as well. "Don't you worry," he said, "there is plenty of time to invent all that." '

'But, Inspector,' I said, 'why are you badgering a respectable young gentleman like Amulya Babu?'

'I have no desire to harass him,' said the Inspector. 'He is not only a gentleman, but the son of Nibaran Babu, my school-fellow. Let me tell you, Maharaja, exactly what must have happened. Amulya knows the thief, but wants to shield him by drawing suspicion on himself. That is just the sort of bravado he loves to indulge in.' The Inspector turned to Amulya. 'Look here, young man,' he continued, 'I also was eighteen once upon a time, and a student in the Ripon College. I nearly got into gaol trying to rescue a hack driver from a police constable. It was a near shave.' Then he turned again to me and said: 'Maharaja, the real thief will now probably escape, but I think I can tell you who is at the bottom of it all.'

'Who is it, then?' I asked.

'The manager, in collusion with the guard, Kasim.'

When the Inspector, having argued out his theory to his own satisfaction, at last departed, I said to Amulya: 'If you will tell me who took the money, I promise you no one shall be hurt.'

'I did,' said he.

'But how can that be? What about the gang of armed men? . . .'

'It was I, by myself, alone!'

What Amulya then told me was indeed extraordinary. The manager had just finished his supper and was on the verandah rinsing out his mouth. The place was somewhat dark. Amulya had a revolver in each pocket, one loaded with blank cartridges, the other with ball. He had a mask over his face. He flashed a bull's-eye lantern in the manager's face and fired a blank shot. The man swooned away. Some of the guards, who were off duty, came running up, but when Amulya fired another blank shot at them they lost no time in taking cover. Then Kasim, who was on duty, came up whirling a quarterstaff. This time Amulya aimed a bullet at his legs, and finding himself hit, Kasim collapsed on the floor. Amulya then made the trembling manager, who had come to his senses, open the safe and deliver up six thousand rupees. Finally, he took one of the estate horses and galloped off a few miles, there let the animal loose, and quietly walked up here, to our place.

'What made you do all this, Amulya?' I asked.

'There was a grave reason, Maharaja,' he replied.

'But why, then, did you try to return the money?'

'Let her come, at whose command I did so. In her presence I shall make a clean breast of it.'

'And who may "she" be?'

'My sister, the Chota Rani!'

I sent for Bimala. She came hesitatingly, barefoot, with a white shawl over her head. I had never seen my Bimal like this before. She seemed to have wrapped herself in a morning light.

Amulya prostrated himself in salutation and took the dust of her feet. Then, as he rose, he said: 'Your command has been executed, sister. The money is returned.'

'You have saved me, my little brother,' said Bimal.

'With your image in my mind, I have not uttered a single lie,' Amulya continued. 'My watchword *Bande Mataram* has been cast away at your feet for good. I have also received my reward, your *prasad*, as soon as I came to the palace.'

Bimal looked at him blankly, unable to follow his last words. Amulya brought out his handkerchief, and untying it showed her the cakes put away inside. 'I did not eat them all,' he said. 'I have kept these to eat after you have helped me with your own hands.'

I could see that I was not wanted here. I went out of the room. I could only preach and preach, so I mused, and get my effigy burnt for my pains. I had not yet been able to bring back a single soul from the path of death. They who have the power, can do so by a mere sign. My words have not that ineffable meaning. I am not a flame, only a black coal, which has gone out. I can light no lamp. That is what the story of my life shows – my row of lamps has remained unlit.

XVI

I returned slowly towards the inner apartments. The Bara Rani's room must have been drawing me again. It had become an absolute necessity for me, that day, to feel that this life of mine had been able to strike some real, some responsive chord in some other harp of life. One cannot realize one's own existence by remaining within oneself – it has to be sought outside.

As I passed in front of my sister-in-law's room, she came out saying: 'I was afraid you would be late again this afternoon. However, I ordered your dinner as soon as I heard you coming. It will be served in a minute.'

'Meanwhile,' I said, 'let me take out that money of yours and have it kept ready to take with us.'

As we walked on towards my room she asked me if the Police Inspector had made any report about the robbery. I somehow did not feel inclined to tell her all the details of how that six thousand had come back. 'That's just what all the fuss is about,' I said evasively.

When I went into my dressing-room and took out my bunch of keys, I did not find the key of the iron safe on the ring. What an absurdly absent-minded fellow I was, to be sure! Only this morning I had been opening so many boxes and things, and never noticed that this key was not there.

'What has happened to your key?' she asked me.

I went on fumbling in this pocket and that, but could give her no answer. I hunted in the same place over and over again. It dawned on both of us that it could not be a case of the key being mislaid. Someone must have taken it off the ring. Who could it be? Who else could have come into this room?

'Don't you worry about it,' she said to me. 'Get through your dinner first. The Chota Rani must have kept it herself, seeing how absent-minded you are getting.'

I was, however, greatly disturbed. It was never Bimal's habit to take any key of mine without telling me about it. Bimal was not present at my meal-time that day: she was busy feasting Amulya in her own room. My sister-in-law wanted to send for her, but I asked her not to do so.

I had just finished my dinner when Bimal came in. I would have preferred not to discuss the matter of the key in the Bara Rani's presence, but as soon as she saw Bimal, she asked her: 'Do you know, dear, where the key of the safe is?'

'I have it,' was the reply.

'Didn't I say so!' exclaimed my sister-in-law triumphantly. 'Our Chota Rani pretends not to care about these robberies, but she takes precautions on the sly, all the same.'

The look on Bimal's face made my mind misgive me. 'Let the key be, now,' I said. 'I will take out that money in the evening.'

'There you go again, putting it off,' said the Bara Rani. 'Why not take it out and send it to the treasury while you have it in mind?'

'I have taken it out already,' said Bimal.

I was startled.

'Where have you kept it, then?' asked my sister-in-law.

'I have spent it.'

'Just listen to her! Whatever did you spend all that money on?'

Bimal made no reply. I asked her nothing further. The Bara Rani seemed about to make some further remark to Bimala, but checked herself. 'Well, that is all right, anyway,' she said at length, as she looked towards me. 'Just what I used to do with my husband's loose cash. I knew it was no use leaving it with him – his hundred and one hangers-on would be sure to get hold of it. You are much the same, dear! What a number of ways you men know of getting through money. We can only save it from you by stealing it ourselves! Come along now. Off with you to bed.'

The Bara Rani led me to my room, but I hardly knew where I was going. She sat by my bed after I was stretched on it, and smiled at Bimal as she said: 'Give me one of your *pans*, Chotie darling – what? You have none! You have become a regular mem-sahib. Then send for some from my room.'

'But have you had your dinner yet?' I anxiously enquired.

'Oh long ago,' she replied – clearly a fib.

She kept on chattering away there at my bedside, on all manner of things. The maid came and told Bimal that her dinner had been served and was getting cold, but she gave no sign of having heard it. 'Not had your dinner yet? What nonsense! It's fearfully late.' With this the Bara Rani took Bimal away with her.

I could divine that there was some connection between the taking out of this six thousand and the robbing of the other. But I have no curiosity to learn the nature of it. I shall never ask.

Providence leaves our life moulded in the rough – its object being that we ourselves should put the finishing touches, shaping it into its final form to our taste. There has always been the hankering within me to express some great idea in the process of giving shape to my life on the lines suggested by the Creator. In this endeavour I have spent all my days. How severely I have curbed my desires, repressed myself at every step, only the Searcher of the Heart knows.

But the difficulty is, that one's life is not solely one's own. He who would create it must do so with the help of his surroundings, or he will fail. So it was my constant dream to draw Bimal to join me in this work of creating myself. I loved her with all my soul; on the strength of that, I could not but succeed in winning her to my purpose – that was my firm belief.

Then I discovered that those who could simply and naturally draw their environment into the process of their self-creation belonged to one species of the genus 'man', – and I to another. I had received the vital spark, but could not impart it. Those to whom I have surrendered my all have taken my all, but not myself with it.

My trial is hard indeed. Just when I want a helpmate most, I am thrown back on myself alone. Nevertheless, I record my vow that even in this trial I shall win through. Alone, then, shall I tread my thorny path to the end of this life's journey . . .

I have begun to suspect that there has all along been a vein of tyranny in me. There was a despotism in my desire to mould my relations with Bimala in a hard, clear-cut, perfect form. But man's life was not meant to be cast in a mould. And if we try to shape the good, as so much mere material, it takes a terrible revenge by losing its life.

I did not realize all this while that it must have been this unconscious tyranny of mine which made us gradually drift apart. Bimala's life, not finding its true level by reason of my pressure from above, has had to find an outlet by undermining its banks at the bottom. She has had to steal this six thousand rupees because she could not be open with me, because she felt that, in certain things, I despotically differed from her.

Men, such as I, possessed with one idea, are indeed at one with those who can manage to agree with us; but those who do not, can only get on with us by cheating us. It is our unyielding obstinacy, which drives even the simplest to tortuous ways. In trying to manufacture a helpmate, we spoil a wife.

Could I not go back to the beginning? Then, indeed, I should follow the path of the simple. I should not try to fetter my life's companion with my ideas, but play the joyous pipes of my love and say: 'Do you love me? Then may you grow true to yourself in the light of your love. Let my suggestions be suppressed, let God's design, which is in you, triumph, and my ideas retire abashed.'

But can even Nature's nursing heal the open wound, into which our accumulated differences have broken out? The covering veil, beneath the privacy of which Nature's silent forces alone can work, has been torn asunder. Wounds must be bandaged – can we not bandage our wound with our love, so that the day may come when its scar will no longer be visible? It is not too late? So much time has been lost in misunderstanding; it has taken right up to now to come to an understanding; how much more time will it take for the correcting? What if the wound does eventually heal? – can the devastation it has wrought ever be made good?

There was a slight sound near the door. As I turned over I saw Bimala's retreating figure through the open doorway. She must have been waiting by the door, hesitating whether to come in or not, and at last have decided to go back. I jumped up and bounded to the door, calling: 'Bimal.'

She stopped on her way. She had her back to me. I went

and took her by the hand and led her into our room. She threw herself face downwards on a pillow, and sobbed and sobbed. I said nothing, but held her hand as I sat by her head.

When her storm of grief had abated she sat up. I tried to draw her to my breast, but she pushed my arms away and knelt at my feet, touching them repeatedly with her head, in obeisance. I hastily drew my feet back, but she clasped them in her arms, saying in a choking voice: 'No, no, no, you must not take away your feet. Let me do my worship.'

I kept still. Who was I to stop her? Was I the god of her worship that I should have any qualms?

Bimala's Story

XXIII

Come, come! Now is the time to set sail towards that great confluence, where the river of love meets the sea of worship. In that pure blue all the weight of its muddiness sinks and disappears.

I now fear nothing – neither myself, nor anybody else. I have passed through fire. What was inflammable has been burnt to ashes; what is left is deathless. I have dedicated myself to the feet of him, who has received all my sin into the depths of his own pain.

Tonight we go to Calcutta. My inward troubles have so long prevented my looking after my things. Now let me arrange and pack them.

After a while I found my husband had come in and was taking a hand in the packing.

'This won't do,' I said. 'Did you not promise me you would have a sleep?'

'I might have made the promise,' he replied, 'but my sleep did not, and it was nowhere to be found.'

'No, no,' I repeated, 'this will never do. Lie down for a while, at least.'

'But how can you get through all this alone?'

'Of course I can.'

'Well, you may boast of being able to do without me. But frankly I can't do without you. Even sleep refused to come to me, alone, in that room.' Then he set to work again.

But there was an interruption, in the shape of a servant, who came and said that Sandip Babu had called and had asked to be announced. I did not dare to ask whom he wanted. The light of the sky seemed suddenly to be shut down, like the leaves of a sensitive plant.

'Come, Bimal,' said my husband. 'Let us go and hear what Sandip has to tell us. Since he has come back again, after taking his leave, he must have something special to say.'

I went, simply because it would have been still more embarrassing to stay. Sandip was staring at a picture on the wall. As we entered he said: 'You must be wondering why the fellow has returned. But you know the ghost is never laid till all the rites are complete.' With these words he brought out of his pocket something tied in his handkerchief, and laying it on the table, undid the knot. It was those sovereigns.

'Don't you mistake me, Nikhil,' he said. 'You must not imagine that the contagion of your company has suddenly turned me honest; I am not the man to come back in slobbering repentance to return ill-gotten money. But . . .'

He left his speech unfinished. After a pause he turned towards Nikhil, but said to me: 'After all these days, Queen Bee, the ghost of compunction has found an entry into my hitherto untroubled conscience. As I have to wrestle with it every night, after my first sleep is over, I cannot call it a phantom of my imagination. There is no escape even for me till its debt is paid. Into the hands of that spirit, therefore, let me make restitution. Goddess! From you, alone, of all the world, I shall not be able to take away anything. I shall not be rid of you till I am destitute. Take these back!'

He took out at the same time the jewel-casket from under his tunic and put it down, and then left us with hasty steps.

'Listen to me, Sandip,' my husband called after him.

'I have not the time, Nikhil,' said Sandip as he paused near the door. 'The Mussulmans, I am told, have taken me for an invaluable gem, and are conspiring to loot me and hide me away in their graveyard. But I feel that it is necessary that I should live. I have just twenty-five minutes to catch the North-bound train. So, for the present, I must be gone. We shall have our talk out at the next convenient opportunity. If you take my advice, don't you delay in getting away either. I salute you, Queen Bee, Queen of the bleeding hearts, Queen of desolation!'

Sandip then left almost at a run. I stood stock-still; I had never realized in such a manner before, how trivial, how paltry, this gold and these jewels were. Only a short while ago I was so busy thinking what I should take with me, and how I should pack it. Now I felt that there was no need to take anything at all. To set out and go forth was the important thing.

My husband left his seat and came up and took me by the hand. 'It is getting late,' he said. 'There is not much time left to complete our preparations for the journey.'

At this point Chandranath Babu suddenly came in. Finding us both together, he fell back for a moment. Then he said, 'Forgive me, my little mother, if I intrude. Nikhil, the Mussulmans are out of hand. They are looting Harish Kundu's treasury. That does not so much matter. But what is intolerable is the violence that is being done to the women of their house.'

'I am off,' said my husband.

'What can you do there?' I pleaded, as I held him by the hand. 'Oh, sir,' I appealed to his master. 'Will you not tell him not to go?'

'My little mother,' he replied, 'there is no time to do anything else.'

'Don't be alarmed, Bimal,' said my husband, as he left us.

When I went to the window I saw my husband galloping away on horseback, with not a weapon in his hands.

In another minute the Bara Rani came running in. 'What have you done, Chotie darling,' she cried. 'How could you let him go?

'Call the Dewan at once,' she said, turning to a servant.

The Ranis never appeared before the Dewan, but the Bara Rani had no thought that day for appearances.

'Send a mounted man to bring back the Maharaja at once,' she said, as soon as the Dewan came up.

'We have all entreated him to stay, Rani Mother,' said the Dewan, 'but he refused to turn back.'

'Send word to him that the Bara Rani is ill, that she is on her death-bed,' cried my sister-in-law wildly.

When the Dewan had left she turned on me with a furious outburst. 'Oh, you witch, you ogress, you could not die yourself, but needs must send him to his death! . . .'

The light of the day began to fade. The sun set behind the feathery foliage of the blossoming *Sajna* tree. I can see every different shade of that sunset even today. Two masses of cloud on either side of the sinking orb made it look like a great bird with fiery-feathered wings outspread. It seemed to me that this fateful day was taking its flight, to cross the ocean of night.

It became darker and darker. Like the flames of a distant village on fire, leaping up every now and then above the horizon, a distant din swelled up in recurring waves into the darkness.

The bells of the evening worship rang out from our temple. I knew the Bara Rani was sitting there, with palms joined in silent prayer. But I could not move a step from the window.

The roads, the village beyond, and the still more distant fringe of trees, grew more and more vague. The lake in our grounds looked up into the sky with a dull lustre, like a blind man's eye. On the left the tower seemed to be craning its neck to catch sight of something that was happening.

The sounds of night take on all manner of disguises. A twig snaps, and one thinks that somebody is running for his life. A door slams, and one feels it to be the sudden heart-thump of a startled world.

Lights would suddenly flicker under the shade of the distant trees, and then go out again. Horses' hoofs would clatter, now and again, only to turn out to be riders leaving the palace gates.

I continually had the feeling that, if only I could die, all this turmoil would come to an end. So long as I was alive my sins would remain rampant, scattering destruction on every side. I remembered the pistol in my box. But my feet refused to leave the window in quest of it. Was I not awaiting my fate?

The gong of the watch solemnly struck ten. A little later, groups of lights appeared in the distance and a great crowd wound its way, like some great serpent, along the roads in the darkness, towards the palace gates.

The Dewan rushed to the gate at the sound. Just then a rider came galloping in. 'What's the news, Jata?' asked the Dewan.

'Not good,' was the reply.

I could hear these words distinctly from my window. But something was next whispered which I could not catch.

Then came a palanquin, followed by a litter. The doctor was walking alongside the palanquin.

'What do you think, doctor?' asked the Dewan.

'Can't say yet,' the doctor replied. 'The wound in the head is a serious one.'

'And Amulya Babu?'

'He has a bullet through the heart. He is done for.'

Additional Notes

These notes supplement the footnotes to the text that were supplied by its translator, Surendranath Tagore.

p. 17. *Bimala*: The name means 'without *mal* or blemish'; clean, pure, immaculate. Cf. Thomas Hardy's subtitle to *Tess of the d'Urbervilles*: 'A pure woman'. Bimala is also often called Bimal for short.

p. 18. *Badshahs*: Muslim term for great kings or emperors, often applied to the Moghul emperors.

Moguls and Pathans: Moghul is now the most common spelling for the Muslim dynasty founded by Babur in 1526. Its Persianized culture penetrated deep into Bengal, and aristocratic families continued to hark back to it during British times. 'Pathans' here suggests an even older culture, as this name for the tribesman of the 'North-West Frontier' region between present-day Pakistan and Afghanistan was also applied to the Delhi sultans (1206–1526), though most of the dynasties of the sultanate were of Turkish origin.

Manu and Parashar: 'Manu the Lawgiver' was the semi-mythical author of the Hindu code of law and jurisprudence (*c.* 600 BC–*c.* AD 300); the 'customs of Manu' would be orthodox Hindu customs. Parashar(a) was the equally mythical sage and Brahmin said to be the author of some of the hymns of the *Rig Veda* – India's oldest and most sacred text. Bimala has thus married into a noble family whose culture is a typically Bengali blend of Hindu and Persian traditions, with a layer of progressive Victorianism on the top.

p. 20 (fn). *zenana*: A 'harem' in a Muslim palace, but in a smaller (Muslim or Hindu) household applied to the inner quarters where women lived in varying degrees of purdah, i.e. behind the *parda* or curtain.

p. 21. *Ranis*: Rani (queen) or maharani (great queen), like raja (king) or

205

maharahja (great king), were used flexibly for anyone from an empress/emperor to the land-owning gentry.

p. 29. *Bande Mataram*: Bankimchandra Chatterjee (1838–94) was the greatest prose writer of nineteenth-century Bengal, very influential not only for having established the novel as a major genre in Bengali literature but also for his Hindu nationalist ideas. He believed that a purified form of orthodox Hinduism was the authentic religion of India, and found in the teachings of Krishna in the *Bhagavad Gita* a supreme ideal. His novel *Anandamath* ('The Abbey of Bliss'), about a revolt in 1882 of Hindu *sannyasis* (ascetics) against the Muslim forces of the East India Company, included a song, *Bande Mataram* ('Hail to the Mother') that was adopted as a rallying-cry by Hindu revivalists and revolutionaries. The song identifies the Motherland with Bengal's favourite deity Durga, wife of Siva, and also with Lakshmi (called Kamala in the song), wife of Vishnu and goddess of beauty and prosperity.

p. 30. *Sandip Babu*: 'Sandip' means 'with *dipa* (light, flame, fire)', so his name appropriately means 'inflaming, exciting, arousing'. 'Babu' was originally added only to the names of aristocrats, but came to refer to any (English-) educated Bengali. It was therefore used mockingly by the British for Bengalis such as the Babu Hurry Chunder Mookerjee in Rudyard Kipling's *Kim*. Its pejorative and its honorific usages survive in India to this day.

p. 31. *Indra's steed*: Indra, king of the Hindu gods, rides on Airavata, a colossal flying elephant produced by the primeval churning of the ocean.

p. 33. *Shakti* (sakti): The creative energy of the universe, associated with Siva's consort, who in Bengal is worshipped as Durga or Kali. A Hindu nationalist like Sandip identifies this power with Bimala herself, with female sexuality, and with 'Mother India'.

p. 34. *Nikhil*: In the Bengali text Nikhil's full name 'Nikhilesh' is generally used. It means 'Lord of the Universe', *nikhil* meaning 'whole', and suggesting harmony and wisdom.

p. 37. *Arjuna won Mahadeva's favour by wrestling with him*: In the third book of the *Mahabharata* (Chs. 38–42), the Pandava hero Arjuna is sent before the final battle to fetch weapons from his heavenly father Indra. On his way through the Himalayas he meets a hunter and gets into a dispute with him over a boar they both claim to have shot. He fights the hunter, first with arrows, then with fists, then by wrestling. The hunter wins, and turns out to be Siva (Mahadeva), who grants him a boon and gives him a special weapon. Arjuna then continues on his journey to Indra's heaven.

p. 38. *Durga*: The form of Siva's *sakti* or consort that is most popular in

Bengal. In October to November the festival *Durga-puja* commemorates Rama's worship of Durga for victory over the demon king Ravana, as mentioned in the medieval version of the *Ramayana*.

p. 39. *'Come, Sin, O beautiful Sin . . .'*: This poem appears to have been written by Tagore specifically for the novel. It does not occur in any of his books of poems, and has not been traced to any other poet.

p. 46. *avatars*: The word literally means 'descent', and is widely used in Indian tradition for a deity (especially Vishnu) taking bodily form on earth. Krishna, Rama, Vyasa (supposed author of the *Mahabharata*) and the Buddha are all regarded as *avatar(a)s* of Vishnu, who was also incarnated as a fish, a tortoise, a boar, etc.

p. 52. *inauspicious Thursday afternoon*: In the original, this is during the *bar-bela* of Thursday. In the Hindu almanac each day is divided into equal parts of three hours (*yama*), which are in turn subdivided into periods of one-and-a-half hours (*yamardha*). Each day has several *yamardha* that are marked as *bar (vara)-bela* – inauspicious for work or action or religious rituals. On a Thursday the seventh and eighth *yamardhas* (which fall in the afternoon) are *bar-bela*, inauspicious times.

p. 55. *the lolling tongue*: The imagery here is reminiscent of Kali, the goddess who represents Siva's *sakti* in its most violent – but also most voluptuous and maternal – form. She has a long, lolling, bloodthirsty tongue, along with skulls strung round her body, snakes round her neck, and weapons in each of her ten arms.

p. 56. *sex-problems*: In the original, the book planted by Sandip treats in 'a very clearly realistic' way *stri-purusher milan-niti* – 'the science (*niti*) of sexual relations (*milan*) between women and men'. Surendranath's translation is fair enough, as precisely what sort of book this is (A sex manual? A book on sexology? Guidance on a perfect match?) is left unclear.

Jayadeva: Regarded as the greatest Sanskrit poet of the Bengal region, Jayadeva wrote in the early twelfth century AD and is renowned for his *Gita-Govinda*, a sensuous poetic drama about the love of Radha and Krishna.

p. 57. *Swadeshi*: The word means 'of one's own *des* or land'. Associated with the (negative) boycott campaign against Lord Curzon's partition of Bengal, it also stood for the constructive promotion of home industries – a cause that Tagore's father Debendranath promoted through his support for the annual Hindu Mela, a festival of national goods and handicrafts that was started in Calcutta in 1867. Rabindranath worked tirelessly to develop Swadeshi projects, on his family estates in the Padma river region in the 1890s, and later at Santiniketan and Sriniketan.

p. 59. *Gita*: The Gita is the *Bhagavad Gita*, the great 'Song of the God' that was inserted into the Bhishmaparvan of the *Mahabharata*. In its eighteen cantos, Krishna urges Arjuna to fight for *dharma* – righteousness – in the imminent battle of Kurukshetra, without concerning himself with the fruits of his actions.

p. 70. *Modern sex-problems*: Again, Surendranath's translation is accurate: a perceptive rendering of *madarn* (the English word 'modern' is used) *kaler stri-purusher sambandha*: 'man-woman relations in the modern age'.

p. 80. *'know thyself'*: One might have expected a scriptural quotation here, as self-knowledge – knowing (in the famous phrase from the Chandogya Upanishad) that *Tat Tvam Asi*, 'That Thou Art' – i.e. Brahman (the Spirit = 'That') is the same as the Atman (Self = 'Thou') – is at the heart of the Upanishads and Gita. But in fact the simple Bengali phrase *apnake jano* ('know your own self') is used.

p. 83. *Ramayana*: Ravana, king of the demonic Rakshasas of Lanka, abducted Rama's wife Sita. The *Ramayana*, Valmiki's great Sanskrit epic, tells the story of her abduction and her rescue by Rama and his brother assisted by the monkey-king Sugriva and the monkey-god Hanuman, Sugriva's commander-in-chief. In his Bengali literary epic *Meghanad-badh kabya*, Michael Madhusudan Dutt (1824–73) made the Rakshasas the 'real heroes' of the story by focusing on their tragic defeat.

p. 84. *Kali*: See note on the 'lolling tongue' of Kali (p. 55). Kali has played a major role in Bengali culture. The name Calcutta (now officially spelt Kolkata) is probably derived from her temple at Kalighat, the famous mystic and guru Ramakrishna Paramahamsa (1836–86) was her devotee, and her worship was central to the secretive and sexualized Tantric rituals that appealed to some revolutionaries. Tagore wrote a powerful early play, *Bisarjan* ('Sacrifice', 1890) attacking the Kali cult.

p. 85. *Vidyapati*: Leading writer of *padas*, songs celebrating the love of the milkmaid Radha for the god Krishna. He flourished in the early fifteenth century AD, and wrote in Brajabuli, a dialect that was a bridge between Bengali and Hindi and became the dominant language of the genre.

p. 87. *Amiel's Journal*: The *Journal Intime* of the Swiss-French writer Henri Frédéric Amiel (1821–81) was translated into many languages and struck a chord with those who, like Nikhil, struggled to find meaning and value in modern life.

p. 88. *pan*: Leaf of the betel-pepper plant, commonly chewed in India with betel-nut (from the betel-palm, a different tree), shell-lime and other spices.

Namasudra: Sudras belong to the lowest of the four *varnas*, the main 'colours' or caste-divisions of Hindu society. *Nama* means 'low', so the Namasudras are a very low-caste, labouring community.

p. 89. *Prince Siddharta*: The name (more correctly Siddhartha) means 'he who has achieved his purpose', and was used by Hermann Hesse as the title for his famous novel about the Buddha (1922).

p. 90. *Ahalya*: Ahalya, famously seduced by Indra, was the wife of the sage Gautama, who, when he found out, cursed Indra, covering him (in some versions of the story) with a thousand *yonis* or vulvas, and turning Ahalya to stone. She revived when Rama accidentally touched her with his foot.

p. 92. '*My lover of the unpriced love ...*': This is a song by Tagore himself ('Amar-nikariya raser rasik kanan ghure ghure'), included in *Gitabitan*, his Collected Songs.

p. 93. *Vaishnava Poets*: The Vaishnava (Vaishnavite) poets here are the medieval authors of innumerable *padas*, songs about Radha and Krishna, in Bengali or Brajabuli (see Vidyapati above, note to p. 85).

p. 97. *Vaishnava Philosophy*: The cult of Radha and Krishna produced an elaborate theology, associated with the saint Chaitanya (1485–1533) and his followers. The philosophy was essentially dualistic, with Radha's love for Krishna being interpreted as human longing for the divine. It was a significant influence on Tagore, especially on his songs, which express *viraha* (romantic/spiritual yearning) in an infinite number of moods and shades.

'*My flute, that was busy with its song ...*': Another song by Tagore himself ('Yakhan dekha dao ni, Radha'). Like the previous one (p. 92) it has Vaishnava echoes, with the singer this time being the flute-playing Krishna himself.

p. 98. *Dewali*: The word (*dipabali* or *dipali* in Bengali) means 'a row of lamps', and is the name for the autumn festival of lamps, which celebrates Krishna's victory over the demon Naraka. In Bengal it often coincides with *Kali-puja*.

Kalidas: Kalidasa is the greatest poet and dramatist of Sanskrit literature. He lived between AD 350 and 600, and his most famous works are the play *Sakuntala* and the poems *Meghaduta* ('Cloud-Messenger') and *Kumara-sambhava* ('Kumara's Occasioning', usually known as 'The Birth of the War-god').

p. 99. *ocean-churning*: In this spectacular myth, the gods have been greatly weakened by a curse from the sage Durvasas, which places them under threat from the Asuras or anti-gods. Vishnu decides that their energy can only be restored if they drink from the milky sea of *amrita* (ambrosia) surrounding him – but it must be churned first. The Asuras are tricked into helping with the churning, which is achieved by the gods and Asuras pulling at opposite ends of the snake Vasuki, wound round the uprooted Mount Mandara.

p. 104. *shoe-beating*: A special insult all across Asia, as shoes are worn in (unclean) public places, never in (clean) domestic areas.

p. 108. *Brindaban*: Bengali spelling for Vrindavan, where Krishna dallied with the *gopis* or cowgirls, stealing their clothes while they were bathing and forming a special attachment to Radha. Situated near Mathura in Uttar Pradesh, the area is full of temples and shrines of immense sacred significance to Vaishnavite Hindus.

p. 109. *bauhinias*: *Kanchan* trees: the Bengali name means 'golden', and is used for several varieties of Bauhinia, whose large fragrant flowers can be purple, white or red but here are described as *golapi* – pink or rose-coloured.

p. 111. *Padma*: The name given to the eastern branch of the Ganges when it enters present-day Bangladesh. The Tagore family had estates at Shelidaha near Kushtia, and Rabindranath spent much of the 1890s managing them.

p. 112. *Marwari*: Originally from Marwar in Rajasthan, the Marwaris of Calcutta (and other big Indian cities) have become one of India's most successful trading communities, synonymous with wealth and business acumen.

Mahomedan: This name for Muslims fell into disuse in the early twentieth century when Muslim reformers complained that it falsely implied that Muslims worshipped the Prophet as Christians do Christ.

p. 119. *Sakuntala*: Although the story of Sakuntala is found in the *Mahabharata*, she is famous mainly because of Kalidasa's play. The latter introduces folk elements such as the ring lost by Sakuntala when bathing, which is found by fisherman in the stomach of a large fish, and which revives the king's memory of her when they show it to him.

p. 123. *Mussulman*: *Musulman* remains the normal Bengali name for a Muslim.

Maratha and the Sikh: Because of their wars against the Moghuls, the Marathas and Sikhs acquired a warlike reputation that led to their being recruited for the British Indian Army as 'martial races'. Calcutta had been sited on the marshy east side of the Hooghly largely as a defence against the Marathas, and under their leader Tatya Tope, hanged by the British in 1859, they played a leading part in the Indian Mutiny of 1857.

pp. 123–4. *Krishna ... and that day he saw the Truth*: The vision is expounded in the *Bhagavad Gita*. Krishna's 'universal aspect' as an incarnation of Vishnu was also revealed to his foster-mother Yasoda when he was playing with his brother Balarama and ate some clay.

When she checked to see if he had cleaned out his mouth properly, she saw the whole universe inside it – heaven, earth and the underworld.

p. 125 (fn). *Upanishads*: The quotation is from the *Mundaka-Upanishad*, 3.1.6: *satyameva jayate*. The translation is controversial. Because *satyam* is a neuter noun, it can be either nominative or accusative. If it is nominative, then 'Truth shall triumph' is correct. This is how it is commonly translated, and is clearly Sandip's meaning here. However, Paul Deussen in his German translation takes it to be accusative: *Wahrheit ersiegt er* – 'He wins Truth [for himself]'. The phrase is used on India's seal of state.

p. 126. *'For my lover will I bind in my hair ...'*: Another song by Tagore himself ('Bandhur lagi kese ami parba eman phul').

p. 128. *zamindars*: Under the Moghul system Bengali zamindars were landholders and revenue collectors, but under the 'Permanent Settlement' of Lord Cornwallis in 1793 they became landowners and the Government's land-revenue demand was permanently fixed. Even in predominantly Muslim areas, most zamindars were Hindus, with houses in Calcutta, and were often absent from their estates. By living on his father's estates in the Padma river area (see above, note to p. 111), Rabindranath was much less absent than most, which makes Nikhilesh, who lives on his estate and tries to do his best for his tenants, something of a self-portrait.

p. 134. *amrita*: Ambrosia, food of the gods guaranteeing immortal life. See 'ocean-churning' above (note to p. 99).

p. 136. *Amulya*: The name means 'without *mulya* or price' – i.e. invaluable, priceless.

p. 138. *mantram*: Normally Romanized as 'mantra': a sacred word or phrase, usually from the Vedas, though sometimes distorted in form or of unknown origin, used in Hindu ceremonies or rituals. A guru traditionally initiates a disciple by imparting a special, secret mantra. More loosely (as here), a magic spell.

p. 140. *Satan*: There is no equivalent to Satan in Hinduism, but as a loose term for malign forces in the world *Saytan* (cf. Arabic *al-Shaitan*) entered Bengali usage through Islamic influence.

p. 157. *'She should never have looked at me ...'*: The first stanza of 'Cristina' in Robert Browning's *Dramatic Lyrics* (1842).

p. 158. *'In the springtime of your kingdom, my Queen ...'*: Another song by Tagore himself: 'Madhuritu nitya haye raila tomar madhur dese'.

p. 159. *Poush cakes*: *Pitha* or *pithe* in Bengali; made of rice-powder, pulse-paste and molasses, these sweetmeats are made and enjoyed during the *Paus Parban* festival in the winter month of Paus (mid-December to mid-January).

p. 161. *Vaishnava ... Shaktas go on with their animal sacrifices just the same*: See 'Vaishnava Poets' and 'Vaishnava Philosophy' above (notes to p. 93, p. 97). Shaktism and Vaishavism are the two main streams of

Bengali Hinduism. Vaishnavas worship Vishnu through his incarnation Krishna and his lover Radha. The tradition is intensely pious and emotional, and stems from the trend in fifteenth and sixteenth century Hinduism known as *bhakti* ('devotion'). Shaktas worship Siva through his *sakti* Durga or Kali (see 'Shakti' above, note to p. 33). Their practices depend more on rituals than on *bhakti*, and *Kali-puja* has traditionally involved animal sacrifice.

p. 162. *Pachur case*: Surendranath's translation here implies a public controversy or even a legal case, but the original just says: 'Haven't you heard about what they did [the trouble they caused] at *Pancure*?' Research has failed to shed light on this: the incident and even the place-name may be fictitious.

p. 169. *Airauat*: Airavata. See 'Indra's steed' above (note to p. 31).

p. 171. *Lakshmi*: Wife of Vishnu. Also known as Kamala: see 'Bande Mataram' above (note to p. 29). Kamala means 'lotus', and Lakshmi sits on a lotus-throne and is also the lotus itself. Kama, god of Love, is her son, and Krishna's lover Radha and Rama's wife Sita are regarded as incarnations of Lakshmi.

Indra's queen: Indrani, wife of Indra, has quite a low profile in Hindu mythology but is admired as a model of beauty and wifely devotion. As Vedic gods, Indra and Indrani are equivalent to Zeus and Hera. They remain as 'King and Queen' of the gods in classical Hinduism, though Brahma, Vishnu and Siva are all more powerful.

p. 173. *prasad*: Prasad is a very resonant word. It means a food-offering to a deity, consumed by devotees after the offering; the remains of food taken by a revered person; and also (more abstractly) grace, favour, blessing, etc.

p. 174. *expiation*: Prayascitta. This can be a formal ritual or expiation, penance or atonement, in order to overcome a sin. Hindu converts to Christianity sometimes underwent a *prayascitta* ceremony in order to reconvert to Hinduism.

p. 183. *Magh*: The tenth month in the Bengali calendar, mid-January to mid-February. There are six seasons, two months for each; Magh is the first of the last and coolest season before the year starts again in spring.

p. 185. *'music of your flute'*: Krishna's flute – so often a symbol of divine, unreachable perfection in Tagore's poetry and song.

p. 188. *amras*: The hog-plum or yellow mombin, fruit of a tree with purplish green leaves that belongs to the cashew family. Its large, fibrous stone is difficult to separate from the flesh. When green and sour, *amras* are used for chutney and pickle.

p. 191. *cakes*: See 'Poush cakes' above (note to p. 159).

p. 201. *Dewan*: Of Middle Eastern origin, the title 'Dewan' (*Deoyan*) in the Moghul system was used for a treasurer or finance minister. On an estate such as Nikhilesh's, the Dewan is the steward responsible for its financial administration – senior to the *Khajanci* or cashier mentioned on p. 139.

p. 202. Sajna: A *sajna* or *sajne* tree has small white flowers growing in clusters, flowering from March to April and faintly perfumed.

I am very grateful to Arun Deb of Konnagar, Renate Söhnen-Thieme of SOAS, and Indrani Majumdar of Delhi for their generous help with a number of details in this new edition. W.R.

PENGUIN CLASSICS

DEAD SOULS   NIKOLAI GOGOL

'It's not a question of the living. I've nothing to do with them. I'm asking for the dead'

Chichikov, a mysterious stranger, arrives in the provincial town of 'N', visiting a succession of landowners and making each a strange offer. He proposes to buy the names of dead serfs still registered on the census, saving their owners from paying tax on them, and to use these 'souls' as collateral to re-invent himself as a gentleman. In this ebullient masterpiece, Gogol created a grotesque gallery of human types, from the bear-like Sobakevich to the insubstantial fool Manilov, and, above all, the devilish conman Chichikov. *Dead Souls*, Russia's first major novel, is one of the most unusual works of nineteenth-century fiction and a devastating satire on social hypocrisy.

David Magarshack's introduction discusses Gogol's plan for a novel in three parts, tracing Chichikov's progress from sin to redemption, and tells how Gogol destroyed part of the manuscript in the grip of madness. The surviving sections, volume one and a fragment of volume two, are translated here.

'Gogol was a strange creature, but then genius is always strange'
Vladimir Nabokov

Translated with an introduction by David Magarshack

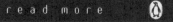

PENGUIN CLASSICS

A HERO OF OUR TIME   MIKHAIL LERMONTOV

'I'm still in love with her ... I'd give my life for her. But she bores me'

Proud, wilful and intensely charismatic, Pechorin is bored by the stifling world that envelops him. With a predatory energy for any activity that will relieve his ennui, he embarks on a series of adventures – encountering smugglers, brigands, soldiers, lovers and rivals – and leaves a trail of broken hearts behind him. With its cynical, immoral hero, Lermontov's novel outraged many critics when it was published in 1840. Yet it was also a literary landmark: an acutely observed psychological novel, narrated from a number of different perspectives, through which the true and complex nature of Pechorin slowly emerges.

Paul Foote's fine translation is accompanied by an introduction discussing the figure of Pechorin within the literary tradition of 'superfluous men' and the novel's influence on Tolstoy, Dostoyevsky and Chekhov. The edition also includes a chronology, explanatory notes and a historical note on the Caucasus.

'Vigorous and audacious ... it retains its power as a psychological study'
Julian Barnes

Translated with an introduction by Paul Foote

PENGUIN CLASSICS

FATHERS AND SONS   IVAN TURGENEV

'Of course you cannot understand me: we belong to two different generations'

When Arkady Petrovich comes home from college, father finds his eager, naive son changed almost beyond recognition, for the impressionable Arkady has fallen under the powerful influence of the friend he has brought with him. A self-proclaimed nihilist, the ardent young Bazarov shocks Arkady's father by criticizing the landowning way of life and by his outspoken determination to sweep away traditional values of contemporary Russian society. Turgenev's depiction of the conflict between generations and their ideals stunned readers when *Fathers and Sons* was first published in 1862. But many could also sympathize with Arkady's fascination with its nihilist hero whose story vividly captures the hopes and regrets of a changing Russia.

Rosemary Edmonds's superb translation of Turgenev's masterpiece is accompanied by Isaiah Berlin's 1970 Romanes Lecture, 'Fathers and Children', which has been acclaimed by scholars as a classic in itself.

'[Turgenev] was, all his life, profoundly and painfully concerned with his country's condition and destiny ... incomparable sharpness of vision, poetry and truth' Isaiah Berlin

Translated by Rosemary Edmonds, with the Romanes Lecture, 'Fathers and Children', by Isaiah Berlin

PENGUIN CLASSICS

THE BHAGAVAD GITA

'In death thy glory in heaven, in victory thy glory on earth.
Arise therefore, Arjuna, with thy soul ready to fight'

The Bhagavad Gita is an intensely spiritual work that forms the
cornerstone of the Hindu faith, and is also one of the masterpieces of
Sanskrit poetry. It describes how, at the beginning of a mighty battle
between the Pandava and Kaurava armies, the god Krishna gives
spiritual enlightenment to the warrior Arjuna, who realizes that the
true battle is for his own soul.

Juan Mascaró's translation of *The Bhagavad Gita* captures the
extraordinary aural qualities of the original Sanskrit. This edition
features a new introduction by Simon Brodbeck, which discusses
concepts such as dehin, prakriti and Karma.

'The task of truly translating such a work is indeed formidable. The
translator must at least possess three qualities. He must be an artist in
words as well as a Sanskrit scholar, and above all, perhaps, he must be
deeply sympathetic with the spirit of the original. Mascaró has succeeded
so well because he possesses all these' *The Times Literary Supplement*

Translated by Juan Mascaró with an introduction by Simon Brodbeck

PENGUIN CLASSICS

THE ROOTS OF AYURVEDA

'One should follow the Middle Way in all things'

Ayurveda, the ancient art of healing, has been practised in India for over two thousand years, and survives today as a living medical tradition whose principles are at the heart of many of the complementary therapies now used in the West. This 'science of longevity' has parallels with Buddhist thought, and advocates a life of moderation through which the three humours of the body will be brought into balance. The practical advice offered here ranges from the benefits of garlic therapy to prayers for protection against malevolent disease deities, from surgical techniques to exercise regimes, and from the treatment of poisons to the interpretation of dreams.

The writings selected for this volume are taken from the Sanskrit medical texts written by the first Ayurvedic physicians, who lived between the fifth century BC and the fourteenth century AD. Dominik Wujastyk's authoritative translation is fresh and contemporary in feel, revealing Ayurveda as a timeless tradition.

Selected, translated and introduced by Dominik Wujastyk

PENGUIN CLASSICS

THE ANALECTS CONFUCIUS

'The Master said, "If a man sets his heart on benevolence, he will be free from evil"'

The Analects are a collection of Confucius's sayings brought together by his pupils shortly after his death in 497 BC. Together they express a philosophy, or a moral code, by which Confucius, one of the most humane thinkers of all time, believed everyone should live. Upholding the ideals of wisdom, self-knowledge, courage and love of one's fellow man, he argued that the pursuit of virtue should be every individual's supreme goal. And while following the Way, or the truth, might not result in immediate or material gain, Confucius showed that it could nevertheless bring its own powerful and lasting spiritual rewards.

This edition contains a detailed introduction exploring the concepts of the original work, a bibliography and glossary and appendices on Confucius himself, *The Analects* and the disciples who compiled them.

Translated with an introduction and notes by D. C. Lau

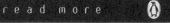
PENGUIN CLASSICS

ON LOVE AND BARLEY: HAIKU OF BASHO   BASHO

'Orchid – breathing
incense into
butterfly's wings'

Basho, one of the greatest of Japanese poets and the master of haiku,
was also a Buddhist monk and a lifelong traveller. His poems combine
'karumi', or lightness of touch, with the Zen ideal of oneness with
creation. Each poem evokes the natural world – the cherry blossom,
the leaping frog, the summer moon or the winter snow – suggesting
the smallness of human life in comparison with the vastness and drama
of nature. Basho himself enjoyed solitude and a life free from
possessions, and his haiku are the work of an observant eye and a
meditative mind, uncluttered by materialism and alive to the beauty of
the world around him.

These meticulous translations by Lucien Stryk capture the refined artistry
of the originals. This edition contains notes and an introduction that
discusses how the life and beliefs of Basho influenced his work.

Translated by Lucien Stryk

PENGUIN CLASSICS

THE RUBA'IYAT OF OMAR KHAYYAM

'Many like you come and many go
Snatch your share before you are snatched away'

Revered in eleventh-century Persia as an astronomer, mathematician and
philosopher, Omar Khayyam is now known first and foremost for his
Ruba'iyat. The short epigrammatic stanza form allowed poets of his day to
express personal feelings, beliefs and doubts with wit and clarity, and
Khayyam became one of its most accomplished masters with his touching
meditations on the transience of human life and of the natural world. One
of the supreme achievements of medieval literature, the reckless
romanticism and the pragmatic fatalism in the face of death means these
verses continue to hold the imagination of modern readers.

In this translation, Persian scholar Peter Avery and the poet John Heath-
Stubbs have collaborated to recapture the sceptical, unorthodox spirit of
the original by providing a near literal English version of the original
verse. This edition also includes a map, appendices, bibliography and an
introduction examining the *ruba'i* form and Khayyam's life and times.

'[Has] restored to that masterpiece all the fun, dash and vivacity.'
Jan Morris

Translated by Peter Avery and John Heath-Stubbs

PENGUIN CLASSICS

THE KORAN

'God is the light of the heavens and the earth . . . God guides to His light whom he will'

The Koran is universally accepted by Muslims to be the infallible Word of God as first revealed to the Prophet Muhammad by the Angel Gabriel nearly fourteen hundred years ago. Its 114 chapters, or *sūrahs*, recount the narratives central to Muslim belief, and together they form one of the world's most influential prophetic works and a literary masterpiece in its own right. But above all, the Koran provides the rules of conduct that remain fundamental to the Muslim faith today: prayer, fasting, pilgrimage to Mecca and absolute faith in God.

N. J. Dawood's masterly translation is the result of his life-long study of the Koran's language and style, and presents the English reader with a fluent and authoritative rendering, while reflecting the flavour and rhythm of the original. This edition follows the traditional sequence of the Koranic *sūrahs*.

'Across the language barrier Dawood captures the thunder and poetry of the original' *The Times*

Over a million copies sold worldwide.

Revised translation with an introduction and notes by N. J. Dawood